They took the bait.

They turned toward him, revealing themselves to Kimmer, and as one goonboy slammed a new magazine home, the other raised his pistol at Rio.

Kimmer aimed between them and took a deep breath. No turning back now. Once she drew blood, she'd be explaining herself to the local law; she'd also drag the Hunter Agency into the mess. From this distance the pellet spread meant she'd hit them both without truly damaging them.

If only the cops were closer.

But now it was more than Hank in trouble. Rio stood within their sights....

Kimmer pulled the trigger.

Dear Reader,

What is a Bombshell? Sometimes it's a femme fatale. Sometimes it's unexpected news that changes everything. Sometimes it's a book you just can't put down! And that's what we're bringing to you—four fascinating stories about women you'll cheer for!

Such as Angel Baker, star of *USA TODAY* bestselling author Julie Beard's *Touch of the White Tiger*. This twenty-second-century gal doesn't know who is killing her colleagues, but she's not about to let an aggravating homicide cop stop her from finding out. Too bad tracking the killer is *exactly* what someone wants her to do....

Enter an exclusive world as we kick off a new continuity series featuring society's secret weapons—a group of heiresses recruited to bring down the world's most powerful criminals! THE IT GIRLS have it going on, and you'll love Erica Orloff's *The Golden Girl* as she tracks a corporate spy in her spiked Jimmy Choos!

Ever feel like pushing the boundaries? So does Kimmer Reed, heroine of *Beyond the Rules* by Doranna Durgin. When her brother sics his enemies on her, Kimmer's ready to take them out. But the rules change when she learns her nieces are pawns in the deadly game....

And don't miss the Special Forces women of the Medusa Project as they track down a hijacked cruise ship, in *Medusa Rising* by Cindy Dees! Medusa surgeon Aleesha Gautier doesn't trust the hijacker who claims he's on their side, but joining forces will allow her to keep her enemy closer....

Enjoy! And please send your comments to me, c/o Silhouette Books, 233 Broadway Ste. 1001, New York, NY 10279.

Sincerely,

Natashya Wilson

Natashya Wilson
Associate Senior Editor, Silhouette Bombshell

Please address questions and book requests to:
Silhouette Reader Service
U.S.: 3010 Walden Ave., P.O. Box 1325, Buffalo, NY 14269
Canadian: P.O. Box 609, Fort Erie, Ont. L2A 5X3

BEYOND THE RULES

Doranna Durgin

BOMBSHELL

Published by Silhouette Books

America's Publisher of Contemporary Romance

SILHOUETTE BOOKS

ISBN 0-373-51373-9

BEYOND THE RULES

Copyright © 2005 by Doranna Durgin

www.SilhouetteBombshell.com

Printed in U.S.A.

Books by Doranna Durgin

Silhouette Bombshell

Exception to the Rule #11
Checkmate #45
Beyond the Rules #59

Silhouette Books

Femme Fatale
"Shaken and Stirred"

Smokescreen
"Chameleon"

DORANNA DURGIN

spent her childhood filling notebooks first with stories and art, and then with novels. After obtaining a degree in wildlife illustration and environmental education, she spent many years deep in the Appalachian Mountains. When she emerged, it was as a writer who found herself irrevocably tied to the natural world and its creatures—and with a new touchstone to the rugged spirit that helped settle the area and which she instills in her characters.

Doranna's first published fantasy novel received the 1995 Compton Crook/Stephen Tall Award for the best first book in the fantasy, science fiction and horror genres. She now has fifteen novels of eclectic genres on the shelves and more on the way; most recently she's leaped gleefully into the world of action-romance. When she's not writing, Doranna builds Web pages, wanders around outside with a camera and works with horses and dogs. There's a Lipizzan in her backyard, a mountain looming outside her office window, a pack of agility dogs romping in the house and a laptop sitting on her desk—and that's just the way she likes it. You can find a complete list of titles at www.doranna.net along with scoops about new projects, lots of silly photos, and a link to her SFF Net newsgroup.

This is for my Nana, who preferred her stories
to be sweet, but whom I'll always think of when
I see this book. In many ways her life was no
less heroic than any Bombshell heroine....

With thanks to Judith's late nights, Jennifer's
smiley faces, Tom's enthusiasm, continuing
conversations in the Things That Go Bang newsgroup
on SFF Net and to Matrice and everyone else
who wanted to see more of Kimmer.

Note: Some of the locations and details are accurate
and really exist, and some of them...don't.
Mwah ha ha! The power of being a writer!

Chapter 1

He's still there.

Still following us, dammit.

Kimmer Reed glanced in the rearview mirror and gave an unladylike snort completely at odds with her shimmery taupe jacquard tunic, her carefully understated makeup and the lingering taste of an exquisite lunch on Captain Bill's Seneca Lake cruise.

The big man filling the passenger seat of her sporty Mazda Miata immediately understood the significance of such a noise. Rio Carlsen turned his gaze away from the picturesque wine country scenery speeding past them—spring-green everywhere—to stretch a long arm across the back of Kimmer's bucket seat, glancing behind them and bracing himself as she took an unsignaled left turn. "Suburban. Big. Old. Can you say 'eat my dust'?"

Kimmer shook her head, short and firm, eyes on the road. She could outrun him…but she wouldn't. She took another left, accelerated down a barely traveled alley on the outer edge of Watkins Glen, shot across a one-way feeder road, and downshifted to take the next left at speed. "This isn't a Hunter Agency assignment. This is my home. There are *rules*."

Rules about how to live…rules for those around her.

Rio's hand strayed from the back of the seat to stroke the hair at Kimmer's nape, a short dark fringe that showed well enough how her hair would explode into curls if she ever freed it from its close cut. A reassuring touch that could turn smoldering in a moment, but right now it wasn't nearly as casual as it might seem. It connected them—and it transmitted his readiness. He said, "Let's go explain the rules, then."

Another glance showed her that the idiot had stayed with her, bouncing along the rough roads on spongy shocks, closing the distance between them. "He's persistent enough. This isn't casual."

Rio glanced behind them. Kimmer knew that quiet tension in his body, the tall rangy strength he hid so well in his amiable nature. "The question is, is this about you or is this about me?"

"Your turf was overseas." The Miata slewed back onto the main road, a two-lane state route between Watkins Glen and Rock Stream. "And you're *ex*-CIA."

"Hey," he said, wounded. "I'm *good* ex-CIA. I might have made an enemy or two. And it doesn't make sense for it to be you. You don't exactly work on your home turf."

"Not if I can help it," she grumbled, not bothering to point out the irony that she'd met him on a job she hadn't wanted simply because it was too close to her childhood home. Her long-buried, long-hated childhood. She blew through a stop sign—not a significant risk on this particular stretch of road— with her eye on the upcoming turn, the one that started off with a decent paved road, turned abruptly to dirt, and even more abruptly came to an end, a service road made obsolete by underground utilities. She thumbed the switch to bring up the Miata's barely open windows. "Check the glove box, will you?"

"God, is it safe?"

Kimmer smiled. "Probably not."

Rio flipped the latch, hands ready to catch whatever spilled out. "Switchblade," he reported, ably maintaining his equilibrium as Kimmer hit her target turn at speed, luring her pursuer along behind…enticing him to carelessness. "Tire gauge. Knuckle-knife thing. And this."

She glanced. "War dart."

He grinned, for the moment truly amused. "War dart. Of course it is."

His wasn't the grin she associated with Ryobe Carlsen, former CIA case officer and skilled overseas operative. No, this particular grin belonged to the man who'd left the Agency after a bullet took his spleen and kidney. Eventually he and Kimmer had collided during one of Kimmer's assignments; eventually he'd turned just this same honest *get a kick out of life* grin on Kimmer. In response she'd turned the fine edge of her no-nonsense temper back on him, and—

And now here he was at Seneca Lake.

Kimmer's car hit the rough seam between asphalt and dirt. She'd gained ground with the turn; she spared an instant to warn Rio with a predatory expression that really couldn't be called a smile.

Rio braced himself.

Kimmer hit the brake, slinging the car around in a neat one-eighty and raising enough dust to obscure the rest of the world. She didn't hesitate but punched down the accelerator, heading back up the road just as fast as she'd come down it. They ripped out of the dust and back onto asphalt, passing the Suburban.

"I think I lost the dart." Rio groped along the side of his bucket seat.

"Got my club," Kimmer said. It was a miniature war club, iron set into smooth red oak wood, sleek with time and use. She handled it with great familiarity and precision.

"You brought your club?" Rio asked. "On our *date?*"

"As if the whole world is about you. Of course I brought it." Kimmer didn't warn him this time; she hit the brake, gave the wheel a calculated tug, and ended up neatly blocking the road. She reached for her seat belt before the car had even rocked to a complete stop. "You coming?"

"Oh, yeah," he murmured, betraying some of the grimness lurking beneath his banter. But he wasn't as fast about pulling his long legs from the car's low frame and Kimmer strode past him as the Suburban's driver—having executed a wide, rambling turn to emerge from the dust and discover himself trapped—came to a clumsy, shock-bobbing stop not far away. The interior of the vehicle filled with a leftover swirl of dust through its half-open windows.

The driver waved away the dust, coughing, as Kimmer stalked his vehicle, alert to any sign that he'd jam the accelerator. The massive Suburban could plow right through her Miata if he wanted it to, but he made no move. As the dust cleared, he seemed oddly mesmerized, watching her with his jaw slightly dropped.

True, she hadn't come dressed for action. She'd come dressed for lunch—the taupe tunic gleamed in the sun, and slimline black gauchos hit just at her knee, offering a low, flat waistband over which she'd fastened a low-slung black leather belt with a big chunky buckle. But her sandals had soles made for walking—or running—and though she held the war club low enough by her thigh to obscure it, he could have no doubt that she held something quite useful indeed.

She didn't give him time to firm up his jaw or to reach for a weapon. Nothing about him set off alarm bells; whoever he was, whatever he wanted, he was well out of his league. She went straight to the door, yanked it open and grabbed his hand from the steering wheel. He yelped in surprise as she flexed it down, levering it against his body to take advantage of the seat belt restraint. "Hello," she said. "Who the hell are you and why are you on my tail?"

"Or my tail," Rio said, coming up on the other side of the window. Kimmer knew that he'd be looking for any signs of a gun, that he'd keep his eye on the man's free hand. He eyed, too, the awkward angle of the man's left arm. "You're not going to break him, are you?"

Kimmer shook her head. "Not yet."

"Hey, hey, *hey*," the man said, and his expression—full of bemusement, floundering in some way Kimmer couldn't understand—didn't fit the situation. Didn't fit it at all. "Ker-rist! Back off, will you?"

Kimmer narrowed her eyes, tipped her head. Thoughtful. There was something about this man…

She knew him.

"Kimmer—" he said, then hissed in pain as her hold tightened.

She knew him.

Not so much the narrow chin and the receding hairline of dark, tight-cropped curls, or the skin, leathery and damaged by sun and cigarettes. Not so much the scowl carved into his forehead.

The eyes. Round, wide-set, thickly lashed. A deep blue, so deep as to look near black unless the light hit them just right.

Kimmer's eyes.

She released the man's hand, slammed the door closed hard enough to rock the vehicle, and turned on her heel, striding back to where the Miata glinted Mahogany Mica in the sun. Maybe, she thought, deliberately taking herself away from this moment, it was time to get that BMW she'd been eyeing. Time to move up.

With the BMW, she could outrun even her past.

Rio came up behind her. In the background, the Suburban's door opened again. Kimmer walked around to the driver's door, brushed dust from the side-view mirror, and slid back behind the wheel. On the passenger side, Rio opened the door, but he didn't get in. He ducked low enough to peer inside. "Hey," he said, a gentle query. "You know him?"

Kimmer didn't look at him. She pressed her lips together, bit her top lip, and was then able to say in an astonishingly moderate tone, "My brother. One of them, anyway. Let's go. We're through here."

She should have known he wouldn't get in. Not with the way he felt about family. He'd never understand her reaction. How could he? For all she'd alluded to her past, she'd never truly explained. He knew she'd turned her life around, remolding herself into the fierce, competent Hunter operative who made her own rules. But she'd never shared the appalling truths of her past.

Because it meant reliving them.

She looked over at him, meeting the almond sweep of his eyes. His Japanese grandmother's eyes, set in the bones of his otherwise Danish family—a face sculpted by the combination. Rio was nothing if not tied to his family, right down to his appearance. And he didn't understand.

A flicker of desperation tightened Kimmer's hands on the steering wheel. "Please," she said. "This is a choice I made a long time ago."

He tipped his head back at the hefty SUV. "It can be a different choice now."

"No," she said tightly. "It can't."

He looked at her for another long heartbeat of time, and then he gave the slightest of shrugs and lowered his tall frame into the low sports car. Kimmer breathed a sigh of relief, thanking him with a glance. They might well talk about this, but Rio had done what Rio did best. He'd let Kimmer be Kimmer, accepting her without trying to change her.

Except this time, just a moment too late. Kimmer's brother crossed in front of the Miata, came around to the driver's window. Kimmer still had time to turn the key, to floor the accelerator—and yet somehow she didn't quite do it. Maybe it was Rio's trust. Maybe she was just tired of running.

Maybe she wanted to think again about pummeling the crap out of a man who had made her childhood miserable.

He stood on the other side of the closed window—not a tall man, nor a bulky one. Like Kimmer in that way. He settled his weight on one leg and crossed his arms. "You don't even know which one I am."

She knew he hadn't changed much, not if he'd tracked her down only to throw that attitude at her.

Of course, he was also right.

"Should I care?" she asked, not unrolling the window. "You all made my life hell. You were interchangeable in that way. Although if I had to guess, the way your ears stick out, I'd say you were Hank."

More than ten years had passed since she'd bolted from Munroville in rural western Pennsylvania. She'd been fifteen and her brothers had been in various stages of older adolescence and early adulthood, still unformed men—their bodies awkward, their facial structures still half in hiding. Hers was a family of late bloomers.

Or never-bloomers.

Her brother colored slightly and lifted his chin in a way so instantly familiar that Kimmer knew she'd been right. Hank. A middle brother, particularly fond of finding ways to blame things gone wrong on Kimmer no matter how minuscule her association with them in the first place. He'd seldom been the first to hit her, but it never took him long to join in. Hank, Jeff, Karl, Tim. They all took their turns.

She started slightly as Rio's hand landed quietly on her leg, only then realizing she'd reached for the club resting beside her at the shift. *You don't know,* she wanted to say to him. *You can't possibly understand.* His family had supported him, surrounded him, welcomed him back home without question when the life he'd chosen had changed so abruptly. Hers had…

A young girl hid in the attic, hands clasped tightly around her knees, face pale and dripping sweat in the furnace summer had made of the enclosed space. She didn't know who'd misplaced the phone bill the first time, or even the second. It could have been between here and the tilted mailbox down the lane; it could have been shoved off the table to make way for one of their filthy magazines. She only knew that today she'd brought in an envelope stamped Final Bill, *and that its arrival was therefore her fault. Her father and brothers had come home before she'd had the chance to slip out the back of the house to the hidey-hole she'd made beneath the barn.*

They didn't know she'd grown tall enough to pull down the ladder stairs and make her way up here. And now she couldn't leave until they were gone. If they spotted her they'd harry her like hounds, shouting and slapping and shoving for something she hadn't done in the first place. She shivered, even in the heat. She could feel their hands, their cruel pinches, blows hard enough to bruise, hidden in places that wouldn't show. And she remembered her mother lying at her father's feet and knew her own life would only get worse as she matured.

A grip tightened on her leg. In a flash, Kimmer snatched up the club, turning on—

Rio.

She withdrew with a noise between a gasp and a snarl. *Never Rio.*

But her brothers had never seen her as anything other than a frightened young girl at their disposal for blaming, controlling and manipulating. A young girl who had highly honed skills of evasion and an uncanny knack for reading the intent of those around her—at least, anyone who wasn't close to her. The closeness…it blinded her instinctive inner eye, kept her guessing.

She'd never been able to read Rio, not from the moment she'd met him. It had terrified her, but she'd learned to trust him. He'd earned it. So now she looked at him with apology for what they both knew she'd almost done, but she wasn't surprised when he made no move to withdraw his hand.

Rio didn't scare easily.

Kimmer took a deep breath and turned back to Hank, the window remaining between them. "I'm not even going to bother to ask why you thought you could or should run me down in a high-speed car chase. Just tell me why the hell you're here."

"I need to talk to you," he said, and his mouth took on that sullen expression she knew too well, a knowing that came flooding back after years of pretending it didn't exist. "You shouldn't have run. It would have been a lot easier for both of us if you'd just pulled over when you noticed me."

"A lot easier for *you*. I like a good adrenaline hit now and then. Or did you really think I didn't know this was a dead-end road?"

Surprise crossed his face; it hadn't occurred to him. "Anyway," he said, as if they hadn't had that part of the conversation, "I had to be sure it was you. Leo told me you'd changed a lot—"

"Leo." Kimmer rolled her eyes, exchanging a quick, knowing look with Rio. Leo Stark, hometown bully and family friend from way back when. Not *her* friend. Not then, and not when he'd cropped up again to interfere with her work just six months earlier. "Damn him. It wasn't enough I gave him a chance to be a hero for Mill Springs last fall? Stop the bad guys, save the country, keep the damsel in distress alive?"

For when Rio had come home to recuperate from CIA disaster, he'd slipped seamlessly back into civilian life, applying a fine hand to custom boat repairs and paint jobs—but only until his cousin Carolyne drew him back into the world of clandestine ops.

Except Kimmer, too, had been assigned to project Carolyne. Of course they'd collided. Disagreed. Worked it out. And now he'd come to cautiously discuss part-time work with the same Hunter Agency that employed Kimmer. Cautious, because he'd been sacrificed on the job once already. But doing it, because Hunter's intense, personal approach was so completely different from his experience with the CIA. In the CIA, one field officer's hubris had nearly killed him, and the chief of station hadn't prevented it. At Hunter, the loyalty between operatives and staff was a given.

Hunter's international reputation for effectiveness was why the agency had been tapped to watch Carolyne, a computer programmer extraordinaire who'd been on everyone's snatch list when she uncovered—and developed the fix for— a security weakness in the current crop of missile laser guidance systems. The bad guys, professionals at the beck and call of those who wanted to exploit that weakness. And Leo Stark's role had been a desperate ploy on Kimmer's part to keep him from focusing on *her.* Because it was Kimmer he'd wanted—Kimmer who'd been promised to him not so much as a wife than as a servant. *Leo. Dammit.*

"He was right, I guess. Must have cost a pretty penny to fix you up like this." He lifted an appreciative eyebrow.

She snorted. "Is that your idea of a compliment? It's supposed to make me stick around long enough to hear what you have to say?"

Hank scowled. "Don't make this harder than it has to be. I've come all this way to find you. That must count for something."

Yeah. It pissed her off.

But there was Rio sitting next to her, knowing only how upset she was and not quite understanding; the puzzlement showed in the faintest of frowns, the only outward sign of his struggle to comprehend the strength of her reaction. And he'd never understand if she literally left Hank in the dust.

You want to know my family, Rio? Okay then.

She raised an eyebrow at Hank. "Coming all this way doesn't count for a thing," she told him. "But let's just call it your lucky day. I'll bet you know where I live, too." She wouldn't have been hard to find once Leo pointed Hank in the direction of Seneca Lake; she was in the phone book. She'd never made any effort to hide who she really was— she'd never expected them to care enough to come looking.

Whyever Hank had tracked her down, it wasn't because he cared. He might still want to control her, he might still want to use her, but he didn't want to renew any kind of family relationship.

Rio would learn that.

Outside the window, Hank nodded. For an instant, she thought he actually looked relieved, but a second glance showed her only the arrogant certainty that she'd see things his way. But whatever had inspired him to invade her world...

It wouldn't be good enough.

Kimmer had little to say on the way home. Full of glower and resentment and anger, she took the curving roads at satisfying speed, reveling in the way the car clung to the road and how it leaped to the challenge when she accelerated in the last section of each swoop of asphalt. She left the Suburban far, far behind and when she pulled the Miata to an abrupt stop beside Rio's boxy Honda Element in her sloping driveway, she exited the car with purpose.

Shedding and gathering clothes along the way, she climbed the stairs to the remodeled second floor of the old house— two small bedrooms and a bathroom turned into one giant master suite—and dumped the lunch outfit on the unmade bed. She replaced it with a clean pair of low-rise blue jeans from the shelves in her walk-in closet, and a clingy ribbed cotton sweater with laces dangling from the cross-tie sleeves. Red.

If Hank thought he was here to see his *little* sister, he had a thing or two coming.

She jammed the war club in her back pocket—Hank would do well to pale if he recognized it, given the events of the night she'd departed—and headed back down the stairs.

Rio puttered in the kitchen, putting away lunch leftovers and the desserts they'd brought home for later. He'd poured them each a glass of bright blue Kool-Aid, his current favorite flavor, Raspberry Reaction. A third glass stood off to the side, filled with ice, waiting to see what Hank preferred. Rio didn't react as she stood in the kitchen entrance, slipping athletic Skechers over her bare feet, but he knew she was there; he pointed at the glass he'd filled for her.

As usual, he seemed to fill the room—he always filled the room, no matter how large it was, though calling her kitchen roomy went beyond exaggeration and straight to blatant lie. He'd gone to lunch in a tailored sport coat over jeans and a collarless short-sleeved shirt, a look he carried off with much panache. Now he'd dumped the coat and still looked…good.

Oh, yeah.

For a wistful moment, Kimmer wished they could simply lock the door and exchange frantic Kool-Aid flavored kisses. Forget Hank, forget family…just Rio and Kimmer, warming up the house on a beautiful spring day.

But Hank was on the way. They had no more than minutes. In fact, he should have been here by now. Kimmer strongly suspected he'd gotten lost. She wished she could take credit for the missing street sign between her street and the main road…it was enough that she'd neglected to mention it to Hank. She sighed heavily and reached for the cold glass.

The sigh got his attention. He turned to look at her, tossing the hand towel back into haphazard place over the stove handle, his mouth already open to say something, but abruptly hesitating on the words. He stared; she raised her eyebrows. He cleared his throat. "I like that sweater."

Kimmer smoothed down the hem. "It's unexpectedly easy to remove," she informed him.

"That's not fair." He seemed to have forgotten he held his drink.

She shrugged at his ruefulness over Hank's impending arrival. "You're the one who wanted me to give Hank his say."

That brought him back down to earth. "But—" He narrowed his eyes at her, accenting the angle of them "—you told me you couldn't use your knack on me."

"I can't," she said, sipping the drink. It wasn't what she'd have chosen, but it was cold and felt good on her throat.

"Ah." His expression turned more rueful yet. "That obvious, am I?"

"Oh, yeah." She gave him a moment to digest the notion, then nodded at the front door. "Let's wait on the porch. I don't want to invite him in."

He followed her outside, latching the screen door against the cat she seemed to have acquired when Rio moved in— an old white marina cat with black blotches, half an ear and half a front leg missing. Rio had seemed almost as surprised as Kimmer when it showed up along with him, muttering some lame-ass explanation about how it was too old to survive alone at the dock. OldCat, he called it.

Big softie. That was Rio, deep down. Too intensely affected by the lives of those he cared about, even the life of a used-up cat.

Though the cat did look comfortable on her front window sill.

Kimmer helped herself to a corner of the porch swing and sat cross-legged, shuffling off her Skechers. Rio took up the rest of the seat and stretched his legs out before him, taking up the duty of nudging the thing back and forth ever so slightly. Down by the barely visible stop sign, a blotchy green-on-green Suburban traveled slowly down the main road, passing by her unidentified street.

Rio settled his glass on the arm of the swing. "You may have to go get him."

Kimmer didn't think so.

After a moment, she said, "When I was little, my mother used to rock with me."

"I thought—"

"Before she died," Kimmer said dryly. "Sometimes my father would be out with my brothers—some sports event, usually. It was the only time we had together. And she spent it rocking me, trying to pretend she wasn't crying. It was too late for her, she said, but not for me. So she spent that time whispering her rules to me. How to survive. Making damn sure I wouldn't end up like she did."

He frowned, hitched his leg up and shifted his back into the corner pillow. They'd been a long time sitting this day; no doubt it was starting to ache. If so, he didn't pay it any close attention. "You've never really said—"

"No. I haven't. Who'd want to?" She felt herself grow smaller, drawn in to be as inconspicuous as a child hiding desperately in an attic. Except as soon as she realized it, she shook herself out of it, deliberately relaxed her legs to more of an open lotus position. "I don't want to go into it right now. I can't. I've got Hank to deal with. But I wanted you to know at least that much, before you watch how I handle this. Every time I say or do something you wouldn't even consider saying or doing to your family, think about the fact that my mother used her most precious private time making

sure I knew no one would take care of me but me. Making
sure I always knew to have a way out. That I always knew
what the people around me were doing. That I always saw
them first."

"You're talking in halves." He prodded her with a sock-
enclosed toe, gently, and then withdrew. "There's so much
you're leaving out."

*She heard the sounds before she even reached the house.
Flesh against flesh. Chairs overturning. A muffled cry.*

*When she was younger, she wouldn't let herself believe it.
But she was eight now, and she had her world figured out.
She flung her school papers to the ground, gold stars and all.
She charged up the porch stairs and through the creaky screen
door and all the way to the kitchen, and she was only an instant away from launching herself onto her father's back,
right where the sweat seeped through his shirt from the effort of hitting her mama, when Mama looked up from the floor
and cried out for her to stop.*

*Startled, her father turned around to glare at her. "You'd
better think twice, little girl."*

She'd looked at her mama, pleading. Let me help. *Her
mama shook her head, right there where she'd fallen against
the cupboard, her lip bleeding and her eye swelling, the
kitchen chairs tumbled around her. She lifted her chin and she
said, "Remember what I told you, Kimmer. Stay out of this."*

And her father closed the door.

"Yeah," Kimmer told Rio. "There's so much I'm leaving out."

Hank's Suburban crawled into her driveway only a few
moments later, as Rio did what only Rio could do—establish
a connection between himself and Kimmer solely with the

honest, thoughtful intensity of his gaze. He'd done so even before he really knew her, baffling Kimmer into temporary retreat. Always it was about trying to understand what lay beneath the surface—and though he usually did a spooky job of uncovering just that, this time Kimmer could see the struggle. He couldn't quite fathom how it had truly been, or how resolutely it had shaped her. "You don't have to understand right this minute," she told him, a quiet murmur as Hank slammed the reluctant door of the old Suburban and made his way up to the porch with misplaced confidence. "Just keep it in mind."

And Rio nodded, going quiet in that way that would leave her free to deal with Hank.

Hank jammed his hands in his back pockets and settled into the arrogance of his hipshot stance. "I get the feeling you're not going to invite me in."

"It's a pleasant afternoon." Kimmer looked out over the yard, where daffodils and forsythia still bloomed. "Why waste it?"

"*Kimmer.* That was Mama's nickname, once. And you're just like her. She didn't know how to take care of family, either. She died to get away from us…you just ran."

She gave a little laugh. "What makes you madder? That I escaped, or that I've done well?"

"Is that what you call this?" He glanced at the little house behind her, the modest yard before her. The Morrows on one side, the Flints on the other.

"Ah." She looked over the yard in bloom, that in which she found such peace. "If this is your strategy to keep me listening, it's not working very well so far." She glanced at her watch. "I've got a meeting to attend, so if you've got something to say, best say it. Otherwise, go away."

Rio knew better than to give her a puzzled glance, even though he knew she had nothing planned for the afternoon, that Hunter had her on call but not on assignment. That she was expected to visit and confer on some upcoming operations, but had no set time for doing so. No, Hunter wasn't what she had in mind. Not with those long legs of his stretched out beside her—not to mention the smudge of Kool-Aid blue at the corner of his mouth. Quite clearly, it needed to be kissed off. Maybe Raspberry Reaction was her favorite flavor after all.

And then Hank blurted, "I need your help."

For an instant, words eluded her. When she found them, they were blunt. "You must be kidding."

"You think I came all the way up here to kid you?" Hank threw his arms up, a helpless gesture. "You think I *want* to be here talking to you and your—"

"Ryobe Carlsen," Rio said in the most neutral of tones. "*Konnichiwa*. We can shake hands another time."

Hank's eyes narrowed, and suddenly Kimmer thought they looked nothing like hers at all. "You were there," he said to Rio. "Leo said there was a man involved."

"There were several, in fact. But I was one of them. I was certainly there when Leo mentioned how you planned to hand Kimmer over to him."

Relief washed through Kimmer. Rio might not truly understand what Kimmer's family did—or more to the point, *didn't*—mean to her, but he knew Hank had a lot to prove. She should have known, should have trusted Rio.

Of course, that wasn't something that came easily. Emotional trust was against the rules.

She took a deep breath, suddenly aware of just how much this encounter was taking from her. Tough Kimmer, keeping up her tough front when all she wanted to do was ease across the swing into Rio's arms. Except—

It was her own job to take care of herself. Her very first lesson.

So at the end of that deep breath, she made herself sound bored. "I can't imagine how you think I can help you at all."

"Leo said…well, hell, you made an impression on Leo. He says you took down the Murty brothers when you were in Mill Springs. And he came back to Munroville spouting stories about terrorists. He said you'd taken them out."

Kimmer flicked her gaze at Rio. "I wasn't alone."

"He said they shot you, and you didn't even flinch."

She touched her side, where the scar was fading. It had only been a crease at that. She shrugged. "I was mad."

"He said," Hank continued doggedly, "that you were *connected.* That your people came into Mill Springs and did such a cleanup job that the cops never had anything to follow through on. Even those two guys you sent to the hospital—Homeland Security walked away with them."

"Leo talks a lot," Kimmer said. But she suppressed a smile. Damned if Hank didn't actually sound impressed. "And you still haven't gotten to the point."

"The point," Hank told her, "is that that's the kind of help I need."

"You want me to get shot for you?" Kimmer shook her head. "Not gonna happen."

"You gotta make this hard, don't you?" Hank shifted his weight impatiently, coming precariously close to Kimmer's freshly blooming irises.

Yes. But she had the restraint to remain silent, and he barged right on through. "Look, I'm in over my head. I let some people use a storage building for…something. They turned out to be a rough crew, more'n I wanted to deal with. An' I've got a wife and kids—bet you didn't even know I had kids—and I wanted out. Except I saw a murder, damned bad luck. They know I want out, and they don't trust me to keep my mouth shut." He looked at her with a defiant jut to his jaw, daring her to react to the story. To judge him.

Kimmer sat silently, absorbing it all. Hank on the run from goonboys. Hank scared enough to track down a sister he'd abused and openly scorned. Hank here before her, asking for help she wasn't sure she could or would give him. *Assuming I believe a word of it in the first place.* Wouldn't it be just like her brothers to send one of them to lure her back down home where they probably thought they could control her?

Out loud, she said thoughtfully, "'Bad luck' is when you're on your way to church and someone runs a red light in front of you. Witnessing nastiness at the hands of the goonboys you've invited into your home is more under the heading of 'what did you expect?'"

His face darkened, something between anger and humiliation. "You gotta be a bitch about it? I'm asking for help here, Kimmer."

"I'm not sure just *what* you're asking," Kimmer told him. Except suddenly she knew, and she spat a quick, vicious curse. "You want me to kill them. You actually want me to *kill* them."

Hank hesitated, startled both by her perception and her anger, and put up a hand up as though it would slow either.

Rio looked at her in astonishment—Mr. Spy Guy, somehow not yet jaded enough to believe this to be something a brother would ask a sister.

But Kimmer, so mad she could barely see straight, still caught the unfamiliar sedan traveling too fast as it passed by her street. She watched as it stopped and backed up to hover at the intersection.

"Dammit, Hank, did you tell anyone you were coming to see me?"

Startled, he at first looked as if he'd resist answering just because he didn't like her tone. By then Kimmer was on her feet, now bare. Rio, too, had come out without shoes. Sock-foot. He never wore outdoor footgear in the house out of respect for his Japanese grandmother's early teaching, even if he didn't use the proper slippers while indoors.

Family. She wanted to snarl the word out loud. She didn't take the time. Hank had followed her gaze and blurted, "Just a few people, but they didn't know why—"

"They didn't have to," Kimmer said, and by then Rio was beside her—and the sedan had turned sharply onto the narrow back street of wide-set houses, the acceleration of the engine clearly audible. "Keys, Hank!"

"What—"

She turned her gaze away from the car long enough to snap a look at him. "Your damn car keys. Hand them over!" She didn't wait for compliance, but headed for him. No time to run inside for any of her handguns, no time to hesitate over anything at all.

"They're in the—hey!"

"They've already spotted it," Rio said, close behind her.

"You don't have to come," she told him, no sting to her words, just simple assessment of the situation as she hauled the door open and climbed into the driver's seat.

"Coming anyway," he said, just as matter-of-factly. And then gave Hank a little shove toward the back door on his way past. In a moment, he sat beside Kimmer. Hank sat in the back, still baffled.

"Where's the shotgun?" Kimmer asked, cranking the engine. It hesitated; she gave it a swift kick of gas and it caught, rumbling unhappily.

"I don't—"

"You *do*. Where?" She wrestled the gear shift into reverse, giving the approaching sedan a calculating glance. *We're not fast enough.*

"Under the seat," Hank admitted, and Rio ducked to grab it. "Why—"

"What did you think?" She snorted, backing them down the driveway. "Have it out right here in my neighborhood, with all these innocent people going about their lives? In my own *house?*"

"I didn't think you'd run!" Hank snapped. "But then, that's what you're good at, isn't it?"

"When the moment's right." Kimmer cranked the wheel to catapult them out into the street, looking back over her shoulder through the rear glass of the big utility vehicle.

Too close. They're way too close.

She couldn't make herself feel any particular concern about her brother's safety, but this moment didn't have to be about Hank. It was about the goonboys, who were now chasing not only Hank, but Kimmer and Rio. Rio, whom she wouldn't allow to be hurt again. With the vehicle still whining in reverse, she locked her gaze on the rearview mirror. There they were. Goonboys, to be sure—guns at the ready, assumed victory molding their expressions.

She wasn't in the habit of letting the goonboys win.

Kimmer jammed down the accelerator and watched their eyes widen.

Chapter 2

The crash resounded along the street. Mrs. Flint popped up from her flower garden next door, horror on her face. Kimmer didn't wait for her rattled head to settle or her vision to clear. She ground the balky gears from Reverse to Drive and jammed her foot back down on the accelerator, bare foot stretching to make the distance.

The bumper fell off behind them. "Son of a bitch!" Hank groused, scrambling to find a seat belt that had probably disappeared between the seat cushions years ago.

Kimmer glanced in the rearview only to discover it had been knocked totally askew, but Rio saw it, too. He looked back and then turned a grin on her. "Nice," he said. "They're stalled and steaming." He racked the shotgun with quick efficiency, counting the cartridges. "Four. And here I was thinking you might have bored out the magazine plug."

"That's not legal," Hank muttered, still in search of the seat belt as Kimmer bounced them along the uneven street, discovering waves in the pavement she hadn't even considered before.

"Oh, please," she said while Rio loaded—one in the chamber, three in the magazine. "You just haven't done it yet. Got more ammo?"

"'Course. Under the seat somewheres."

"Find it." She hit the brake, found it soft and unresponsive, and stomped down hard to make a wallowing turn uphill. "This thing drives like a boat."

"Needs new brakes," Hank said. He pawed through the belongings in the backseat, tossing take-out food wrappers out of his way.

"Needs brakes," Kimmer repeated. "You don't say." And to Rio, "How's it look?"

A glance, a resigned grimace. "They're on the move again. You have a plan?"

"One that doesn't include outrunning them?" she said dryly, glancing at the speedometer. Just forty miles per hour—fast enough in this rural-residential area. "Yes. Get the high ground. Pick them off if we have to. Hope my neighbors called the police."

"I love that about you," he said. "So efficient. Bash the bad guys—"

"BGs," she reminded him.

"—and get the cops in on things at the same time."

"Cops?" Hank popped up from his search. "If I'd wanted to go to the cops, I woulda called 'em from my place and saved myself the trip!"

"Quit whining," Kimmer said shortly. "And find that box. Unless you just want to get out now? I can slow down—"

"This isn't my hunting vehicle, you know. Dunno that I'll find—whoop!"

Kimmer had no doubt that without his seat belt on that last hump of road, he'd been riding air. White picket fence flashed by the side windows as they hit a washboard dirt road and another incline. She spared a hand to grab quickly at the rear-view mirror and straighten it. The road made perfection impossible, but now she could get her own glimpses of their pursuit.

Too close. She made a wicked face at the mirror. "Dammit."

"Still going with Plan A?"

"There isn't a Plan B. Besides, the last little bit is completely rutted—" this as she manhandled the Suburban around a turn that took them from dirt-and-gravel to dirt-and-grass— "and I don't think they can make it." They'd left the last farmhouse far behind and now climbed the road over a mound with picturesque spring-green trees. At the crest of that hill the road faded away into a small clearing, one that bore evidence of being a lovers' lane, teenage hangout and child's playground. Condoms, beer cans and a swinging tire.

On the nights when Kimmer couldn't sleep, she found it the perfect target for a fast, dark training run. Less than a mile or so from home, a good uphill climb and at the end a perfect view of the descending moon on those nights when there was a moon at all.

The Suburban creaked and jounced and squeaked, and then abruptly slowed as Kimmer carefully placed the wheels so they wouldn't ground out between ruts. A glance in the rearview mirror and...*ah, yes.* The sedan had lost ground. Pretty soon they'd be walking, unless they didn't realize this road dead-ended and gave up, thinking the Suburban would just keep grinding along, up and over and down again.

Though if they stuck around long enough, they'd hear the Suburban's lingering engine noise.

Kimmer crested the hill, swinging the big vehicle in a swooping curve that didn't quite make it between two trees; the corner of the front bumper took a hit.

"Hey!" Hank sat up in indignant protest, scowling into the rearview mirror when no one responded to his squawk. Kimmer finally put the gearshift in Park, unsnapped her seat belt with one hand and held out the other for the shotgun. "Keep looking for those shells," she told Hank.

"And Plan A is…?" Rio asked.

"I can get a vantage point on them. See if you can find something else in this heap that we can use as a weapon. Tire iron, maybe. Any other nefarious thing Hank might have collected. I've got my club, too." She twisted around to look at Hank. "I changed my mind. Get your ass up here and turn this thing around. It's going to take time we won't want to waste if they do come up here on foot."

"Jeez, when did you get to be such a bitch?" Hank gave her a surly look. "I came up here for help, not to get pussy-whipped."

"You've got help." Kimmer assessed the semiautomatic, a gun made for a bigger shooter than she'd ever be. No surprise. "You just thought you were going to call the shots. Well, guess what? Wrong." She slid out the door. Rio was already out and at the back, rummaging around. "Watch your feet," she told him. "There's broken glass up here."

"Got it. And got the tire iron. I'll keep looking."

With little grace, Hank climbed down from the backseat and up into the driver's side. With exaggerated care he began the long back-and-forth process of turning the SUV around.

Kimmer took a few loping steps to the nearest tree, the

maple with the tire swinging from a branch made just for that purpose. A lower branch on the other side acted as a step. She pulled herself up one-handed, climbing the easiest route to the branch from which the tire hung. From there she looked down on the road they'd just traversed. It passed almost directly beneath the tire before the hairpin turn that ended at the top of the hill. From there the area spread out before her—small farms and then the smaller tracts of her neighborhood in neat, topographically parallel streets.

The pursuing sedan sat barely visible through the trees, not moving. With the grind of the Suburban swapping ends and gears in the small space behind her, Kimmer couldn't hear anything of the men who'd been in the sedan, and she couldn't yet see them.

She waited. Her toes flexed on smooth maple bark, her fingers warmed the wood stock on the shotgun, and she waited, plastered up against the tree to put as much of herself behind the trunk as possible. Beneath her, Rio came to stand beside it—a second set of eyes. And Hank finally finished turning around and cut the engine.

Blessed silence. And then in the roadside not far below them, a flock of kinglets exploded into noisy scolding, flittering from bush to bush like parts of a perpetual-motion machine. Kimmer rested the shotgun barrel on a tree branch and snugged it into place against her shoulder as Rio eased back behind the tree. She raised her voice to reach those slinking below. "That's far enough."

The birds hopscotched away through the brush. An annoyed voice asked, "Who—*what*—the hell are you?"

"I haven't decided yet, but I'm still young," Kimmer said airily. "Hank will tell you I'm a bitch, though, and I suppose that's really all you need to know. Plus I bashed up your nice

car. I also have you in my sights and this is double-ought
buckshot, too. It's gonna sting, boys. Where do you want I
should aim it?"

The reply came as something inarticulate and disbelieving, a strong Pittsburgh accent in play. Kimmer glanced down
at Rio, who looked up with perfect timing to raise an eyebrow
at her.

"Hunter's going to hate this," Kimmer told him. "They really want us to play nice in their backyard."

"Look, sputzie," said one of the BGs. "We only want the
scrawny guy we followed here. There's no need for you to
get hurt."

"No need at all," Kimmer agreed, hoping she heard the
sound of small-town-cop sirens in the distance. Unless these
suited goonboys took off across country on foot, they couldn't
leave this little section of Glenora without meeting the cops
on the way out. And Kimmer would be on their tail…squeeze
play. She saw a rustle of movement and carefully sighted a
foot in front of it, squeezing the trigger of the twelve-gauge.

The spring brush exploded in bits of leaves and twigs.
Damn, that thing has a kick. But she'd been prepared and
stayed firmly in position, braced between the spreading
limbs. The goonboys scrambled wildly into the bushes, cursing copiously. Kimmer saw a glint of metal. "Here it comes."

A quick volley of shots from someone who obviously felt he
had ammo to spare, and Kimmer ducked behind the tree trunk.
She was sure they were out of pistol range, but even goonboys
got lucky. They'd take turns laying down cover to dart up the
side of the road, getting closer…maybe getting close enough.

Rio knew it, too. "I'm going to draw them off," he said.
"I doubt I can get their interest more than once…better not
waste it."

Blam! Blam!

"Won't," Kimmer told him. *Won't waste anything.*

"What the hell?" Hank growled loudly from the SUV between gunshot volleys. "Don't play games with these people, Kimmer! Just...*do* something!"

Blamblamblam!

"Nice," Kimmer told him, her cheek still pressed against smooth bark. "You don't even have the guts to say it. What is it you want me to do, Hank? Exactly?"

Blam! Blamblamblam!

"Whatever it takes!" Hank's voice crept toward panic. "Just stop them!"

Uh-huh.

Blamblam—click!

"Reload," she said, but Rio was already away, running crouched just behind the crest of the hill and heading for another tree. He made a god-awful amount of noise and then took position behind the tree, holding the tire iron up to his shoulder so the sun glinted along its length.

They took the bait. They turned toward him, revealing themselves to Kimmer, and as one BG slammed a new magazine home, the other raised his pistol at Rio.

Kimmer aimed between them and took a deep breath. No turning back now. Once she drew blood, she'd be explaining herself to the local law; she'd also drag Hunter into the mess. From this distance the pellet spread meant she'd hit them both without truly damaging them. It wouldn't end this confrontation unless they took it as the warning it was and withdrew.

If only the cops were closer.

But now it was more than Hank in trouble. Rio stood within their sights, drawing fire for her. Drawing it from Hank, who deserved no such sacrifice.

Kimmer pulled the trigger.

They both went down, tumbling away in surprise, losing ground downhill away from the road. Good. That bought some time for the cops to close in. Not much time, but—

She and Rio startled in unison as the Suburban's engine revved. *Hank! That puny-assed—*

Rio reacted immediately, running for the vehicle with long strides, dirt sticking to his socks and the tire iron in hand. The SUV swung past him, building speed, and with a grunt of effort he managed to draw even to the open tailgate and fling himself into the back. For an instant Kimmer thought he'd bounce right out again, but he must have found something to grab on to; his feet disappeared inside.

And that left Kimmer. Kimmer, sitting in a tree and staring stupidly at her stupid brother's stupid break for it. So much for the plan to sandwich the BGs between Kimmer and the cops she'd so fervently hoped would arrive in time.

No way in hell was she leaving Rio to take this one alone. Not when she had the only gun.

Though maybe while he was bouncing around in the back, he'd find those shotgun shells they needed so sorely.

The shotgun had a sling strap. She pushed the safety on and ducked through the strap, freeing her hands so she could climb swiftly out on the branch and then down the rope to the tire. She could just barely push off the side of the hill while crouching in the tire and she did it, swinging back closer to push harder, propelling herself into the open air over the road as the BGs struggled to pull themselves together, smarting and bleeding but still well-armed.

And here came Hank, hauling the Suburban around the hairpin turn from the clearing, forced to slow down for the rutted section. Kimmer adjusted the arc of her swing, leaning to the side and pushing the tire around until she hung precariously out over nothing, high enough to see nothing but sky.

Time to let go. And if her timing was off, to go splat.

Kimmer landed with a painful klunk, denting the roof under the luggage rack. The shotgun smacked her in the back of the head, the metal smacked her bare feet and palms, and her forehead made contact with…something. She squinched her face up as if that would clear her head, clinging to the luggage rack as the vehicle bounced beneath her.

"Kimmer?"

That was Rio's voice, filtered through metal and glass and creaking shocks, and she thumped the roof twice in affirmation. She wanted to bellow to Hank that he should slow down—hell, he should just plain stop—but he'd already scraped the Suburban by the sedan in a painful screech of metal and she knew better than to think he might give her shouting a second thought. Best to just hang on.

Yeah. So much for Plan A.

The road grew a little smoother, giving Kimmer the wherewithal to turn around and watch their back.

And here came the sedan. Backing down a road it hadn't been built to climb in the first place, and doing it with the careless haste that said the driver had already decided it would be sacrificed to the cause.

Which was killing Hank. And now, killing Kimmer and Rio.

She flattened out over the luggage rack, wrenching the shotgun around into a useable position. Eventually the road would get smoother. Eventually she wouldn't have to hang on with all her fingers and toes just to keep from being jounced over the side.

They hit pavement. The sedan lost ground with a hasty three-point turn but then more than made up for it with the increased speed of forward movement. Hank responded with a lead foot, and they screamed downhill toward the residential area far too quickly for the sake of playing children or loose livestock. *You fool. I took us away from this area for a reason.* From inside the vehicle came the sound of raised voices, Rio's emphatic and Hank's shrill and defiant. The Suburban wove back and forth, wildly but briefly, and then continued as it had been. Kimmer, a little vertiginous at the landscape speeding backward past her, took the activity to mean that Rio had tried but failed to wrest some sort of control from Hank. And then they hit a series of turns for which she could only clutch to the luggage rack, grateful for its presence and cursing centrifugal force.

He couldn't have any idea where he was going.

Nor did Kimmer, until she finally got a glimpse of the Dairy Queen on the way by and knew the road they traveled, and where it went.

Where it stopped.

The docks.

Kimmer could only imagine Hank's cursing when he realized he'd driven into the asphalt equivalent of a box canyon. Quaint, bobbing wooden docks all around them on this little jetty, populated by a plethora of gently rocking boats— sailboats, pontoon boats, a speedboat or two. No launching bay; this area was meant for cars to back up and unload. Not even enough room for the Suburban to turn around without backing up to the wider parking, bait sales and gas and propane refill area they'd just passed.

No time for that.

The Suburban rocked to an uncertain halt. Kimmer gave two sharp knocks on the roof beneath her, letting Rio know she was still aboard. She uncrimped her fingers from the luggage rack and pushed up to her elbows, bringing the shotgun to bear.

The sedan, unsteady on its wheels from the abuse it had taken, shot around the corner into the parking area. The goon-boys were just mad enough to keep accelerating when they could easily have crawled to a stop and still had the same result.

The Suburban was trapped at the end of the lot with only one place to go.

Seneca Lake.

With perfect timing, an old station wagon loaded to the fenders with kids and fishing gear and flotation devices came ambling around the corner, not far behind the sedan.

And this, Hank, is why I took us up the damned hill.

Two cartridges left and no other way to warn the innocent bystanders on this family-run dock. With a wicked curse, Kimmer jumped to her feet, legs braced wide, toes finding purchase on the roof rack. Only peripherally aware of the vehicle's sway beneath her as Rio disembarked, she pointed the shotgun at the sky and pulled the trigger.

The station wagon screeched to a halt; the figures within made emphatic gestures at her and each other. Other people on the edge of her vision reacted, withdrawing. Someone shouted at her.

And the sedan kept coming.

One cartridge left.

With deliberate movement, Kimmer resettled the gun at her shoulder, perfectly aware of the dramatic silhouette she made standing braced on top of the SUV. She considered it fair warning. She'd fired on them before; they'd know she wasn't bluffing. She could see their silhouettes: big, dark blots, the passenger with his gun held ready. They'd be out and shooting as soon as they stopped—or out and grabbing up prisoners, which could only lead to shooting in the end. They didn't know her. They must be counting on her nerve to fail in this peculiar game of chicken.

Wrong.

Kimmer pulled the trigger.

Someone screamed. The windshield shattered and the car veered wildly. For a moment Kimmer thought it would plow right into the Suburban. She crouched, ready to leap away from any collision, and then the car sheered away toward the side of the parking lot and the clear path to the—

"Kimmer!" Rio shouted, and Kimmer dove for him, perfectly willing to use him as a landing pad to get behind cover because *anysecondnow*—

The goonboys and their car ran smack into the propane storage tank, smack at the juncture of tank with intake and outflow pipes. The initial impact of metal against metal preceded the explosion by just enough time to distinguish one sound from the other.

Kimmer hit Rio and Rio hit the ground and the ground rocked beneath them. Shrapnel struck the Suburban in a series of staccato pings; jagged shards of tank metal dug into the asphalt and the wooden docks beyond. The station-wagon family and any other spectators were long gone. The dizzying blast of noise settled into the roar of flames as the sedan burned. From inside the Suburban, Hank muttered a long string of profanities, making free and repeated use of the phrase "fuckin' crazy bitch."

Kimmer pushed herself off Rio's chest. She found it a good sign that he helped, disentangling their arms to support her shoulders. She found his eyes, the warm sienna irises almost hidden by pupils wide with shock and anger and concern. She grinned down at him. "Hey," she said. "Was it good for you?"

Owen Hunter, Rio thought, had used remarkable restraint. At the time Rio had been too pumped to appreciate it, stalking around with the impulse to pick up the damned tire iron even though there was nothing left to hit and the cops would have taken him down for it anyway.

Or they would have tried.

"How's your back?" Kimmer had kept asking and he'd repeatedly said it was fine, knowing it would be a lie once the adrenaline rush faded, but for the moment, true enough. Besides which, another six months of physical therapy had made the difference; he hadn't expected further improvement at this point but he'd gotten some anyway.

All a good thing, for by the time the fire department, the cops and Owen Hunter had hashed out the situation to everyone's temporary satisfaction—meaning the fire chief was unhappy, the cops were disgruntled but willing to discuss things further without making outright arrests and Owen Hunter had displayed his remarkable restraint any number of times—Rio had stiffened up considerably and was thankful for the heating pad now tucked between the side where his kidney had once been and the oversized, overstuffed recliner of Kimmer's he found so comfortable.

More comfortably yet, Kimmer sat sideways in his lap, curled up to flip through the style magazine she'd finally fessed up was a guilty pleasure after he'd found it tucked behind the cookbook she never used. Not quite under the mattress, but she blushed enough so it might as well have been.

He liked that she'd blushed. She wouldn't have been that vulnerable with anyone else. She'd have kicked his ass for snooping around.

Not snooping. He lived here now. For now. Him and the battered, failing OldCat he hadn't been able to leave on his own back at the Michigan dock. For now and for...who knew? Kimmer's wasn't a large house, and her personality filled it. Claimed it. Made Rio aware of how hard she'd fought to get here, and that unlike himself, she'd never shared space with a loving, squabbling, all-for-one family.

Just the hard, cruel family which included the man now watching ESPN in the small TV room, a space meant for a dining room but where Kimmer had chosen to isolate the television so she could have this den for quiet moments. Perfect, quiet moment, turning the pages of her magazine while Rio rode the edge of sleep beneath her, arms loosely around her waist, hands clasped against her hip, feeling the rise and fall of her breathing, her slight movements as she scanned the pages, the occasional nearly silent snort of derision at some piece of haute couture for which she saw no use, the movement of her shoulders when she grinned, laughing under her breath at some joke within the pages. Eventually she rested the magazine on the fat arm of the chair and let her head tip against his shoulder, her short curls soft against his neck. Dark curls, so short they never grew sun-streaked. Intense, like Kimmer herself.

After some moments, she murmured, "Sleeping?"

"Yes."

She moved slightly against him. *Oh, yeah.* Wuh. *Like that.* And then she said, "No, you're not."

He smiled without opening his eyes. "Honey," he said, "I could be almost dead and *that* would still happen."

Her cheek moved against his shoulder as she, too, smiled. "Okay, then," she said. "Just checking."

"Nice shooting, by the way."

"Had to be. Last cartridge. I wasn't expecting the whole propane-tank thing, though."

"I wasn't expecting Hank to identify the men as the ones running his chop shop." Rio kept his voice low, although the televised sound of car engines and crowds—and his sporadic couch coaching—inspired little concern that Hank would actually hear them. "Boom, the end of all his troubles. He never lifted a tire iron, never touched the trigger. Just a victim."

"I never expected anything else," Kimmer said, and traced Rio's collarbone through the fabric of his T-shirt in a way that made him want to rip it off. Okay, *that,* Hank might notice.

Too damn bad they'd both decided the unpredictable man was best kept close to home—a decision Owen had emphatically endorsed. For although the Hunter Agency had taken only a generation to expand from a small missing-persons agency to the current elite collection of international undercover operatives, it remained more than discreet on its wine-country home turf. It was invisible.

And Owen wanted to keep it that way.

"We'll be okay," she added. "The cops aren't happy, but they know what Owen does for this town—that his operatives go out of their way to keep the area safe. We've pitched in on plenty of their difficult cases."

"They owe you? That's not exactly how the law is supposed to work. Turn the other cheek is more of a civilian option."

"Trust me, we'll earn it when we go in for our little discussion at the station tomorrow. They'll pry every detail from us, write it all down and look it over as carefully as they

would anyone's. They'll know Hank isn't telling the whole
story about why those guys were after him, but they don't
have anything on him here. And when there are legitimate
choices to be made, they'll give us the benefit of the doubt.
Nothing happened out there today that wasn't self-defense.
And they know I tried to draw the action away from anyone
else. *Tried* being the operative word. And come on, there
were so many other things the goonboys could have hit besides that propane tank. That wasn't fair."

"Probably the very last things that went through their
minds."

"Yuck."

Hank's voice rose above the sound of his television pro-
gram. "Hey, Kimmer, bring some coffee this way."

Kimmer stiffened. In that moment she stopped being the
woman who showed him glimpses of a gentler, playful self,
and returned to being the woman he'd first met. Hard. A
woman with edges. A woman who had no intention of being
ruled by her past, in whatever form it came. She no longer fit
perfectly into his lap; she just happened to be sitting there.
And she said, "You want I should make up some sammitches,
too? Call up some girlfriends to keep you company? And I
got a little bell you can ring anytime you need something,
how about that?"

Rio winced.

She knew it; she felt it. For all the ways her knack of reading people failed her when it came to Rio—when it came to
anyone close to her, for good or bad—she'd learned to com-
pensate. To observe and know him. She withdrew, sliding off
his lap to stand before him. "It's not the same and you know
it."

Rio's grandmother had ruled her Danish-Japanese children, and then her grandchildren. His *sobo* had instilled her courteous, often ritualized ways through the entire family— and those who had married into it soon found themselves murmuring courteous phrases, taking off their shoes at the door, providing slippers to guests…and going out of their way to make guests feel at home. In *Sobo's* household, failure to anticipate a guest's needs—so much as a cup of coffee—was a profound failure indeed. Those in Rio's generation were more relaxed about such things, but still respectful, still attentive. And though during the years away from home—the CIA years, as Rio thought of them—Rio had adjusted to myriad cultures, he'd easily returned to most of his old ways once he'd come home.

Well, his old ways if you didn't count the constant adjustments he made for that spot where his kidney used to be, and all the not-so-well-adjusted muscle and tendon that had also been in the way of that bullet.

Rio looked up at Kimmer, found her defiant and hard— that same demeanor that had drawn him in, the one shouting *I don't need anybody* when in fact she needed everything. Someone to accept and love her for who she was, just for starters. Petite but carrying hard, toned muscle, lightning-fast in reaction and as quick in improvised strategy as she was on her feet. Features saved from being *cute* by the hard line of her jaw and the look in her deep, clear blue eyes. And because being honest with Kimmer was the only option, Rio said, "No. Hank is not a good guest, or a welcome one. But it's not about him, it's about you."

"Exactly." She gave an assertive nod, and if Rio didn't know her so well he might have missed that faint tremble in her chin. "It's about me never forgetting the things my family taught me—even if they didn't mean to." Not entirely true; Rio knew by now that Kimmer's battered mother had deliberately left her with a set of rules to live by. "And I guess there's no hope if I haven't at least managed to learn that men like Hank will own you—if you let them."

"That's not—" Rio started and then stopped, because he could see that the conversation was over, that Kimmer had gone to that place where her past very much ruled her, even if in a way she'd never acknowledge. She hesitated a moment, clad in lightweight drawstring pants and a French-cut T-shirt, and Rio's experienced eye saw vulnerability beneath that hard edge. When she turned away, it was to stalk out to the front porch on bare feet that had been wrapped in sports tape at heel and ball to cover the damage the day had wrought—tree bark, asphalt, gouging bits of stick and gravel had all left their mark.

Rio had thrown his socks away, but they'd lasted long enough to leave him with little more than a few pebble bruises.

He lost himself in the appreciation of watching her walk away, and then he tipped his head back and closed his eyes, trying to call up the moments when he'd had her in his lap and they'd manage to forget—mostly—that Hank was here, and all the things he'd brought with him. Goonboys. Troubled past. A really bad attitude. And then he sighed and told himself, "Walk the talk, Ryobe Carlsen."

That meant switching off the heating pad and getting up to walk silently into the next room, where he interposed himself between Hank and the television and said, "I'll make some coffee. Go out and talk to your sister."

Hank couldn't have looked more startled. His gaze flicked past Rio to the television and then out to the front porch. Rio made his point by turning off the television. Before Hank's open mouth could emit words, Rio jerked a thumb at the front porch. "Go. Talk. She saved your ass today." And then, as Hank slowly, uncertainly, stood, Rio added a low-toned, "And be nice. Don't crowd her. Don't boss her. Just try saying thank you."

Of course Hank had to open his mouth. "Kinda looks like she's got you pussy-whipped."

"You think so?" Rio cocked his head to consider it. "You know what? I don't. Maybe you and I will have a talk about that another time. For now, you want that coffee? You go be nice."

Hank shook his head, a gesture of disgust—at just exactly what, Rio wasn't sure. And didn't care. Hank headed for the front porch—and Rio found himself walking in the wrong direction to make coffee. He found himself following Kimmer's brother, stopping to hover within earshot through the screen door.

Hank, diplomat and master of subtlety, let the screen slam behind him, shattering what peace the porch might have offered Kimmer. "There you are," he said, and it somehow sounded accusing, as if Kimmer had deliberately inconvenienced him by choosing to sit out in the cool spring night. Rio could see her there in his mind's eye—on the porch swing, her shoulders wrapped with the crocheted afghan she kept out there. "I guess what ol' Leo said was right, then. You sure did handle those guys. I was kinda hoping to avoid the cops, though."

"So was I," Kimmer said dryly. "Gee, I wonder where we went wrong?"

"Rio's making coffee." Another accusation, his tone indicating she should be the one in the kitchen. Rio moved closer to the door—close enough to see out—knowing Kimmer had likely detected his presence already.

Kimmer rose from the swing, the afghan still enclosing her shoulders. "And he sent you out here to make nice, didn't he?"

"Jeez, Kimmer, you turned into a real ball-buster. I don't even know you anymore."

"That's for the best, don't you think?"

From Hank's expression, he hadn't caught the exquisitely dry tone of Kimmer's sarcasm, but nor did he quite know how to take what she'd said. He finally shook his head. "Maybe you should come back with me. Get to know the family again."

Kimmer snorted. "I know what I need to know. I think I've made that clear enough."

Hank went squinty-eyed. Together with the thin flannel shirt left open over a dingy white T-shirt, worn jeans made ragged with the rip they'd received sometime today and chin scruff too old to call stubble and not old enough to call a deliberate beard, it wasn't a good look on him. "You've changed, Kimmer."

That, too, was an accusation.

She responded with a cool, even look. "And thank goodness for that."

He reached for her then. *Damned fool.* Rio stiffened, wanted to run out and intervene—but didn't. He just stood there, watching Hank's abrupt and harsh movement stagger short as Kimmer executed a swift stop-thrust, the heel of her hand hitting the sweet spot just at the bottom of Hank's breastbone and then withdrawing so quickly that Hank was left to gape—and to gasp at the impact, hunting for the air she'd knocked out of him. "You don't touch me," she said. "You got that? You never, ever touch me."

Hank made a garbled noise, not quite ready for speech.

"Look, Hank. The only reason you're still here is because my reputation—and my boss's mood—depends on getting this mess cleared up. Because it's best if we do that as quietly as possible. One day, maybe two, and you'll be out of here. You can go back to Munroville and you can tell everyone what a bitch I am and how ungrateful I am and how pathetic I am. You can even tell them I grew a mole, one of those great big black ones with hairs coming out of it. Whatever floats your boat. But as long as you're here, in *my* house, you won't touch me and you won't treat me like your personal slave."

So much for meddling. So much for *be nice* and *say thank you.* Rio hadn't quite been able to imagine Hank's capacity for boorishness…or Kimmer's simmering anger. He'd never imagined Hank would try to grab her, try to intimidate her here in her own home, the very same day he'd seen her take down his two personal goonboys. And while part of him ached to charge out there and bodily lob Hank into the street, the rest of him churned at this very graphic demonstration of why he and Kimmer would never look at their lives—or their families—in quite the same way.

Chapter 3

Not so young anymore. Wiser.

But not wise enough.

Or simply too tired to be wise, walking through the hall to her dark, tiny bedroom without hesitation, without pausing to listen. Without pausing to smell the cheap beer in the air.

They grabbed her as she took that last, no-turning-back step, blocking her so she couldn't squirt right back out the door. Rough and hurtful hands—hands that had once only randomly yanked and pulled and jerked her around, now targeting forming breasts, pinching hard. Stabbing cruelly at every private, personal spot a growing teen would want to protect.

Not this time. *Kimmer made no attempt to fight them off. She ground her jaw closed on what wanted to be whimpers of pain and renewed fear—for the boys were getting worse, and she knew where this would end up one day. Maybe today.*

Maybe this time they had Leo here with them again—it seemed always to be Leo's idea—and maybe this time they'd wear her down and get her pants off.

So she didn't fight them. She didn't try to escape back out the door. Squirming, dropping her books and shucking the ragged sweatshirt on which they had such a secure hold, she darted forward. She landed on her twin bed and shoved off from her knees, sliding over the edge and onto the floor with the bed between her and the boys.

At first they laughed; they mocked her for thinking she could hide under the bed.

At first.

Because although she did dive under the bed, she came back out again. And she had a bat.

An old bat. A cracked bat salvaged from the school garbage bin. A bat heavily taped along the handle. But when Kimmer came out from under the bed she sprang to her feet and even in the darkness those boys could see the bat, see her ready stance, see her willingness to fight back with a vengeance.

It bought her the time to escape out the window. That, too, was ready—unlocked, already cracked up past the sticky part so she could merely fling it open. Out onto the roof, over the dormer and down to the lowest corner, racing them—for they knew her escape route. She lobbed the bat to the ground and hung down, dropping off for a hard fall, rolling…reclaiming the bat and running with every ounce of speed she had. Into the woods, over to the barn. As long as she had enough of a head start, they wouldn't follow.

No doubt they were laughing anyway, bragging about the cruelties they'd managed while they'd had the chance—the soft feel of her breasts, the tug of her wild, unruly hair, the warmth between her legs. No doubt they'd locked her bed-room window, thinking themselves victorious in that.

But Kimmer was thirteen, and she'd learned her lessons well. She knew the rules. She had a metal shim tucked away behind the shutter, and she knew how to wield it silently and swiftly to get back inside.

Kimmer Reed knew how to take care of herself.

"Whoa!" Rio's voice came from the bedroom darkness like a slap in the face. Kimmer jerked back from the sound and froze, battling the inner conflict of past and present, the overwhelming urge to strike out with the abrupt awareness that this was *Rio*.

The lights blazed on overhead, revealing Rio stretched out to reach the switch, one arm and his head through a cable sweater, concern on his face.

And Kimmer realized how very close she'd come to striking him, to hitting him hard. Her arm still hesitated halfway through the motion, the heel of her hand ready for the impact, her body already positioned to follow through with a low side kick that would have taken out his knee. Slowly, she straightened. "Oops."

"Yeah," Rio said. "That would have been an *oops* all right. At least, from my point of view. You okay?"

Kimmer cleared her throat and said, as lamely as it got, "You startled me."

Rio worked his arm through the sweater and tugged it down into place. No great mystery what he was doing; the evening had turned chilly, and the threat of rain hung in the air. He'd not bothered to turn on the lights; he'd left that sweater on the bed this morning and probably planned to be out of the room in a matter of seconds. "Uh-huh," he said. "Doesn't answer my question. You okay?"

Kimmer looked away, surprised at the sting of tears. The contrast between the past and the present wasn't something she could truly reconcile. It made the past that much worse and the present that much more unbelievable. And though she searched for the words to answer him, she couldn't find any.

He took a step closer, and she realized he was waiting for her to nod, or to gesture, or even just to tell him it was okay. She lifted her head a little—a defiant movement attached to the acknowledgment for which he waited—and when he stepped in close it was to cup his hands around her shoulders and kiss each eyebrow. With his mouth still brushing her forehead, he murmured, "Hang in there."

Of course, hang in there. When had there ever been any other choice?

By the time they left the small police station in Watkins Glen proper the next day, the rain was coming down in a steady drizzle and Kimmer's stomach growled a constant reminder that they'd had an early breakfast and talked through lunch.

"So that's that?" Hank said, hunching his shoulders against the rain. If he had a rain slicker, it was in the Suburban—which was in for repairs, acquiring just enough in the way of fixes to make it roadworthy again. It had actually held up pretty well, right up until the propane explosion had put a piece of shrapnel through the radiator. "No charges being filed?"

"Not yet, aside from the fine for discharging a weapon in a public area. It could still happen." Kimmer pulled the bill of her cap down closer to her eyes. She'd dressed no-nonsense today—good jeans, a gauzy fitted vest over a stretchy black turtleneck, black post earrings. Rio wore a dark slate sweater, a fine silk knit that fit just right under a tailored collarless jacket that would have looked as good over dress slacks as it did his jeans, though it hadn't been made for this weather. She admired the view a moment, unwilling to let any conversation with Hank deprive her of such indulgence. "But you know, I'd stick to the speed limit on the way out. The chief seemed to understand pretty well how the action ended up on the docks, and I don't think his people will cut you any breaks."

"It's not my fault I don't know the area," Hank said, sullen rebellion in his voice and resentment on his face.

"I'm still not sure why you came to me for help at all." Kimmer headed for the little group that had split off from them—Rio, Owen Hunter and the lawyer who'd flown in from Albany the night before. Owen hadn't been taking any chances. "You sure didn't trust me to handle the trouble you brought along."

"I didn't know—" Hank started, but stopped as they reached the group and the other three men looked over at him.

Kimmer couldn't read Rio—nothing new about that—but she could instantly see that Owen and the lawyer didn't welcome Hank's presence. Whatever conversation they'd been having stopped, and Owen started a new one. "Kimmer, I'd like you to come into the office this afternoon. I think it'd be a good idea if we got you on an assignment as soon as possible."

Kimmer narrowed her eyes at him, flicking a glance at the lawyer to see from his face that it had been his suggestion. "I'm on leave," she said, though she knew he knew it. A couple of well-earned weeks, for though Rio had moved down a month and a half earlier, she'd almost immediately gone out of the country for several weeks. This was their time to settle in together, and it hadn't been long enough.

"Things change," Owen said, and though his rugged face held understanding, his voice was firm. Most of the Hunters were lean of body and aesthetic of feature, the same basic mold for each sibling. Owen had turned out craggy and rugged with a heavyweight boxer's physique; he had only the Hunter nose, and even that was broader than the aquiline nose of his siblings. Kimmer sometimes wondered if he understood what it was to be the black sheep—except that Owen had otherwise followed in his family footsteps, leaving his younger brother Dave to break the mold.

"What he means," Hank said, a smirk in place, "is that you screwed up, and now you've gotta get out of town so you don't rub off on the agency."

Kimmer sent a cool look his way. Then she told Rio, "I'm going to go grab a couple of subs. You want that horrible pastrami thing again?"

"With mustard," Rio answered promptly. And he waited until Kimmer had moved almost out of earshot—but not quite—to say, "What Owen meant, Hank, is that you screwed up, and you rubbed off on Kimmer."

Hank snorted. "She can take care of herself."

And Rio didn't bother to hide his pride. "Yeah. She can. But that won't stop me from stepping in if I think I need to."

Men. All posturing and saber-rattling. But Kimmer found herself smiling all the same.

When she returned with the subs, Owen and the lawyer had left, and the drizzle had stopped. Hank sat on the bumper of Rio's midsize SUV, and Rio waved, standing by the half-open car door as he fished his cell phone from his pocket, glanced at the caller ID, and picked up the call. "Hey, Caro. What's—"

When Carolyne Carlsen cut Rio off, Kimmer instantly

wondered if she'd gotten herself into another situation. As far as Kimmer knew, Carolyne still handled security issues on some of the federal government's most sensitive systems—the same job that had gotten her into trouble the previous fall.

But Rio glanced over, saw Kimmer's attentiveness, and gave the slightest shake of his head. He could still read her like the proverbial book, dammit. And it still shook her sometimes; she still wasn't used to it. No doubt he could tell just how she felt about Hank, even if Hank himself wouldn't ever pick up the depth of her true feelings, not even if they came attached to a clue-by-four. "Caro, slow down. Is she…" he stopped, didn't seem to be able to use the words he'd had in mind, and finally finished, "…still in the hospital?"

Kimmer knew, then. It had to be Rio's grandmother. His beloved Sobo. Had it been anyone in his nuclear family, his cousin wouldn't be passing the news along. Though for Rio, of course, "nuclear family" encompassed as many layers as the average extended family.

Kimmer thought of her nuclear family in terms of single digits. One. Herself.

"Who's she staying with? Mom and Dad? Good. Mom won't let her do anything more strenuous than flower arrangement. Do they need—"

Quiet Carolyne was overwrought indeed, to keep cutting Rio off in midsentence. "Okay. Okay. I hear you. I promise. I won't go. Not without checking first. And I'll give them a day or two before I call. Yes, I promise. I won't even send an e-mail."

That, Kimmer knew, was calculated to get at least a small laugh out of Carolyne. For as much as Carolyne was connected and interconnected to the online community—wireless satellite connections for every machine she owned and then some—Rio was disconnected. He hadn't yet gotten his hand-me-down laptop to work with Kimmer's slow rural dial-up. Now the worry on his brow smoothed a little, and she knew the tactic had been at least partially successful. But his voice, when he spoke again, was as intense as Rio got. "Listen, Caro, you call me if anything changes. I mean it. Okay. Look, we'll talk later. Soon. Thanks for letting me know." And he listened another moment or two, nodding before a final goodbye.

"Did you ever notice," Hank said into the silence that followed, into the connection Kimmer and Rio had established, a silent communication during which she let him know she'd followed and understood the development, "that people on TV sitcoms never say goodbye? They just hang up."

"Here." Kimmer thrust the sub sandwich bag at him, and he pushed himself off the bumper to reach for it. "I got you turkey and onions with mustard." An old favorite. Ick. "There's a soda in there, too. I thought you might be hungry enough to eat on the way home." *I thought I might be hungry enough to eat on the way home, but if it keeps your mouth busy, first dibs are all yours.*

And then she cranked the window down to let fresh air dilute the stinging odor of onions.

Once home, Kimmer didn't linger. Owen expected her at Hunter, and she wanted to get it over with. She also wanted to escape Hank. And mostly, she needed time to consider Rio's situation.

The blunt truth was that she had no idea how to respond to his grandmother's illness, a conjecture he confirmed in a few murmured words before she threw her tough black Eagle Creek bag in the Miata and headed the twenty minutes to the

Full Cry vineyards and winery. Sobo had been diagnosed with mild congestive heart failure, briefly hospitalized and was now adjusting to a new regime of medicines while her family made hasty arrangements for the partial nursing care she'd need until she stabilized. And it was killing Rio to be down here, to be away from them…not even to call them. But Carolyne had said they needed the space to make the necessary arrangements, and that he should wait.

That left Rio in limbo. He couldn't go rushing off to save the situation as he had so many times in the past, he couldn't pull off his casual laid-back average-guy mode to continue life as normal, and he wasn't made for sitting around doing nothing.

Kimmer didn't know what to say to him, what to do for him. She didn't have the faintest idea what it felt like to have family—people known from childhood, people immersed in and part of her life—in crisis.

So she didn't linger. She stayed long enough to see Hank set up in front of the television and to see Rio changing into shorts, a cut-off sweatshirt and running shoes, and she didn't say anything absurd like "It'll be okay," because who knew? She just ran a hand down his arm, waited for him to notice, and said, "I'll be back as soon as I can."

Full Cry Winery was nestled between two of New York state's southern tier Finger Lakes, near the shore of Seneca Lake. Kimmer knew the winding road between her Glenora hilltop home and Full Cry well enough to make navigation second nature—and to sail past the speed limits when occasion warranted, slowing down only for the tiny town of Rock Stream.

At midafternoon, the area's surfeit of farmers and grape

growers were at work, but few of them took to the road and Kimmer had command of it to travel south in record time. She pulled past the lot of the old barn converted to a visitor's center and around behind to the addition and modern outbuildings where working areas of the fully functioning winery were located. The double-level cellar started beneath the business offices and ran under the barn. Kimmer liked to walk it in the hottest part of summer and absorb the stringent smells of tannin and crushed grape and wine and damp concrete.

Not far from the parking lot sat the Hunter family home, a surprisingly modest structure. And snuggled away behind the winery's business section, buffered by discreet security measures, the Hunter Agency maintained its own entrance to its offices, one that was, without fanfare, labeled Viniculture Development.

Kimmer reached it and flipped up the weather cover over the security pad next to a steel door that gleamed even in the darkness, pressing her thumb against the glass. It gave a brief blue glow and then issued an invitation with the quiet *thunk* of disengaging locks.

As she pushed through the door she considered this abrupt change of plans. Hunter maintained an extensive string of operatives, from part-timers to those who lived undercover, and although they all had specialties, they were also widely cross-trained. Kimmer herself fell in the middle of the spectrum— a full-time operative who went from job to job, usually undercover. "Chimera," they called her, because she was so adept at reading people that she could live up to their expectations, going undetected. She could be all things to all people.

Hunter made good use of her knack to suss out people and

situations, using her where their background intel had failed, inserting her into quickly developing situations to assess personalities and even clients. Often their game plan developed around Kimmer's reports.

Kimmer went down the curving, carpeted concrete stairs. They spit her out at the end of a long hallway, where she had to navigate another security feature, this one a chamber of bulletproof glass that let her in but only let her out when it was satisfied about her identity. The whole handprint this time.

Gadgets. You gotta love 'em. Personally she trusted her own judgment over any gadget, and she was just waiting for the time one of their own became stuck in this flytrap.

With a pneumatic hiss, the door slid aside and released her into the Hunter Agency proper, a place of no-nonsense but quality furnishings, never metal where warm oak would do, everything oiled and polished. No doors squeaked; no dust dared settle or fingerprints linger. She went straight to Owen's office, through the small area occupied by his secretary during "normal" working hours, and rapped lightly on his door before opening it and inviting herself in.

He looked up from his desk, expectation on his craggy features. He raised a heavy, dark brow at her. "What took you so long?"

Since she'd basically taken no time at all, Kimmer ignored him. She cared more about the fact that he was annoyed and trying to hide it. "I see you," she told him, sitting in the chair across from his desk. They both knew she wasn't talking about his mere physical presence. *I see your hidden stress and anger.*

Owen sighed, acknowledging the annoyance as he shuffled the papers he'd been studying aside. "Bad timing," he said.

"Is there ever a good time to blow up a propane tank and a couple of bad guys with it?"

That got a wry smile out of him as he leaned back in his chair. "Point well taken. And I do realize you did what you could to contain the situation."

"Given that I had zero notice." Kimmer scowled at the thought of Hank's arrival, and then again at the way he'd rabbited from the hilltop. "If he'd just stayed on the damned hill where I put him…"

Owen shrugged. "I'm not sure I blame him. I think your brother was in way over his head."

Kimmer thought back over the events of the previous day. "He came here hoping I would kill them. He thinks I'm the kind of person who'll just…do that. And damned if I didn't turn them both into toast. Never even had a chance to talk to them." She frowned at the situation a moment. "There's no telling if they'll ever be able to ID the guys. You can bet Hank's not telling."

Silence fell between them, until Owen said, "And how's your brother strike you?"

Kimmer blinked. "What do you mean? You know I can't read him. A fact for which I'm almost grateful, I should say."

"I'm not sure it adds up, that's all," Owen said. "If Hank saw someone killed, why is it safe to go back?"

"He told me the dead guys were the only others to know about it. I gather it wasn't a large organization. Just a few guys running a chop shop under the cover of Hank's salvage business."

"Hmm." Owen gave a thoughtful rub of his chin. "Would have been nice to have talked to those two men."

"Too bad toast doesn't talk." Pieces of toast, to judge by the condition of the sedan after the explosion. "Wildly scat-

tered" was an understated way to have put it; identification
would be impossible unless they'd been in the DNA database.
No wonder Owen felt he needed to appease the local law
agencies. "Tell me you're not sending me away."

"I'm not sending you away."

"Because I really can't—" Oh. She looked at him, realized
she'd been about to say she couldn't leave Rio right now, not
again. Not with his grandmother sick. Then she realized she
didn't actually know if that was best. Maybe Rio just needed
to do his thing. "Okay, then what's up?"

"You're going to put your unique abilities to work right
here."

She tipped her head at him, an unspoken *is that so?*

"The governor is making his rounds across the state this
spring," Owen said. "Election year prep. I've offered Hunter's
services as backup security. You won't be the only one. I want
you working undercover as he comes through Watkins Glen
next week. From arrival to departure, I want you in the background. Watching."

Because if someone aimed to cause trouble, she'd spot it
before anyone else. He didn't have to say it. Hunter had taken
advantage of her knack often enough that such things had
been said many times before.

"The others?" she asked.

"Three other agents. Also in the background, but in an obvious security capacity. You won't have to interface with
them. You'll be reporting straight to the chief of police. You'll
also be blending in to their arrangements, not the other way
around. The point is to provide a seamless extra layer of pro-
tection without causing them any extra work."

Kimmer tapped her fingers on her knee. "Are we expecting trouble?"

"Not at all." Owen smiled at her, the look he got when he was happy at how he'd worked things out. "It was an offer I made to take some of the pressure off the department. A gesture of goodwill, you might say. Or even by way of apology."

Some gesture. Hunter Agency time didn't come cheap. Kimmer winced.

Owen raised a hand. "Look at me," he said. "I want you to know I'm not trying to pull one over on you here. The truth is, it's good for us to make these gestures now and then. We want the local law to think of us as people who work with them and within their boundaries. We want them to understand that this is our home, too."

Kimmer looked. She found him unfazed by her scrutiny...possibly even slightly amused. She made a grumbling noise and settled deeper in her chair. "So when—?"

"The end of the week. Give the chief a call first thing tomorrow." He tossed a business card across the desk—one of his own, but he'd scrawled a phone number on the back. A real high-tech moment.

Kimmer stretched forward to scoop up the card...and then she sat there, deep in the chair, flipping the card back and forth in her fingers.

After a moment, Owen raised his eyebrows. "This isn't about the new assignment." When she shot him an annoyed look, he just grinned. "You know, the rest of us are able to make observations and deductions, too. I know you well enough for that. More than well enough, for all you don't like to hear it. So spit it out—what's bothering you?"

Kimmer hesitated as something on his flat screen computer monitor caught his attention. He turned to type in a few quick words and then turned back to her, expectant.

Damn. Maybe she should have run while she had the chance.

But she hadn't, so she took a deep breath. "You have a family…"

"A rather large one." Owen smiled a compressed and crooked smile.

"Then…when you get bad news about one of you…"

After she'd hesitated long enough, he prompted, "Bad news as in 'Dave's breaking away to do his own thing instead of following the family business,' or bad news as in someone's dead?"

"Jeez, Owen, you've got to let that thing with Dave go," Kimmer said. "He's still in the family business. He's just doing it differently."

"Excellent use of distraction," he said. "Two points. And minus two points for evading the question."

Kimmer gave him a sulky look, just because she knew she could get away with it. "As in bad news, someone's sick. Someone *old* is sick. Someone who means a lot to the whole family."

"Got it. What about it?"

"What's…someone else supposed to do? Oh, screw it. Me. I. What am *I* supposed to do? I don't get the whole family thing. I don't get hanging together through thick and thin. I don't get how you drop everything and try to make things right even if you know you can't. I don't *get* any of it! How am I supposed to do the right thing?"

Owen cleared his throat. "Rio has had some bad news, I take it."

Kimmer nodded. "I feel like I'm supposed to do something about it. But I can't fake it. I can't even truly believe it—that his family could be that close."

Owen hesitated for a long, long moment, looking at Kimmer until she felt uneasy. He thought she should have this answer. And at last, he gave it to her. "What if it were your mother?"

She almost jumped right to her feet. To prevent herself, she froze, stiffening enough that she thought she might even creak. "That's not fair, Owen. It's not the same, not the same *at all*." She and her mother had been bonded by abuse and adversity. They'd never had a normal relationship—just an intense one. "My mother taught me how to survive. But she also married my father in the first place…and then she left me with him. I don't have a relationship with her, I have a memory *of* her. And I learned the very hard lesson that even the people who might love you still end up leaving you." A long speech for her, especially when it came to this topic.

Owen shook his head. "You can't truly believe that. Or why invite Rio down here?"

That was easy. "Because he was willing to take the chance." She relaxed slightly; it was either that or turn into one giant body cramp. "Don't get me wrong. What we have is…something I'd never even considered for myself. But that doesn't mean it's forever. As soon as he sees an advantage in being elsewhere…" She stopped herself. She hadn't meant to say that much. Not nearly that much. In fact, she hadn't even realized she believed it possible of Rio until she heard her own words.

Maybe she was just afraid of it.

Owen regarded her for a good long while—one of the few people comfortable enough with himself that he could do that, knowing of her knack. Most people fidgeted, wondering what she saw. Owen held himself quietly, with the unusual dignity he carried around like an extra jacket. "As to your original question," he said finally. "Think of your mother in those days when she was the most important to you. When she could still protect you. And then think what would have made you feel better when you were frightened for her."

Not to wonder if my damned father would come for me next. But that was the easy answer, the smart-ass answer that while perfectly truthful, also didn't plumb the question as deeply as could be done. So she nodded. "You think I don't have to get the whole family thing in order to…be there…for Rio."

"I think you don't," he agreed, and then, totally unexpectedly, reached into a drawer for a set of keys and tossed them her way. "These belong to Hank's Suburban."

"It's fixed already?" Kimmer eyed the keys in disbelief.

"Consider it a favor," Owen said dryly.

"I cannot imagine you wanting to do my brother a favor after all of this."

Owen snorted, as coarse a response as he ever made. "The favor was for you," he said. "And come to think of it, for me, too. I need your head on straight next week."

"My make-nice week," she murmured, and reached for the keys. "Don't worry, Owen. From the way Hank's acting, he's had enough of me, too."

Chapter 4

The house clanged with the sound of free-weights landing on the thin, cheap basement carpet over the concrete floor. Kimmer hesitated just inside the doorway, tossing her girly red ostrich tote on the nearest chair and her matching red driving cap on top of it. Otherwise her outfit was demure enough: black stovepipe jeans with elaborate stitching on the calves, a black silk turtleneck and a gauzy vest over it all. Just the red at her wrist—her watchband—and the red detailing on her flat, open-toe sandals.

Just enough to peek out at the world in a sassy way, and to leave her brother in the position of snatching surreptitious looks when he thought she wasn't paying attention. For his mouth to open as though he might say something as she drove him to Full Cry Winery to pick up the Suburban, and then to close again on those words unspoken.

She'd pulled into the employee parking lot near the back

end of the Suburban, and she hesitated without turning off the engine—without even putting the vehicle in Park. "Look, Hank," she said as he reached for the door handle. "Now you've seen me. Now you can go back and tell the others that I'm up here, but I didn't turn out the way you wanted and I can't be convinced to change and I don't want anything to do with you. Any of you. Whatever power you once had over my life is long gone."

Hank grunted in an unconvinced way. "Maybe not. But you didn't turn me away."

"I didn't have the chance." Kimmer kept her tone flat. "Don't make the mistake of bringing trouble to my home twice."

Hank shook his head. "You've got your nice car and your house and you think you're better'n all of us now, but you still haven't learned the first thing about what it means to be a family."

"Wrong." She smiled at him, showing teeth. "I know what it means to you, and I want none of it."

With that he'd gotten out of her car, hauling his cheap nylon duffel from the backseat. He threw her a sarcastic, half-assed salute and headed for his own vehicle, and Kimmer laid down a satisfying strip of rubber on the way out.

And now Kimmer stood in the entry of her house, thinking that it seemed like forever since she and Rio had been here alone and not just a handful of days.

"Kimmer?" Rio's voice filtered up from the floor beneath her.

"Here," she said. "And alone."

He muttered something she couldn't quite catch and didn't really need to, and there was a final clink of shifting weight before he climbed the old wooden stairs leading from the basement, creaking on those fourth and seventh steps as usual. He came out of the kitchen with a towel around his neck and one of those T-shirts with the cut-off sleeves that showed his biceps to perfection, and that pair of shorts that hugged his ass just right.

"You're wearing those on purpose," she said, narrowing her eyes at him. Worry dogged his eyes, but the tough-guy-I'm-working-out expression let her know he wasn't interested in talking about it—about his grandmother—just now.

He grinned, convincingly enough. He'd been drinking that Kool-Aid again, leaving a smirch of blue at the corner of his mouth. "Do you think so?" He stalked closer, hands on either end of the towel, an exaggerated prowl. Sweat blotted his shirt here and there, but not so much as to cry out for a shower.

She didn't answer. She told him, "Hank is gone. And Hunter's not sending me anywhere."

That diverted his prowling a moment. "No?"

"I've got some local spy-girl duty," she said. "Maybe I'll have the chance to throw myself in front of an important political figure in the line of duty."

"The governor's visit," he guessed. "That's not bad. It's barely more than a drive-through."

"As penance goes, I'll take it. But sooner or later, I'll go out on assignment again."

She didn't have to say any more; he shook his head. "I still haven't decided if I want to go back to that kind of work," he said. "I've been burned badly enough. I don't have that need anymore, the drive to go out and take care of the things no one else even knows about. Make the world safe, *blah blah blah*. Been there, done that…and there are others better qualified than I. You, for instance."

"You were driven enough last fall."

"That was different. That was family. You know that. And you know I hardly blend into the crowd. I found ways to use that to my advantage with the agency. I was good for drawing attention away from other case officers when they needed it."

She could well imagine that. At six-three and with that bright blond hair, those striking angles in his features, the natural warmth of his rich brown eyes, he'd drawn her attention quickly enough.

"I can be hidden, but...it's not what I'm best at. And my back means there's no way Hunter could use me in their more...active assignments. I'm done with paramilitary. So..." He shrugged. "I can find work with boats here, too. I don't have any problem with that."

"It's less of a commitment," she guessed, surprised that it hurt to say it. It was common sense, that was all. Dabble your toes in the water before jumping in. If she hadn't just had that conversation with Owen she wouldn't think twice about it. That conversation in which she realized that she still fully expected Rio to walk away when it suited him.

Who could blame him? It wasn't as if Kimmer herself had ever been anything but a loner, using her personal interactions as transactions and trade-offs.

And Rio just shrugged, a gesture that neither confirmed nor denied but simply didn't get into it.

Kimmer took a deliberate breath. "Okay," she said, letting go of the subject quickly enough to surprise him. "Besides, anyone would need time to recover after meeting my very suave brother. Did he leave you any of those fried pork rinds?"

"OldCat loves 'em," Rio reported.

Kimmer shuddered with exaggeration. She tipped her head back and scrubbed her fingers through her near-black hair—not long enough for the curls to do any more than suggest soft waves along her head and a few wispy, feathery curls at her nape, but still long enough to ruffle under her fingers. She shook like a dog, shoulders all the way down to her fingers, torso down to her hips, making a rolling-*R* noise of a shivery nature. "There," she said, straightening to find Rio watching her with interest. "All those Hank vibes...gone."

"Do that again," he said.

"Do which? The whole—?" and she shook her arms to demonstrate.

"More the part with the hips."

She gave him a speculative look from beneath half-lidded eyes; his own widened. She had no idea how he'd ever been a spy guy.

Because what he shows you isn't what he'd ever show anyone else.

He swallowed visibly. A flicker of tension ran up his arm, a brief clench of muscle. Kimmer murmured, "You goof," as if it were actually an endearing phrase, and then a moment later it occurred to her that she was kissing him and *had* been kissing him for who knows how long. Pressed up against his slightly damp shirt, fingers pressed into the hard muscle of his arms, hips against his and angled to connect most intimately. She pulled back long enough to tell him in her most serious voice, "You must use this power only for good," and then to laugh with pleasure at the dazed expression already glazing his eyes.

Somewhere in the back of her head Owen's words trickled through, and she followed his advice the only way she knew how. A long, slow kiss that said *I'm here for you.* A lick and nibble at the corner of his jaw, *I care.* A delicate nip at his ear, one that made him groan, made his knees buckle down in the way they sometimes did, made him surge back up again to hold her more tightly, lifting until her toes merely brushed the floor. Slow kisses, her fingers skimming his back beneath the shirt and down, caressing cheeks that clenched under her touch. *I'm here. I care. I love, as best I can.*

A quick hitch-and-lift and he pulled her higher, high enough so she could wrap her legs around him, pressing against him so snugly, so intimately, that they might not have been clothed at all.

Except for one thing. "Damn seam," Rio panted, his mouth muffled against her neck.

Kimmer threw her head back to laugh, trusting him to hold her, her arms only loosely around his shoulders. He took the opportunity to lick her cleavage right through the silk turtleneck, a whispery caress that sent shivers down her spine and turned the heat up between them. "Stairs," she told him, suddenly just as breathless as he.

He headed for them, for the bedroom. But the stairs were as far as they got, a tumble of motion and sensation and need. And when Rio finally cried out in completion on the heels of Kimmer's gasps, his voice held emotional pain as well as physical joy. Afterward he held her for a long time, cuddling on the stairs as though they were the grandest feather bed while dusk crept in around them and made shadows to hide the things they weren't sure they wanted the other to see.

Worry. Doubt. Vulnerability.

Desperate hope that two people of such wildly disparate backgrounds could somehow maintain their fledgling bonds in spite of it all.

* * *

Kimmer stood in the doorway of her guest room and looked in on the bed still rumpled from use, every detail revealed in the cheery morning sunshine slanted across the end of the bed and across the dirty sock hanging from the post of the open footboard. No, the sheets weren't pulled from the bed and quietly piled for the laundry. No, the guest towels hadn't been gathered from the tiny guest bathroom. Not a surprise. The bed had waited three days before she'd felt like dealing with it. She'd seen it already. Now she picked up the sock between two fingers and dropped it in the wastebasket.

Upon tackling the bedding she discovered a pair of dirty briefs. Boxers or briefs…*I didn't really want to know.* Those, too, went into the trash, and then she stuffed the linens down the laundry chute and gave in to the impulse to wash her hands.

He was married and had two daughters, he'd said. She hadn't asked about the woman, hadn't asked about the kids. Hadn't wanted to know. But now she wondered who would possibly marry such an unrepentant, unmitigated male chauvinist, a man who didn't even hide his abuse behind a public mask of nice.

Then again, her mother had married her father, hadn't she? She'd told Kimmer that he'd been so sweet to her at first, so solicitous, so caring. Until the caring slowly turned to controlling…and then once he'd hit her, he had to tear her down in order to justify himself. By the time Kimmer came along, it was a way of life—and her mother, who had desperately hoped to avoid bringing a daughter into the situation, finally ran out of luck.

Hank had never been sweet. He'd probably got some girl pregnant and had leveraged his way into marriage. That was his style. Nothing clever, just brute force thinking itself sly.

So what had he really been up to during his time here? He hadn't truly wanted a family reunion—he'd left as soon as he was able. He hadn't paid any attention to the undeniably charming countryside, hadn't availed himself of any winery tours....

Kimmer snorted to herself. If Hank drank wine, it was the kind that came in a gallon carton.

Hank had certainly been in enough trouble upon his arrival, but who would care enough to chase his sorry ass all the way up to the Finger Lakes in person? It seemed to her that if someone had a car-theft ring and chop-shop thing going, there ought to be enough goonboys hanging around to send a couple after Hank.

But according to Hank, they'd cut the head off the monster—ended the threat. He certainly hadn't seemed worried as he'd driven off in his newly gleaming vehicle, the CD player blasting an old Conway Twitty album. Not even with the potential of more police questioning lingering over his head, and the fainter potential of accessory charges in the goonboy toasting.

Hmm.

Kimmer pulled her nightshirt over her head and tossed it down the laundry chute as well, padding naked through the second floor and wishing she'd find Rio to pounce upon, but he'd gone out early, checking out a sailboat being sold at the dock she'd nearly blown up. Serendipity and all that. Didn't matter. She was headed south for Watkins Glen. She'd spoken to Chief Harrison several times, checked in with her fellow Hunter agents, and now needed to go scope out the small park in which the governor would make his short speech and appearance. A few trees, a gorgeous smattering of lilacs in bloom, some strategically placed park benches, a bandstand for the governor himself, and the center of town closed to vehicle traffic. A morning of lurking, an hour of listening and watching, a few staged photo ops, and then the governor would drive away to be someone else's concern.

Although *concern* was a mighty strong word in relation to the actual threat level here, which was, in Kimmer's estimation, zero.

Still, she'd play secret weapon for Owen and the chief. Chimera.

Today Chimera was no one special, just a young woman on a walk through the center of town. She might even renew her driver's license while she was down there. No one had to know she was wearing Pooh Bear underwear beneath the wide-legged tan utility-style cords she'd pulled on, or that the wine-colored top, long sleeves tied off with drawstrings and shoulders shirred at the edge of a wide neckline, hid a multitude of whitened scars, thin and old—except for the still-pink furrow low on her side where saving Carolyne the previous fall had cost her a bullet.

They especially didn't know that her back pocket held a small, stout toothpick knife, that her abstract leaf necklace unfolded into another blade, or that she had a .38 secured in a SmartCarry holster between Pooh Bear and the cords. A conundrum of contradictions, Rio had called her once—but he'd done it with that smile that meant he liked her that way. She dumped her things into a one-shoulder contoured backpack and made sure to include the handmade miniature war club that had been her first reliable weapon.

She didn't expect to need any of it today. But they were all old friends, and only completely abandoned at airport security.

To all of that she added her small digital camera, the

latest spiffy FinePix. Focusing on the world through a camera helped her to isolate the important parts, to burn the moments into her memory. She might never print the images, might not even download them to her computer. She certainly never considered anything so trite as an album. Just taking the pictures often did the trick.

OldCat jumped on the bed, as subtle as stripes and plaids together and no more graceful. He settled into place with his front legs curved in before him, neatly hiding the missing lower leg, and stared at her with eyes narrowed beneath the absurd blotch of black partially covering his eye and the ragged remainder of his ear. He should have looked ridiculous, but of course he didn't. His gaze seemed distinctly accusing.

Kimmer stared back in the same manner. She'd fed him, Rio had cleaned the litter box, there were catnip toys secured in various places the humans weren't supposed to know about and the front window sill was cleared for his use. "So what's your problem?"

OldCat made a half-audible squeak of a meow, an amazingly silly sound to come from his broad-headed tomcat self. And Kimmer rolled her eyes. "Whatever," she told him, but bent to kiss the top of his head anyway. OldCat purred, closed his eyes with cat satisfaction and gave her permission to leave.

"There's a reason I've never had a cat before," she informed him, and went.

She tucked the Miata away at the edge of town, using street parking and pushing her luck near a fire hydrant. Lafayette Park was a brisk but pleasant ten minutes away on foot, past various charming historical buildings—the First Baptist Church, the brick Schuyler County courthouse with its central white cupola. Someday she'd sneak her way up into that cupola just for the view. Kimmer stopped to frame the park entrance with her camera—black wrought iron gates between massive brick pillars that had no actual fencing to make them functional, the bandstand looming directly beyond—not bothering to snap the picture. The governor and his party would come through here, on a sidewalk barely wide enough for such an entourage. They'd probably spill over the edges; if there were any sort of crowd, it would cause movement. Confusion.

Prime opportunity for anyone who wanted to move in on the man.

She wandered the area for a while, viewing it from all directions, assessing the dangers that could come from each. Just one of several people in the park—a plain young woman eating a yogurt from a park bench, a jogger swinging through the green zone on the way out of town, a man through the trees on the other side of the park feeding rats-on-wings pigeons.

She sat on one of the benches for a while, just absorbing the park. She knew this place, had been here before. But she hadn't looked at it through her Chimera eyes, and now she did. Looking, then closing her eyes to recreate what she'd seen in her mind's eye—trees and greenery and benches and the bandstand and a water fountain, all carefully arranged within the neat rectangular confines of the street block. When she finally stood and stretched, she could visualize the entire park in a sweeping inner panorama. Come tomorrow, she'd know at a glance if something felt out of place.

Like now. There, in the corner of her eye. The fellow with the pigeons was still there. He'd either had a significant amount of stale bread to dispense, or he had other reasons for hanging around.

Come to think of it, the pigeons didn't look very interested in him. And he no longer looked interested in them. A more focused glance revealed his boredom.

Waiting for anyone in particular?

Kimmer settled her backpack in place, but not before slipping her little club into her back pocket, smooth wood finding the worn spot where it often resided, the smooth, hard business end obscured by her pack. She took a leisurely walk around the park, completing her memorization work, and kept an eye on Pigeon Man.

He didn't leave the birds, but as she walked the park perimeter he rotated his body on his park bench to keep track of her.

Waiting for me?

Hmm. At first she'd pegged him as another advance scout—someone on the governor's staff, maybe even a reporter. Or security. Another layer of safety, smart enough to peg her as not-just-another-visitor, not enough in the know to realize she was official. If so that puts us in the same spot. Both blinded by the need-to-know approach.

Well, she'd get a picture. Owen would have the resources to ID the guy if he was working for the side of right, and probably even if not. Facial recognition software was a wonderful thing. Kimmer headed down the side of the big rectangular park and cut across on a diagonal that would bring her close enough to use the camera still in her hand. She watched Pigeon Man's body language change from surprise to realization to annoyance and then *snick* she had his picture. *Smile, you're on Chimera Camera.*

She'd been prepared for some sort of reaction, but not the instant cover-breaking anger as he shot to his feet, scattering indignant pigeons in all directions.

What the hell? Who the hell—? But by then Kimmer was running. Big lopey strides, not caring if she, too, had broken her cover as a random park visitor. If this man meant trouble for the governor, he might well just take his trouble elsewhere now that she'd taken his picture. She pulled the backpack around on the run, jammed her camera into it, zipped it tight and ducked her head through the strap so she didn't have to worry about losing it. When she glanced back she saw Pigeon Man had not emulated her big lopey strides, but—although not a natural sprinter, with awkward form and wasted motion—was making an obvious effort to catch up with her.

Kimmer did a mental eye roll. *Really not subtle, fella.* But if that's the way he wanted it, then she needed to take things to a more private arena. No one here needed to be hurt…and Owen would be unhappy indeed if she created another big stinky scene. She rounded the corner from 4th Street to North Franklin, banking with her speed and skipping around a neat lineup of preschoolers clinging to a rope; their startled teacher stopped short and then got her charges moving again in a "nothing happened there, move along" tone of voice. By then Kimmer was half a block away, and she listened for the inevitable encounter between children and Pigeon Man except…

It didn't come.

She glanced back. No one. No sign of him. She slowed, jogging to a stop, wide tan pant legs whapping against each other with the change of stride and then going silent as she downright stopped.

Nope. Gone. No Pigeon Man anywhere.

Well, then. Wasn't that exciting. Kimmer gave her backpack—and the camera within it—a pat. No need to hunt down Pigeon Man and risk one of those big stinky scenes.

She had his picture, and even if he hadn't been identified before the governor rolled into town, every security officer, cop and Hunter agent would have his image at hand. If he was smart, he was already running away. She'd take a nice roundabout route back to her car and head straight for Full Cry Winery.

Behind her, someone took the turn from 4th to North Franklin too fast, tires squealing against asphalt. Kimmer automatically gave the vehicle a look, and then looked back again as she realized its speed and realized even more abruptly that it was veering toward the curb and then in another heartbeat that the driver had no intention of stopping, curb or no curb. He was, of course, headed straight for her.

Run, Kimmer, run.

And run she did. She angled away for the first alley, a little thing not on the map, and a turn she hoped was too acute and too narrow for Pigeon Man—for heaven forbid it was someone other than Pigeon Man, a second BG on her heels—to make. Hoped, in fact, that he would splat himself all over the sturdy brick corner of the building on the other side of the alley.

Then again, she'd also hoped to find the alley full of good hiding places—trash cans, cellar stairs, a fire escape or two leaning down to offer her a hand up and out of the way.

Cleanest damn alley in the history of mankind. Nothing but struggling grass over old, old cobbles and the occasional collection of back-door recyclables in a bin too small to hide anything but her feet and ankles.

Behind her, the car muscled around, backed up and by-bloody-damn squeezed right into the alley, the driver fast gaining confidence and speed.

Kimmer ran.

But it didn't matter that she had a good sprint in her or that she could maintain a marathon pace for miles. Not when a car was the other runner in this race, the engine noise coming up fast behind her so she didn't even bother to look, legs pumping and arms pumping and heart pumping, gaze frantically sweeping the tightly featured back walls—red brick with light stone windowsills in neat rows far over Kimmer's head, shallow doorways that wouldn't protect her if Pigeon Man chose to risk a little paint and swoop in close to pick her off.

With the car so close she wasn't sure why she hadn't yet felt the brush of the bumper, Kimmer took a wild leap and caught the edge of the windowsill, legs cranked up at the knees and out of the way, hoping to hold on just long enough for the car to pass beneath her but immediately slipping—

Her fingers burned against stone, fingernails breaking and she landed hard on the sedan's roof just as Pigeon Man stomped the brakes. *Damned slippery little hump of a roof.* No handy luggage rack, nothing to keep her in place when he started to move. No room to bail over the side and hunt an open window, and if she fell off the back he'd just turn her into road pizza. Alley pizza.

She'd make her own damned window, then. As Pigeon Man found the accelerator again, Kimmer grabbed the war club from her pocket and slammed it into the back window, watching the glass spiderweb and dent. The car lurched forward and Pigeon Man must have turned to look behind himself, because he ran the corner of the bumper into brick. He backed up in a jerk of movement as Kimmer slipped around on the roof, all her concentration on slamming the window again and again.

Here I come, Pigeon Man—

Turf spun out behind the vehicle as the tires chewed through thin turf to cobblestone and the car shot forward, dumping Kimmer on the hard surface. She sprang to her feet, ready to run—but Pigeon Man had had enough. Or maybe he'd just seen the flashing yellow lights at the street end of the alley—not a cop, but an interested witness sure enough. His car bobbed away down the uneven ground of the alley, already too far away to get even a partial plate. Surely it wasn't that her head was spinning.

Kimmer stuck the club back in her pocket, straightened her backpack, and gathered her dignity to stride out of the alley in her most matter-of-fact fashion. She'd gathered a little crowd, drawn by the unusual parking choice made by the tow truck; the driver himself met her as she emerged.

"Are you all right? I saw the car turn, but there's no traffic allowed back there anymore. Holy shit, you people filming a movie or what? 'Cause I called the cops. That looked serious!"

"Yes," Kimmer said, putting on an absent expression. She had to get out of here before the cops arrived.

He pushed back his billed cap and said, "But where—"

Cameras. Of course, cameras. "Just a run-through," Kimmer said brightly. "Thanks for your concern. Gotta go!"

"Good makeup," someone in the crowd muttered from behind him. "Looks just like blood." And a male voice with an *I'm important* tone said, "Movie, bullshit. Don't let her just walk away!"

The tow truck driver had a you-gotta-be-kidding sound in his voice. "After what I just saw? *You* stop her."

Kimmer smiled to herself and kept on walking.

Chapter 5

Kimmer grabbed a take-out lunch at the edge-of-town mom-and-pop diner, where the Watkins Glen racetrack inspired the decor inside and out. She barely looked at the take-out window attendant, paying more attention to her camera as she waited for her food. To judge by the battered exterior of her backpack, it had taken some hits. The camera lens cover had a slight crack, but the display on the back still functioned. She found a mighty nice image of Pigeon Man captured for posterity.

Who the hell was he? Advance for the governor? Trouble in waiting, scoping out the site?

Kimmer suddenly realized that the young woman at the window held out a soda and food, impatient in a way that meant she'd been waiting—and then, as Kimmer finally reached to take her order, those impatient eyes widened slightly. Huh. *Whatever.* Distracted, Kimmer took her food and pulled out onto the road, unwrapping her burger to eat with one hand as she drove. She headed back north along the lake, not bothering to savor the taste but knowing better than to head for Full Cry Winery without fuel on board. Owen expected her, though he wouldn't greet her news with any glad cries. More likely a nice long discussion about discretion on the job even as he sent the photo out for identification.

And to think Kimmer had hoped for a quiet afternoon at home. A little time for the flowers, a little time to nudge information out of Rio…the kind of information she could simply perceive in anyone else. But no matter how she'd learned to read the nuances of her lover's expressions, it still wasn't the same as using her knack. And lately she wondered if he wasn't doing it on purpose—hiding himself. Hiding his concern for his *sobo*—because he felt she wouldn't understand.

But this afternoon wasn't likely to offer any opportunities. Nor tomorrow. Perhaps the next day….

Kimmer swung into the employee parking lot at Full Cry Winery, putting the car in Park, yanking the keys from the ignition and stepping out of the Miata in nearly the same motion. She took a moment to brush lunch crumbs away and slung the backpack over her shoulder, stepping out in strides long for her height.

She rounded the corner of the main building and ran smack into a winery tour. She knew the guide as she knew most of the employees here, all part of her vague cover as a viniculturist. Her status as a Hunter agent hadn't even been revealed to the local law until the incident with the propane tank. *Yet another reason for Owen's annoyance.*

"Kimmer!" said the guide, looking startled but swiftly shifting into tourism mode. "Um…this is one of our viniculture research experts, Kimmer Reed. Tough day wrestling with the vines, Kimmer?"

Kimmer took a look at the tourists—a group of seven, with various expressions of startlement and one man with a leer he was trying to hide—and said blandly, "That graft with the Venus Flytrap just isn't working out." She gave them a smile and neatly sidestepped the group just in time to forestall the guide from asking for a few quick words about her work. "Enjoy the tour!"

And they would, for it would end in the convincing ambiance of the tasting room, a refurbished area of the original barn that gleamed with tradition and good care. Whereas Kimmer was headed for the hidden technological wonders of the agency offices. The thumb print ID pad had to think about admitting her; she spat on her thumb and scrubbed it off on her pants, and that did the trick. She pushed her way through the other entrance tricks and then fairly jogged down the carpeted hall to Owen's office. No need to go through his admin assistant in the adjoining office; Owen figured that anyone who made it this far was welcome to knock directly on his office door.

So Kimmer knocked, knowing better than to barge in when the door was securely closed, and in a low voice she said, "Kimmer."

And then she waited. Impatient, shifting from foot to foot, indulging herself in a way she wouldn't, were anyone there to watch. Finally Owen said, "All right," and Kimmer entered the office with enough haste to betray herself.

But she stopped short at Owen's expression—an expression she'd already seen several times this afternoon. He said, as dryly as possible, "And here I was just reassuring Chief Harrison that none of my people had anything to do with the bizarre little disturbance in town not so long ago."

Kimmer dropped the backpack on the chair in which she wasn't quite ready to sit, and finally looked down on herself. Smudged, dirty, bloody around her fingers. She ran a hand over her face, but felt no bruises.

"No," Owen said. "Look down. Look *under.*"

Under—? Finally Kimmer realized the one spot to which she didn't have easy visual access and pulled the snug shirt down and away from herself. Sure enough, there was a nice big rip, one that had followed the curve of her breast. That explained the tourist's leer. She gave a little snort and said, "At least I wore a bra today."

"You'll go out of here with something else on," Owen said. "I don't want anyone connecting you with the incident in town."

She decided not to tell him about the tour. "You're assuming I did have something to do with it."

"Yes," Owen said, no apologies there. "I am."

"It wasn't my fault. I didn't start it."

"That," said Owen, "is what I expect to hear from my three-year-old." Kimmer winced and he waved it off. "Just tell me what happened."

She pulled the camera out and handed it to him. Owen connected it to his computer as she quickly summed up the encounter. "I don't get it," she concluded. "I can imagine someone coming out to heckle the governor tomorrow, but Pigeon Man is a lot more than a simple heckler. He risked a lot to get my camera."

"It sounds very much like he was trying to keep you from reporting back to anyone while he was at it."

"Well, he failed on both counts. And you owe me a camera."

"*Another* camera," Owen murmured, saving the image to

his hard drive and immediately starting the identification process by kicking it out to one of his tech folks. "I'll have to fess up that you were involved in the ruckus downtown…but given what started it I think I can make a case it was for the best. Good work in spotting him. But try to avoid playing matador with cars, will you?"

"The thing that bothers me," Kimmer told him, ignoring the matador comment, "is that whole 'more than a simple heckler' thing. Whoever's behind Pigeon Man might not be put off by our little encounter. And whoever it is might have someone else to send out tomorrow."

Owen nodded. "I'm going to pull a few more people into the situation. And I'd like you to get there first thing in the morning. For now, grab a scrub shirt, go home and get yourself a good night's sleep."

Home.

Home to a house with someone else in it, and looking forward to it. Kimmer hadn't ever expected that day to come.

Showered and powdered and lotioned with Lush's Red Rooster citric and cinnamon, Kimmer pulled on an oversized T-shirt and curled up on the bed with a cotton throw over her shoulders, her attention focused on the photo album propped on her pillow.

Rio hadn't brought a great deal with him when he'd come. Some of his things were in storage in his brother's boat garage, but mostly he just seemed to travel light. Socks, jeans, a variety of shirts that fit neatly into her walk-in closet, one suit that tailored well enough over his tall, strong frame to make any woman drool. A heating pad, though she'd had one. A bunch of ice packs. He'd left his weights because she had those, too, along with a membership in the small Watkins

Glen health club. A batch of crossword puzzle books that quickly spread throughout the house, along with his thoughtfully gnawed pencil stubs.

And this album. A photo album not created by any man's hand. His mother, Kimmer assumed. It was one of those memory books with sparkly-pen captions written in a neat hand, fancy hand-scissored borders and loving touches of boyish stickers in the right places. Footballs. Frogs. Unlaced sneakers. Less of that as the pictures ranged from boyhood to the gangly young man who would ultimately fill out to be Rio, but no less care with the captions and the photo placements.

It wasn't just Rio. In fact, it was rarely just Rio. The pictures were crowded with family members, and though Kimmer frequently recognized a young Carolyne, the others she could just guess. His brother, probably, with the same general cast of features but a more barrel-chested build. His sister, who looked a lot like Carolyne but had more refined features in her oval face. Others, aunts and uncles and cousins and who knows who, she just skimmed over, making no real effort to identify them. And then of course there was Rio's *sobo,* an elderly lady who didn't seem to change much over time. Her skin grew more translucent and her eyes slowly disappeared behind aging epicanthic folds, but they were set at an angle that reminded her of Rio's eyes, and in her serene smiles Kimmer imagined she saw a hint of what lay behind Rio's engaging grin.

She returned to the front of the album, running her fingers along the edge of one of the first pictures, then giving in to impulse and lightly tracing her fingertips over the protected surface. A proud young woman and her child, sitting in a rocking chair and draped in baby blankets. Kimmer conjured up an image of the same picture, had it been taken in her household. *A tired woman and her child, sitting in a rocking chair, the baby blanket ragged. The woman, her bruises showing at the edges of her short sleeves, murmured, "I never wanted to bring a girl into this world."* The same words she'd said to Kimmer as she grew older, more bruised and even more weary, trusting Kimmer to understand that she'd always known a girl would have to fight to survive in this family of hers and never considering what it would be like to hear those words as a very young girl.

And later, here was a picture of the boys still in single-digit years, already showing their strength and their long legs. Rio and his brother proudly held their older sister aloft; she lay on her side with her head propped on her hand and utter confidence on her features while they grinned great big toothy grins, arms up overhead and hands carefully placed to keep her balanced.

Kimmer could see herself in that same position. *Four brothers, scrawny and triumphant, doing their best to keep their younger sister balanced overhead while she squirmed and fought. When they put her down it would be into a slop of mud or the cold river during winter or over the edge of the hayloft with very little on the floor below to break her fall.*

Oh, and this one was good...a family portrait. Predictably stilted pose, but their smiles were real enough, and something about the look in Rio's eyes made Kimmer think he'd just pulled some sort of silliness on the photographer. He looked so young, even in his midteens; his beautiful bright wheat hair fell over his brow just as it did today, but the angles of his face were still forming—the basic structure present, but the lines not yet clean, not hardened into the masculine beauty she had first seen in a roadside gas station in rural Pennsylvania, back when she thought she could avoid meeting him altogether.

Family portrait. At that age, no mother, just a blank spot. And there she'd be, edging away from her brothers while her father bestowed upon her a mighty frown. The only question in Kimmer's mind was whether the picture would be snapped before or after her father reached for her.

She put her head down on the pillow, fingers still tracing the edges of the pictures no longer within her line of sight, and tried to use what she'd seen in those pictures to imagine what it was like to be Rio and to be worried about his grandmother.

Nope.

Still couldn't do it. Not for lack of trying. She could see it, as though viewing those emotions from a distance. She could almost reach out and pull those feelings toward her. But ultimately, she just closed her eyes and fell asleep.

Rio hadn't expected to find her here. He'd seen her car, knew she was home, but still hadn't actually expected that to be the case.

He'd been out driving. Thinking. *Don't come,* they'd said. *We need to keep things as simple as possible while we sort things out.* The medication, the home nurse visits, the relearning of Sobo's limitations and abilities.

But he wanted to go. He wanted to go, now.

Being good sucks.

But being observant was useful, so when he'd come inside to none of the usual puttering noises Kimmer made while at home, he'd gone quiet and gone looking.

Unlike Rio, Kimmer scarcely ever simply sank into a chair for reading or even helping with one of his crosswords. She'd offer suggestions, but she'd do it while she was working with the weights or cooking something decadent or refinishing furniture or…

Perpetual motion machine. That was Kimmer on her own turf.

But now she was still. Sleeping. Her mouth relaxed and lips just barely parted—and so much more appealing in its natural color than in the bright lipstick she'd used in her undercover persona when they'd met. She must have showered; the scent of cinnamon lingered in the room, and her dark curls, even this short, had the untamed look that meant she'd hadn't brushed them out when they were wet. He took another step toward the bed, but still out of reach, for he'd come to appreciate more and more how ill-conceived it was to startle this woman. Sleeping or just distracted, she came back fighting first, asked questions later—and she kept herself in training and condition to do just that. Her very sweet little ass peeked out from an oversized T-shirt and the cotton throw in a bare-cheeked way that made him look twice.

Hoo boy.

And her legs—not long and runway-model lean, but at Kimmer's height, legs didn't often come in *long.* They did come perfectly proportioned, muscled even in repose—and were those bruises?

Rio shifted, moving closer to the side of the bed instead of the end of it, taking advantage of the early evening light from the window. Yes. Bruises. Deep ones. He couldn't make out the nature of them; couldn't think of anything she might have been doing today that would have involved such scuffling. Ouch.

What he could do was see that she'd been looking at the memory book his mother had made. He doubted Kimmer could recognize the touches that spoke of Sobo—the white space every bit as important as the photos, the photos never crowded on the page, the captions placed just so—but to Rio they were every bit as important as the memories the photos invoked.

He didn't have to guess what she'd been doing.

Trying to understand.

Just as he was trying to understand how she could so thoroughly cut the ties to her own family, never knowing whether her brothers had grown out of their cruelties, whether her father still lived, whether any of them ever regretted contributing to a life that had driven Kimmer away so young. Thinking of Hank, Rio made a face. The man had been frightened. Awkward. Out of his league and knowing it…and then embarrassed at the extent of his salvation at Kimmer's hands.

But he had a wife. He had children. Who knew how many other nieces or nephews Kimmer had by now? She hadn't asked Hank and he hadn't volunteered. Mostly he'd hidden out in front of the television, although he'd learned very quickly that casual demands for service or food had done little good. Kimmer had made the food easily available and left it at that.

Rio had his own nightmares—betrayal, the death of friends, the agonizing injury that had ended his career and almost his life, the long recovery—but he wouldn't want to be in Kimmer's place.

A sudden shift of light foretold sunset. Rio moved to the other side of the bed. Pulling off the thick cable sweater made some noise. He removed his watch and belt and let that make noise, too. Kimmer stirred by then, and he said softly, "It's me." She smiled and would have turned to him, still half-asleep in that relaxed way that let him know she understood perfectly well who it was, but he leaned over the bed and put a hand on her shoulder, and she settled. He ran that hand from shoulder down the curve of her back and into the dip of her waist, and let it come to rest on—yes, on that sweet little ass. Always good for a moment of appreciation. His body sighed happily, in complete agreement.

Then he lifted the end of the cotton throw and slid in underneath, spooning up against Kimmer. She wasn't slow to realize he came mostly dressed, still in a T-shirt over the loose-legged jeans he preferred. And it must have suited her on this particular night, for instead of turning over to undress him, she inched back against him, lifting her arm just enough so he could slide his hand in over her ribs, letting it come to rest quite comfortably over her just-right breast. The rest of him responded immediately but not with any intense urgency…just savoring the sweetness of lying there with as much of Kimmer as possible tucked up against as much of him as possible. Her head and its cinnamon-scented curls tucked in under his chin, but only after he'd kissed it. Thoughtfully. Very much aware that they'd had few of these quiet moments—that Kimmer allowed very few of them.

Perpetual motion Kimmer, always keeping herself busy. Not, he thought, because she was so driven by her past. Aside from the days since Hank's arrival, he'd seen little sign that it actively bothered her anymore. She'd come to some sort of peace with who she was on that very assignment on which she'd met him, enough peace to let someone in her life for the first time.

Someone. *Him.*

Now all they had to do was make it work.

We'll figure it out.

We have to.

* * *

Kimmer faced Governor Day stiff with bruises. The whole bouncing off a car trick hadn't been her best thought-out ploy ever, but it had worked—and those on the governor's team now had a clear photo of the man involved, even if he hadn't yet been identified. Any minute now, the governor would arrive. The Hunter Agency would save the day and return to being nothing more than a benign local presence. Kimmer could go back to sorting out her life—to building something new for herself.

Today she wore professional bland. Black tailored blazer, black slacks, black dress shoes comfortable enough for running. Her silk V-neck shirt came in deep forest-green, and no one had to know that she'd painted her toenails in something closer to lime—or that they matched her underwear. Her scent of the day had almost been mentholated muscle rub, but she'd opted for a more subtle ginger destiny powder. Unlike the others working security here, Kimmer had a tiny walkie-talkie in her pocket but no coil of wire up to her ear. Nothing nearly so obvious. She was Hunter's secret weapon, and the coil of wire was really obvious.

She'd left Rio preparing for a real estate run, drive-bys of those properties that had intrigued him from the listings he'd been gathering. Her house had never been meant for two. Not when they consisted of one woman fiercely protective of her turf and a man who had longer legs and a larger personal presence than most.

But she had mixed feelings about the results of his search. She loved her little house, the remodeled interior built just to her tastes. She loved drowsing in the same bed and sitting in his lap to do his crosswords, even if she rarely sat still long enough to make it through a whole puzzle. She wasn't sure she wanted to give up any of it.

Moving easily through the edges of the crowd which now waited with growing impatience, Kimmer spotted the man who didn't want to be there but who'd been towed by his significant other, the woman who had a crush on the governor, and the older woman who waited, intense and ready to deride everything the man had to say. Kimmer slipped a sinus-tingling mint into her mouth and checked her watch. Any minute now.

And then she looked up and met the eyes of the man for whom she'd been watching. Not a face she knew, not features she knew. But a man waiting for the right moment, poised for action and impatient in spite of his apparent outward repose. She saw his eyes—muddy brown even from fifteen feet away—widen slightly.

Knows I've pegged him as trouble....

Just what kind of trouble she didn't know or care—she couldn't let the governor walk into it. She pulled her tiny radio from her pocket and put it to her mouth. "Chimera here. Abort, abort. Hostile spotted." But as she held the device to her ear, the crowd noise swelled and a spatter of applause built to as much enthusiasm as a small crowd in a small park in a small town could generate. She didn't think the governor had actually appeared—no, a quick glance showed her he'd merely been spotted on the far side of the bandstand—and though he'd stopped and bent his silvered head to listen to the brief words of his escort, the audience still anticipated his imminent arrival. The escort gestured out toward the crowd and the governor gave a sharp shake of his head.

"Chimera, report!" the radio crackled, barely intelligible over the crowd noise no matter how closely she held it.

The man hadn't moved. The crowd surged briefly around him; he held his ground. Ugly brown suit, blue tie that didn't match. Muddy brown eyes that did. Hand dipping inside his coat in a move Kimmer knew too well—a move she couldn't make sense of. Why give himself away? If he knew he'd been spotted, he might well have tried to quietly walk away before she could reach him. If he didn't know, why expose himself before the governor was anywhere near the range of a handgun?

Her own hand twitched for her waist, where a streamlined belt holster held the equally streamlined SIG Sauer she carried in dress mode. But the crowd, spontaneously renewing its applause, changed her mind. She slipped her hand into the wide flat pocket of her blazer and retrieved the war club from where it subtly ruined the lines of the tailoring.

Brown Suit had to know she was carrying. Had to. What the hell was he up to? He still stared her way and Kimmer's expectations warred with her observations until she finally gave up and followed her knack.

He wasn't here for the governor.

He was here for *her.*

Rio lay on the floor, back against the braided rug and legs propped up on the big recliner, pencil stub between his teeth. OldCat purred on his chest, quite successfully giving the impression that Rio was actually in OldCat's way and that the purring was a complete coincidence.

Working on the crossword puzzle that had recently ended up wrinkled between the two of them pretty much seemed a lost cause. He rubbed a finger on that spot between OldCat's eyes where the short, stiff hair met from all directions and contemplated the real estate properties he'd seen that morning. Contemplated the chances that Kimmer would want to leave her home to make a new one with him. Contemplated the fact that he even doubted.

He hadn't doubted when he'd packed up to move down here. He knew they had much to learn, much to build. But until now he hadn't truly absorbed Kimmer's bitterness about her family. And while he accepted that as well as he could, he couldn't accept the thought of watching her apply those same standards to his own family.

OldCat squeezed his eyes closed, pretended not to notice Rio's perfectly placed scritching. Purred. Purred so loudly that Rio almost missed the slight click of the doorknob.

Not Kimmer. Kimmer wouldn't be back for hours. Kimmer wouldn't open the door slowly, carefully, uncertain if it would squeak and betray her.

Rio dumped OldCat. The creature gave a scolding meow, smacked him with blunt end of the stumpy leg, and lurched away with his tail held high. By then Rio had rolled to his feet, bare soles silent on the hardwood floor. He stayed low, crouch-walking to the old-timey glass-paned door that separated this reading room from the entryway when it was closed. As he hesitated there, the intruder walked right into the entry and stopped to take stock without even realizing Rio crouched a mere arms-length away, half-hidden behind the reading room entrance.

And Rio came nose to nose with the man's stun gun.

Aw, not again.

He'd had his fill of stun guns down in Mill Springs not so very long ago. This one filled the man's hand, held with easy familiarity and an obvious willingness to use the thing, but it wasn't nearly as big as the one Rio had encountered in Mill Springs so up close and personal. Its presence likely meant the man wasn't here to harm—and in fact didn't want to harm—but that he had some other mission.

Still. No, thank you.

Rio removed the pencil stub from his teeth, stuck it between his fingers point out, and gave the back of the man's hand a quick pop, lightning-fast, full of focused impact.

The man made a noise somewhere between a howl and a snarl. Though the stun gun went flying, the man turned his reaction into a perfect pivot, bringing his knee up into Rio's face. Rio staggered backward, landed on his ass and scrambled awkwardly around to find his hands and knees, ready to launch himself forward—

And faced the man from the photograph Kimmer had taken the day before, an image she had left in hardcopy on the kitchen table this morning.

Here we go again.

Chapter 6

Me.

He's after *me*.

Kimmer had barely slipped her hand through the club's thong when Brown Suit's expression changed—and not for the better. The *backup has arrived* expression, never a good thing. A child came capering out of the crowd between Kimmer and Brown Suit, a donkey-imprinted balloon in tow. Kimmer shifted gears and tried to peel off to the side, knowing there was someone behind her somewhere—

Too late. Dammit. She could see it in Brown Suit's face, knew an instant before the hands descended upon her from behind that someone had reached her—and knew from the very breadth of those hands that it was someone big. He clamped his hands on to her arms just above the elbow, pinning them to her sides and neatly evading the blind kick she lashed at him, and then as she hissed frustration between her teeth, he yanked her arms back, sliding his grip down to her wrists.

So he can pin them together with one hammy hand. So he has one hand free to do…whatever.

I don't think so.

Then think fast, Kimmer. Think very fast. Brown Suit headed their way, smug and needing to be hit, his quick glances taking in everything about the situation—her helplessness, the rising disturbance of the crowd as they realized the governor had stopped on the verge of making an appearance, the staticky blast from Kimmer's pocket as her radio demanded attention. *Report, Chimera.* Yeah, right. "Pay attention, you idiots!" she snapped at the blameless radio. "Try *looking* this way!"

Even if they did, they'd never make it here in time. And the crowd, though alarmed and making noises of protest, still kept its collective distance.

Up to me.

Same old, same old.

Hammy Hands held her wrists, not her hands. Kimmer flipped the war club around on the thong so the handle—the narrow, delightfully solid hardwood handle—aimed outward.

Then she rammed herself backward.

And she aimed low.

Hammy Hands dropped with a gut-wrenching groan—and he took Kimmer down with him. But now she had the room to kick at him, twisting in his grip to land several swift blows in succession. "You're supposed—" *kick* "—to let—" *kick* "—GO!"

And finally he did, and she bounced to her feet and found herself face-to-face with Brown Suit.

Face-to-face and something quite abruptly poking in her

belly. Inwardly she snapped off a searing curse; outwardly she smiled sweetly. "I don't suppose you're glad to see me."

His face took on a tight amusement. "I suppose I am. So glad, in fact, that I'd like to prolong our conversation."

Kimmer didn't even have to glance around to see that the crowd had withdrawn, giving them wide berth but still not certain what was going on. *That's okay. Me neither.* Or to know that sooner or later, one of those who had drawn in to protect the governor would be here by her side.

Or to know that she couldn't chance the possibility that her resistance would result in the injury or death of someone in this crowd, some of whom seemed about to interfere. They couldn't see the gun, held so tightly between Kimmer and Brown Suit. "A chat," she said. "How lovely. And it looks like we have so very much to talk about."

His hand closed over her arm. He'd chosen the one with the club still hanging discreetly by its thong, hobbling her without even knowing it. *Figures.* Didn't mean she couldn't still manage an offhand draw of the SIG, as awkward as it would be.

It wasn't as if she hadn't practiced.

But not here. She let herself be steered away from the crowd, hoping that the first security personnel on the scene would be Hunter agents, that they would know to approach with discretion when they saw her leaving without resistance. Leaving, in fact, like two friends walking away from a no-show governor in the park.

"You're not here for our friendly politician," she said. "This isn't Plan B, using me to walk away. This is Plan A, isn't it? Although I doubt your friend expected to get left behind." *Then again, I doubt he expected me to take him down.*

"He can take care of himself," Brown Suit said, but when

Kimmer tried to glance back to see, he jammed the gun hard into her belly.

"Sheesh," she said. "One belly button is plenty."

Brown Suit shook his head in her peripheral vision. "I heard you were a smart-ass."

"Did you?" Kimmer felt unexpectedly pleased as they passed through the open iron gates. Headed for a car somewhere, and then headed for…it didn't matter. She knew she didn't want to go there. He hadn't searched her yet, but there was no way he'd shove her into the car until he'd handled that detail, and she had too many backup systems to lose. "That's funny, you know. No one's ever said anything to me about you."

"Nice try, but I'm not answering questions today." He steered her down the Decatur Street sidewalk, away from the park. Pretty, charming downtown Watkins Glen, seen at gunpoint. It gave her an entirely new perspective. Beside her, Brown Suit snorted, amused by his own thoughts. "Next you'll try to convince me to let you go because you don't know anything. Well, guess what. Your brother has been known to squeal like the proverbial pig. He thinks he's saved his hide, but he's really only taken you down with him. He'll know that before this is over. He's not nearly as smart as he thinks he is."

"Tell me something I don't know," Kimmer muttered, furiously yanking her suppositions about the situation to another, totally unexpected direction. This wasn't about her work with Hunter. This wasn't about the governor.

Hank. It was somehow still about Hank.

Dammit.

Owen was going to spit.

She wiggled the fingers of her hand, finding them tingly

and clumsy from his tight grip. They'd have to do. She could still feel the club, and Brown Suit—one hand busy with his gun and the other clamped around her wrists—couldn't. That was all that mattered. "About Hank—"

"We'll have this conversation later," he said shortly, yanking her to a stop, not beside the sedate sedan she'd expected, but an old Escort that must have come from the nearest Rent-a-Wreck. He shoved her back against the car, and kept the stubby gun barrel jammed into her stomach—good old S&W .38, she carried one herself sometimes—as he fished around in his pocket.

Oh, good. Handcuffs. He was going to be so sorry, oh yes… Kimmer smiled blandly at him, thinking it was too bad he didn't notice. Then he might have been prepared. He might have at least been more wary, although considering what she'd done to Hammy Hands she figured he'd had his warning.

He held out the cuffs, giving a jerk of his chin toward her hands. "Put 'em on."

Kimmer took the cuffs, but only long enough to drop them. She made a noise of dismay as they clattered to the asphalt by the curb and immediately knelt to get them, her hand already shoving her blazer aside to reach for the SIG.

He must have been wary after all. He didn't even hesitate before lashing his foot up in a kick that was meant for her face but landed on her shoulder as she desperately twisted aside, cursing herself for underestimating him.

But he'd thrown himself off balance and had no follow-through. When Kimmer slammed back against the car she bounced right back at him, swung the club at the side of his weight-bearing leg, and rolled forward on momentum. She scrambled out of his way as the joint went crack and he screamed and fell, all pretty much at the same time. She dropped the club and snatched up her gun, and just that quickly their positions were reversed. "You better hope my collarbone's not broken," she snarled at him.

She didn't think he heard her. Which was fair enough, because she suddenly didn't hear him, either. She suddenly realized that if they'd sent two men to find her here at the park, they might well have sent someone else to her house.

And Rio had no warning at all.

The man had trailed Kimmer yesterday, come looking for her today. *Three strikes, you're out.* And Rio didn't particularly care that his math didn't add up. He launched at the man's legs, happy enough to take advantage of the height and breadth he had on the guy. Pigeon Man. It was a solid hit and they both went flying, skidding down the hardwood floor of the hall and taking a small rug with them. For a few murky moments the struggle deteriorated into high school antics, each of them trying for the upper hand without actually finding any opportunities. Rio heard a hiss and spit, made no sense of it, and ignored it. Then his weight won out and he got enough control to sit briefly on Pigeon Man's chest, snatch his very nice suit jacket at the lapels, and put him through a few lift-and-bash head-slammers. Pigeon Man strained to reach something—Rio didn't care what it was, only that if Pigeon Man wanted it, Rio didn't want him to get it. He jerked them back down the hall again, using Pigeon Man as a sled. Then he rested two curled fingers against the man's throat, knuckles strategically placed against cartilage.

Rio leaned forward, all his weight on those knuckles. Although the man had a hand free—the other being neatly tucked under Rio's knee—he stiffened, and didn't follow through on his evident intention to batter at Rio's head.

"What are you doing here? What do you want from Kimmer?"

"Camera," the man managed, his eyes bulging just a little.

"Ah." Rio nodded, finally identifying the location of the low, constant growl in the background as just inside the kitchen. "It's broken. And you're too late. Your photo is pretty much in the hands of every cop, agent, bodyguard, National Guardsman and Boy Scout in this part of the state. Probably the Girl Scouts, too."

Annoyance shot through those murky brown eyes, and Rio rolled his knuckles slightly. "Take it easy there, fella. Because guess what, it can't do you any harm now. I've already *got* you." And as soon as he called the cops, Rio would just as quickly lose him. Pigeon Man would disappear into the system to be questioned by the authorities—and not by one ex-CIA agent who hadn't even yet committed himself to working part-time with the Hunter agency. Sooo…

Let's not call the cops. Not just yet.

"You wouldn't want the camera if you hadn't been up to no good in the first place. So tell me what's so fascinating about Lafayette Park that you found the need to case it so thoroughly, and that you had to come after an innocent—" Okay, that was stretching it. The man would know as much after his alleyway encounter: car vs. woman and woman wins "—after Kimmer." *And how did you know where she lives?*

He realized that part almost too late. *Getting slow, Rio.* He let it show on his face before he could stop it. *Getting stupid, Rio—*

The man bucked, straining to crawl out from beneath Rio, his free hand reaching and grasping for anything to latch on to and pull; his fingers scrabbled at the end corner of the hall-way, clawing into the kitchen to the tune of a rising growl.

None of that. Time to secure the bastard and *then* talk. Rio lifted the man, ready to give him a good swift couple of thumps against the hard floor—enough to buy him the time to fling open the junk drawer in the kitchen and snatch up the cable ties.

But with a final surge of motion, a grunt of effort, and an amazingly animalistic snarl, Pigeon Man lurched forward just enough to snatch up what he'd been reaching for.

Rio, ready to disarm him and expecting the wayward stun gun, stopped short at the sight of a furious scruff-gripped Old-Cat.

He realized his mistake in that instant. The hesitation. The transference of initiative.

"Now we'll talk," the man said, his voice still croaky from the knuckling he'd received. "You dumb bastard. What did you hope to accomplish? Showing off for your bitch of a girl-friend? We owed her before and now we've got plenty of rea-son to see that she pays. Now get the fuck off me or this mangy cat goes facefirst into this wall."

Rio should have said something smart, like *he's had a long life* or *he's still got three lives to go* or *he's not even my cat,* but instead he froze, a moment of startled reaction while he calculated ways to keep OldCat safe or at least free from im-mediate demise.

Pigeon Man snatched the initiative and flung OldCat not into the wall but at Rio's face.

OldCat shrieked a feline curse and landed with claws set to shred—but immediately leaped away, tail double its nor-mal size and sticking straight up in the air as he yowled his fury. And when Rio looked down at Pigeon Man, ready to let the man know he'd done nothing but really make Rio mad, he suddenly recalled Pigeon Man's frantic movement beneath him, and just as suddenly realized what it had to mean, giving himself just enough warning to try to throw himself away and out of range but not enough warning to actually do it.

The wayward stun gun came into action, stabbing at his leg and then a second jolt directly on the tender skin of his side, exposed where his shirt had ridden up. His body jerked into an involuntary cry; his vision turned gray and sparkly and his ears roared. He fell to the floor feeble and twitching, his face mashed uncomfortably against the hardwood and his muscles feeling like so much overcooked noodle.

Stun gun. Dammit. Again.

Pigeon Man left him that way, disentangling himself to head straight for the kitchen to shuffle around the few items sitting out on the counter, and then to the tiny dining area to clear the messy table in one sweep, scattering the contents so coins and former pocket contents came rolling to a stop by Rio's nose. The man made a cursory search through it all and demanded, "Where is it?"

Rio tried a few words. They didn't work. Just as well; they hadn't been words the man would like. Carefully, slowly, parts of him still quivering from the electrical assault, he stated the obvious. "'Sbroke!"

The man kicked him—more like an afterthought than a deliberate, targeted blow, and Rio was glad he didn't hear anything crack. "Moron. I'm not talking about the camera. I mean the recording."

That was enough to get a surprised grunt from Rio, a wordless, "What?"

"The *recording*," Pigeon Man repeated in rising impatience. "Hank said it was in the kitchen. A nice cozy brother-sister chat detailing our operations. On keychain memory."

If Hank had said even that much—as absurd as it was—then he must have been in trouble. Or desperately trying to get out of it. Rio fought through his bleary mind, just as desperate to put two thoughts together.

He didn't get the chance. The phone rang, an urgent and startling sound. And again, from the kitchen floor where Pigeon Man had flung it in his mad search. Pigeon Man hesitated, as if whoever was calling would leave a message such as "Rio! I left the keychain memory stick under the mattress!"

At the fourth ring, the answering machine clicked on. "Rio, heads-up!" Kimmer, out of breath and obviously on the move. "BGs on the loose. I'm on my way—" and then the honk of a horn, the distant squeal of tires and Kimmer's muttered curse as the line went dead. Eventually the answering machine clicked off and commenced the every-fifteen-seconds beeping noise it would make until Rio was insane or until he got to his feet and shut it up.

Pigeon Man stood frozen for a few indecisive moments, then dove into the living room and tore through the neat contents of drawers, shelf and beneath cushions. Change clinked on the floor; something broke. Rio rolled to his side, slowly gathered his legs to where he might consider rolling over on those, too. Twitchy, tingly muscles, still zinging with nerve pain. In a brief moment of silence in the search-caused destruction, the answering machine beeped.

Look, little man. Search away. Given another moment, and Rio would be back on his feet. A moment longer and Kimmer would pull into the driveway. She might not even brake before reaching the living room.

But Pigeon Man had a keen awareness of the time. He gave up on the living room and ran back to Rio, disrupting Rio's newly found balance by snatching his sweater—an attempt at lapel-grabbing, except the sweater mostly just stretched. "Where's the goddam record—"

Rio drove himself up with every bit of still-uncoordinated strength he had, and his head connected with Pigeon Man's face. Pigeon Man flailed wildly and fell back, and Rio would have pounced on him had he not also bounced back from the impact. By the time he untangled himself, Pigeon Man had spewed a string of blood-spitting curses and bolted for the still-open front door.

Oh, no. No, you don't, you sonuvabitch. Rio clawed to his uncooperative feet and staggered after Pigeon Man, determined to at least get a license plate number and stumbling down the front porch steps upright more by coincidence than design—just in time to see Pigeon Man hot-footing it between two houses across the street. No license plates here, not even any cars. Rio's knees gave up the fight and he didn't try to stop it, just gave thanks he was on the lawn and not the concrete of the sidewalk. And that's just where he was moments later when Kimmer's Miata slewed to a stop at the bottom of the driveway.

Kimmer saw him from down the street and accelerated the short distance to her driveway, coming to a controlled skid of a stop even as she shoved the stick into neutral and yanked the parking brake. Rio on his knees, bright blond hair in severe disarray, eyes glazed and a puffy bruised abrasion along one of those magnificent cheekbones that almost obscured the set of deep parallel scratches there. She dropped to a crouch before him, taking in the open front door, the quiet neighborhood. In the distance a car engine gunned to a peak, dropped into the next gear and faded away. "What happened?" she demanded.

"Sonuvabitch," Rio muttered, and Kimmer suddenly knew where she'd seen that look on his face before. *The floor of a remote building, with Carolyne sobbing beside him.* Stungunned. She saw, too, the fury lurking in his dazed brown eyes and she knew then that he was all right. She patted his cheek gently and stood, extending a hand. "C'mon," she said. "We've got places to be."

"House," he said, somewhat apologetically. He took her hand and let her put some muscle into getting him to his feet. Once he was there she slipped her shoulder under his and took him as far as the porch step railing.

She glanced at the door. "Pretty bad?"

"Bad enough." He sounded more like Rio, then. Getting over it.

Kimmer bounded up the stairs and closed the door. No point in letting OldCat out. "Then we'll have something to do when we get back."

Rio snorted most expressively, and she helped him out to the car.

Kimmer left the scene somewhat more sedately than she had arrived, but not by much. She blew through Watkins Glen before Rio stirred in the passenger seat, making subtle adjustments to the seat belt she'd buckled for him. When he glanced over at her he finally looked alert, if still mad. "Where are we going?"

"Schuyler Hospital in Montour Falls. Hammy Hands got away, but Brown Suit ended up in his own damn cuffs." She glanced over, assessed him as ready to listen, and gave him a quick recap of the events in the park. "Owen's there, and so's Chief Harrison. They're…not happy…that I ran off to check on the house." *To check on you.* "Doesn't matter. Even if I wasn't expected there, I'd want this. Brown Suit will probably need surgery on that knee, and I want to talk to him first."

"Pigeon Man wanted a recording." Rio looked a little surprised that he was only now remembering to relay this information. "A USB keychain stick. He might go back to the house—"

"Let him." Kimmer navigated hilly Route 414 with familiar confidence, pushing the speed limit to a significant degree and ignoring the casually gorgeous scenery. "What's he going to find? And I gather the place is already a mess."

"Gomen nasai." Rio touched two fingers to his abraded cheek in a rueful gesture along with the apology. "You looked like an avenging goddess, running up that lawn."

Kimmer snorted gently. "That was stun-gun haze," she told him. "What do you know about this recording? Anything? Neither of my guys said anything about it."

"Only that Hank said it existed. Supposed to be a record, and I quote, 'detailing our operations.'" He checked his ribs, gave a dismissive little shrug.

"Hank." Kimmer felt her voice go hard, her body stiffen, her fingers tighten on the wheel. "Brown Suit said something about Hank." About squealing like a pig. About going down with Kimmer. "That's why I've got to talk to him."

"Does Owen know?"

Kimmer shrugged, managing to release the angry tension she'd gathered. "Depends on what Brownie has said since I left him." They headed into Montour Falls and quickly hit the light at Steuben, where she turned left and drove along the hospital complex, already hunting a parking spot as they approached the turnoff. "If not, he's about to find out."

The E.R. held only a smattering of people. One early drunk, reeking from across the room and apparently left to sleep it off. A young woman with a tearful toddler whose cheeks were flushed with fever. An uneasy uniformed cop who spotted Kimmer and came to attention, his thumbs tucked in his laden equipment belt. She went to him.

"Ma'am," he said. "They're in the back." His formality came from offense rather than respect; he thought her a trouble-maker.

Well, he was right.

The cop gave Rio a wary eye but said nothing, and Kimmer could see him forming the decision to let the chief handle this one. He'd just do his job and get Kimmer to the right room.

Enclosed rooms in the small E.R. were rare enough, but Brown Suit had been given one. The cop opened the door, stuck his head in to murmur a few words and then stepped back to indicate that Kimmer should enter. Rio followed as a matter of fact, nodding to Owen and the chief.

Kimmer kept her initial attention on Brown Suit. An air brace encased his knee, and handcuffs secured him to the hospital bed. Kimmer wondered if they were still his very own cuffs. He'd been stuffed into a hospital gown, and his expression had a tight, resistant look that spoke of his pain and his determination to avoid revealing anything. He'd probably refused pain meds for that very reason. She turned her attention to Owen, giving him a nod that said she knew they'd talk about all this later. And then turned to the chief, a very tall fellow who might or might not have to duck under the average ceiling fan. Middle aged, but not showing it except for the gray at his temples and the creases at the corners of his eyes, he had one eyebrow raised and an expectant expression.

And reasonably so. "This is Rio Carlsen," she told him. "He's had some experience with law enforcement."

And Rio, bless him, did that polite bow that his grand-mother had drilled into him, shallow enough so as not to seem entirely out of place in American society but effective all the same. He also held out his hand and answered the chief's obvious unspoken question. "Ex-CIA," he said. "No inclination to get in the way."

The chief shook his hand, offering a brisk nod in return. He might have asked what Rio was doing there at all, but let it go, even as his eyes raked the scratch'n'abrasion combo on Rio's face.

Maybe later.

Owen said, "We've just begun our conversation with Mr. Doe. There was some delay while they checked him for damage."

"Oops." But Kimmer didn't even feign regret.

"You might want to have an X-ray or two yourself," the chief suggested, not particularly kidding. "You were on our watch. We don't take injuries in the line of duty lightly."

"Nor do I," Kimmer assured him. "I'm fine, but if you'd prefer I have someone take a look, that's fine, too." And it was. Out in the field, she could operate in a damaged state for as long as she had to…or at least for as long as her body let her. But when it wasn't necessary, playing macho got her nowhere. She couldn't afford to have her body fail her through negligence.

By now Brown Suit wore a wary expression tinged with annoyance. "If you'ns aren't planning to talk to me, maybe you could take this elsewhere?"

"Tsk," Kimmer told him. "Crabby without that morphine, aren't you?"

And the chief gave her a startled glance as if about to ask her how she knew; Owen only smiled slightly. But Harrison left the question behind and got to the point with their prisoner. "Mr. Doe," he said, putting a dry twist on the title, "We've got your prints. I'm comfortable with the notion that they're on file. We'll figure out who you are. Once we do, we'll also figure out the identity of your accomplice. You've got nothing to lose by telling us his name...and everything to gain."

Brown Suit snorted, then winced. "Don't see how you figure that."

"Because," Kimmer said, easily filling in the chief's train of thought, "if you make us jump through the hoops, we're going to be intensely irritated with you. And if you cooperate...there are so many ways your life could be easier."

Another startled glance from Harrison, this one more successfully concealed. He nodded to himself. It looked like approval to Kimmer; she relaxed slightly.

Brown Suit feigned boredom—not an easy task under his physical circumstances. Kimmer had to give him points. He wasn't, she thought, so unwilling to talk. Not personally. But he had reasons to avoid it. Beneath his tension and pain peeked a glimpse of fear.

Harrison said, "You can thank Ms. Reed for the fact that we're not simply throwing the book at you. If you'd completed your attack on the governor, you'd be in a much different position right now." Brown Suit barely stifled his surprise—but then, Kimmer knew he hadn't been there for the governor, and she hardly needed her knack to see that surprise anyway. The chief missed it. He said, "We need to know the identity of your accomplice. I suppose once the feds get here they'll want to know what you hoped to achieve. The governor is hardly a figure of controversy."

Not exactly true; there was the whole abortion issue. But

not relevant, either. By now Brown Suit was settling into complacency, finding security in the chief's misunderstanding.

Time to rattle him.

Kimmer said, "Your friend didn't find what he was looking for."

She got his attention. She got Harrison's attention. She got Owen's attention. Only Rio remained relaxed, watching Brown Suit closely. Kimmer added, "But we have his photo, as I imagine you know. Or should I say, as I imagine *you'ns* know?"

Owen stood a little straighter, an obvious change in a man of his robust nature. He inclined his head at Harrison and said, "We're here as a courtesy." *Don't step on any toes.*

"Actually," Harrison said dryly, "I just wanted to keep an eye on her."

Given the last week or so, Kimmer could even appreciate that. She watched him, waiting for him to verbalize the decision his body language told her he'd already made, while Brown Suit waited with hope, expecting turf wars to win out over cooperation and knowing full well it was to his own advantage that they do. Finally Harrison nodded. "Run with it," he said, and he, too, was watching the unspoken curse reflected on Brown Suit's face.

She circled to the other side of the bed so Brown Suit would have to split his attention while Harrison could watch them both. "You didn't even know the governor would be here until you came looking for me," she told him. "You and your friend in the park and the incompetent muscle who tried to nab me yesterday and who came looking for the photos today. Didn't you do any recon at all? Or did you just rely on tracking my car?"

"Those aren't real questions," Brown Suit said disdainfully, but the glint of worry in his eyes told her she'd gotten it all right. "If you want to tell stories, try pediatrics."

"Here's a story," Kimmer said. "Someone sent you. Someone big enough that you don't dare reveal your ties to him, because whatever we can do to you, he can do worse. Your goonboss. Well, guess what? When we figure out who you are and who you're working for without your help, that person is still going to blame you. And when we do figure it out, it's going to hit the news. You boys didn't do yourselves any favors with your timing."

"In fact," Harrison said, a bit of a drawl in his words, "you've drawn quite a bit of attention to yourselves."

The thought alarmed Brown Suit, and Kimmer capitalized on it. "By now there must be statewide news flashes—and the national news is already poking around for footage. Or did you think no one would notice when the governor ran back to his limo surrounded by bodyguards? Did you think no one there would have cameras?"

She was guessing, but Harrison's quick glance in her direction told her she'd hit the mark. There was footage, all right. Kimmer and the BGs, clinched in battle. Owen shifted, exchanging his own glance with Kimmer. For Chimera's sake, he'd have to find a way to suppress national exposure of any footage that showed her face.

Or steal it, if he had to. Hunter was as zealous about protecting its own as any international agency.

"It's us or them," Kimmer told Brown Suit. "And I think you know which way you're better off." She stopped, considered her words a moment, and smiled a feral smile at the man. "At least, as long as you're not where *I* can get you."

Chapter 7

*K*immer threw the knives one after the other, an old piece of plywood set up against the inside of the barn as her target. Two of the cheap knives thunked into the wood and stuck; the third clattered dully against the dirt floor. She'd had the knives ordered from a catalog she found on the counter of the sporting goods store in town. She'd told the proprietor they were a gift and he'd done nothing more than warn her that the inexpensive nature of the knives would make them harder to learn with....

He'd been right. But she kept working on it, and she slowly got better, and she saved her money for some real knives. Once she was good enough, she'd let her brothers catch on to her covertly acquired skill...she might even have to sacrifice a knife or two to demonstrate. But it would be worth the expense if they kept their distance.

She looked down at herself, uneasy. Even baggy hand-me-

downs no longer disguised the fact that she'd changed this last summer. Those were real breasts now, and not just little buds. And even if her hips would never bloom into a truly womanly figure, the curves were obvious enough. She ran a hand from collarbone to hip, feeling the changes—areas of softness over the tight muscle she cultivated with her own fierce training. Some of the girls in her class had lost their interest in boyish games, but Kimmer threw herself into every gym class, every opportunity to sneak into the school's tiny, smelly weight room.

And now she'd used what time she considered safe for her knife practice, and she gathered them up and hid them away, flipping the plywood over to look like the scrap it was. She badly wanted to draw a man-size target on it, but doing so would only truly give away her game if it were found. So she hid the knives and turned to the battered workout bag she'd made—a feedbag stuffed with dirt and straw, hay twine criss-crossed up and down its length just to keep it together. She put old socks over her hands to protect her knuckles from the rough material, grateful enough that the bag had been left alone. Her brothers liked to use it, she thought. Otherwise they'd tear it into bits.

It creaked underneath the pounding she gave it, swaying gently on the long sisal rope that swung from the rafters. She'd done some reading. She'd learned to strike at a point just on the other side of the bag, to drive her energy through. She practiced kicks until they seemed natural, learned to balance on one leg as easily as two, learned to keep herself centered. She drove herself at the bag until her arms burned and her thighs tingled and her feet and fists ached from impact.

Because now…now Kimmer had something to protect. Those breasts, those hips…. They might not be much com-

pared to what the other girls of her age were showing off, but they were all hers.

"Hey, Pizza."

Kimmer whirled, her feet planted, her fists up and ready. "Jeff," she said flatly. Oldest brother, still not come into his growth, but then, none of them looked like they'd get much bigger.

Normally she heard them coming. Normally she slipped out through the ragged spot in the corner, or under the floorboards by the feed room. Today she'd made a mistake...she'd lost herself in the pure physical exertion, in the thrill of feeling that in this one thing, she had control. She'd given him the chance to come up behind her, to call out to her. Pizza, for the port wine birthmark over the side of her face. Short for Road Pizza.

Except today Jeff was alone, and though he'd been heading her way; when she whirled on him he stopped short. He had a slightly puzzled expression, as though he'd run into someone other than who he'd expected to find here.

Kimmer realized, with a tiny bloom of triumph, that he was actually uncertain of her. That in the absence of Hank and Tim and Karl and even the oft-present Leo, he actually hesitated to approach her.

But she didn't push it. She didn't let him see her awareness. She dropped her gaze and her fists and she took a step back. Just as suddenly, Jeff's normal bravado slid into place. He grew an inch or two and habitual scorn dropped on to his features. "Get to the kitchen," he said. "There's dishes piled up."

Kimmer nodded mutely, standing off to the side as was her habit, carefully waiting for Jeff to leave—and he knew she wouldn't try to come past him. But beneath her cowed pos-

ture, she examined that nugget of empowerment, the thrill of knowing that for that one instant, she'd been the one with the edge. She ran her thoughts over that feeling in the same way she might run her tongue over the sharp edges of her teeth— probing, finding the strength...finding the satisfaction. She pulled that feeling deep inside, determined to nurture it. To savor it as fuel for the next moment she—

Rio's voice reached her dimly. "Not now."

Kimmer realized that her feet pounded against the treadmill footing, her pace fast, her bruised leg aching and everything else reaching that peak between burn and wobble that let her know she'd done enough if she wanted to be in good form the next day.

"Not kidding," Rio said, his voice gone a little flat. "Not now."

The treadmill. In the gym. In Watkins Glen. The day after her fight in the park. Brown Suit hadn't been identified yet, Hammy Hands and Pigeon Man had stayed out of sight. And life went on. She was at the gym running on the treadmill because she didn't feel like running in the morning rain.

But the anger still burned within her, fueling her body, fueling her awareness that she'd ended up in the middle of something that hadn't been her doing. Not her choice.

Enough is enough. Kimmer flicked a wrist sweatband across her forehead before thumbing the treadmill down to a fast walking pace with a quick, familiar manipulation of the control keypad.

"Hey," Rio greeted her, still running along on the treadmill beside hers. A slower and more deliberate pace than the one she'd been lost in. His face looked terrible but the rest of him looked oh-so-fine. "You're back."

"Such as I am," she agreed, and blew a drop of sweat off her upper lip.

Rio nodded over his shoulder, and Kimmer, still walking out her warm-down, turned to the figure who'd been in the corner of her eye.

The woman took it as an invitation. She wore a spiffy gray pantsuit, the jacket of which didn't quite fit her correctly, but the pink camisole peeking out the front was just the right color to bring out her peaches-and-cream complexion. If only she hadn't…what *had* she done with her lipstick? Two enhanced peaks topped the woman's lips, and it was all Kimmer could do to keep from staring as though she were a child seeing her first disfigured person. She tore her gaze away to take in the rest of the young woman—sleek hair, big blue eyes and an expression of eager calculation that pretty much gave her away.

Reporter. No doubt a young television reporter looking for that first big break.

She wasn't going to get it here.

Kimmer picked up the towel hanging off the treadmill handrail and mopped her face and neck with it, still walking; the reporter took it as permission to approach and said, "Hi, I'm Shara Ingleswood from WEFL. I was at the park yesterday."

"Wasn't everyone?" Kimmer kept her voice flat, her tone uninviting. *We are not friends.*

Shara smiled; it had that reporter smugness to it. "But not everyone got pictures of the real action."

Kimmer gave a silent groan. Owen was supposed to have taken care of this. Then she gave the reporter a second glance and saw the determination, the little extra kick that came from defiance. Ah. She'd been told to drop this and she'd decided it was worth the potential consequences to see it through. Even if the potential consequences would be paid by someone else.

Shara confirmed it in the next moment. "I figure," she said, "that there must be a good reason for suppressing the First Amendment."

Kimmer snorted, and pressed her face into the towel. When she emerged she'd managed to take most of the sharpness out of her tone. "Don't even go there," she said. "No one's taken your film. Sometimes it's to your advantage to work *with* a situation instead of against it. Or to trade off an interesting but meaningless picture for the promise of more interesting pictures down the road. Your station manager knows that." Or else Owen would have been in touch, warning Kimmer that her picture was about to hit the paper.

"Or maybe he's just too…busy…to see what's in front of him. A whole photo series of a woman taking on a man twice her size and leaving him on the ground. And then being escorted away under obvious duress. And yet, here you are. It's an exciting mystery…I'm sure our viewers will be interested. I know I am."

Kimmer wrinkled her nose. "Your life must be pretty boring, then."

"Perhaps compared to yours." Shara let the comment stand for a moment, watching as Kimmer slowed the treadmill another increment but kept walking. "The most interesting thing, of course, is why you'd try to keep this incident under wraps at all."

Kimmer firmly pressed her lips closed on the word *idiot*. Surely it was obvious enough. Then she looked straight at Shara's big blue eyes, bypassing her impossible lips. "Because publicity will impair my ability to do my job. And my job is helping people."

"So is mine. Keeping information openly available allows the public to make wise decisions." Shara threw the words at her like a righteous challenge. Not listening. Not listening at all.

Kimmer took a deep breath. "Think this through, Shara. This is real life. The people who will be affected by airing that film are real people. Not just me, but everyone who works with me. Everyone we might try to help."

"You're the one who put yourself in a position to be news."

Still not listening.

Enough with the *nice.* Kimmer didn't need her knack to see that this woman had no intention of dropping the story— no matter the consequences, no matter what her manager had dictated. "Drop the photos, Ms. Ingleswood. It's a no-brainer. I get to keep helping people, your station gets brownie points with my boss—who, as it happens, has no little influence in this region."

The impossible lips tightened. "That sounds like a threat. You should know that a threat would only convince me there was something worth investigating."

Kimmer thought she heard Rio groan. She eyed the reporter; the woman was taller than she and perched on heels that added another several inches, her shoulders padded by the suit—a woman used to having a physical presence. She probably considered Kimmer to be small.

Kimmer stopped the treadmill and leaned back against the handrail to rake Shara with the same assessing, no-holds-barred gaze she would use on any man she intended to take down. The reporter raised her chin slightly, and then ruined that defiance by taking a step back. Kimmer said, "No, *this* is a threat. Those men in the park wanted something. An item. They still want it. I wonder what they'd do if I told them I'd given it to you for your story?"

Shara sucked in what she probably hoped was a silent

breath, but Kimmer heard it. Saw it, too, in the sudden stiffness of the reporter's spine. Kimmer didn't give her much time to think about it. "This isn't a game. You want the full story on what's going on? I can make sure you get it. But there's no halfway. You either leave this alone and let me continue with my work and my life, or you're going to jump right into the deep end." She smiled, a hard expression. "Even if I push you in myself."

When Kimmer's cell phone rang, Kimmer couldn't help another smile. Just the right timing...let Shara Ingleswood step back and think about things. And Kimmer, too, needed the moment—to convince herself that even if Ingleswood blew her local cover wide open, the worldwide community would hardly be watching the Watkins Glen 11:00 p.m. news. Three seconds of fame. It wouldn't matter.

Except that it would. She'd never be able to go into a job secure in her cover, not unless she was heavily disguised. And her covers were usually long-term, depending more on understatement than *Mission Impossible* magics. She wouldn't quit...but she'd always wonder.

And she had Hank to blame for the whole mess.

She pulled the phone from her lightweight workout jacket folded neatly behind her, and didn't recognize the phone number displayed on the Hunter-enhanced phone. Forget games and fancy gadget features, this phone was laden with function. Enough function so her caller ID could not only display the number, but also the location.

Phone booth in Seneca Falls. Well, this should be good then. Especially as her phone number wasn't listed. She picked up the call and lifted the phone to her ear to say, "Make it good."

The very tone of her voice caught Rio's attention; he stopped pretending he wasn't there and left his treadmill to lean on the handrail of hers from the outside, stretching his legs back as Kimmer heard a brusque male voice say, "We know you've got the recording. We want it. And we'll tear your life down around you to get it if we have to."

"That would be stupid," Kimmer told him. "I'd hardly want to talk to you then, would I?"

Shara Ingleswood stood up very straight, her fingers clutched around her purse strap at her shoulder. If her ears could have swivelled forward, she'd have done that, too. Kimmer lifted her chin in acknowledgment. *Yes, this is them.* The men still at large from the park. The men with whom she'd just threatened the reporter. The mean growly voice responded in irritation. It sounded like just the kind of voice that should come with Hammy Hands. "Don't *you* be stupid," it said. "Either way you'll lose your house. Just hand over the recording and we're done with this."

"Hold, please," Kimmer said, using her most officious secretary voice. She pushed the mute button and raised an eyebrow at Shara Ingleswood. "He wants me to hand over the object they covet. Shall I tell them I've already handed it over to you?"

"No!" Ingleswood blurted, blowing the cool out of her attitude. Truly, she was young. And perhaps hungry enough to make her way closer to the top than this small station, but not on Kimmer's back.

Kimmer caught and held the reporter's gaze as she thumbed the phone back to life and cleared her throat. "Sorry," she said blandly. "The terror of the situation overwhelmed me for a moment. All better now. And I don't have what you want. If I did, you'd be feeling the heat from it already. But if you'd like to leave me your number, I'd be glad to give you a call if I run across anything interesting."

The voice offered a few words of anatomically impossible advice. Kimmer held the phone away from her ear to wrinkle her nose at it. "Bo-ring!" she said, a singsongy voice, and then cut the connection. She'd relay the phone number to Owen. With luck before the day was out they would know if the call was charged to a credit card and whose, though Kimmer had odds on an anonymous phone card.

"You bitch!" Shara Ingleswood finally managed to gasp. "You really would have—"

"That's right," Kimmer said. "You keep that in mind, because your soft little underbelly is all mine, anytime I want it. Now do we still need to talk about those pictures? About pursuing this story?"

Ingleswood looked as though she'd just bitten a lemon. Her mouth twisted; her eyes narrowed. And she finally spat a reluctant, "No. I'll leave it alone. For now."

"Forever," Kimmer told her. "And now you've caused yourself another problem. If film shows up on any other station in this entire state, I'll assume you put them up to it." She wiggled her fingers at Ingleswood, a little *go away now* gesture. "So nice meeting you. The pleasure was mutual, I'm sure." But after the woman had turned and stalked away on her long legs, the sway in her hips meant for Rio's eye, Kimmer turned around to lean back on the same handrail on which Rio propped himself up from the other side, their elbows touching. "We need to talk to Owen," she said. "These guys aren't going to stop until they're caught—and they obviously aren't concerned that their friend is going to talk."

Rio caught the significance of that, lifting his brown eyes to meet her gaze. "Then we'd better talk to the chief," he said.

"Until they get Brown Suit out of that hospital and behind bars…"

Kimmer grabbed her water bottle and her jacket and headed for the shower. "He's probably dead already."

Owen looked as disgruntled as Kimmer had ever seen him—annoyed at the news of Shara Ingleswood's potential interference, and personally offended by the Hunter Agency's failure to pin down the identity of the goonboys at large. "I hate to say it," he said, "but I think we've underestimated them."

Rio sat casually in the chair opposite Owen's desk; Kimmer hadn't taken a seat at all, but prowled restlessly over the thick carpet, wishing she felt as relaxed as Rio looked, his legs stuck out before him and crossed at the ankles, his ankle-high sneakers laced only two-thirds of the way up and his worn jeans sporting a discreet rip over the knee. But his eyes gave him away. His eyes were darkened with wary concern, no matter that he'd briefly massaged them with his fingers before speaking. "In other words, Kimmer made it all look easy enough that we didn't give them credit for their extreme badness."

"They know how to cover their tracks, if nothing else." Owen tapped the eraser end of a well-sharpened pencil against the open folder with Brown Suit's records in them. "Or more likely, whoever's behind them is big enough and influential enough to do it for them. Mr. Albert Wolchoski is made of Teflon. Arrests across the board, and all of them dropped for lack of evidence."

"Let me guess." Kimmer stopped behind the empty chair that should have been hers and gave the files an upside-down glance. "No drugs, no prostitution, but if you want an enforcer with finesse…" She looked over at Rio and added, "Hammy Hands filled the brute strength slot."

"So I gather." He nodded at the neat stack of photos on Owen's desk—stills taken from the news footage the station had declined to hand over, but of which it had provided a copy along with its "let's work together" attitude. "But Brown Suit—I mean, Wolchoski—is still with us?"

"Alive if not kicking. And with one of our own on the way to the hospital to help keep him that way." Owen's mouth twisted slightly. "Schuyler County doesn't exactly have the kind of manpower to guard the room around the clock."

Kimmer sighed. "I'm sorry, Owen. I know you don't like to tinker with local issues. If I'd had any idea what Hank was bringing with him, I'd—"

"You didn't exactly have a choice," Rio said, looking up at her from under a frown, dark brows shadowing his brown eyes toward black.

Yes. I did.

But she didn't need to drive that point home. He wouldn't—couldn't—understand it.

So instead she said, "They had to have followed me from home when Pigeon Man showed up at the park, figured out what I was up to and used the governor's visit as a diversion. And they had my phone number, Owen. They had to have gotten it from Hank."

"Probably," Owen agreed. "The question is, under what circumstances? When he left here, he seemed to think his troubles were over. I'm not sure events support that belief."

"Just because his troubles slopped over to us doesn't mean he wasn't right," Kimmer said. "You can't believe he'd hesitate even for a second if, for instance, Hammy Hands sidled up to him and wanted my phone number."

But Owen shook his head. "Too many loose ends on this one. Why the story about a nonexistent recording? Whatever's going on, it's more than we first thought. Wolchoski hails from Pittsburgh—no doubt the other two came up with him. He certainly didn't acquire them in this area."

"Or maybe we're overreacting." Kimmer shrugged. "Wolchoski is fine and I've gotten nothing but a lame threatening phone call. There's no question Hank didn't tell us everything…but that doesn't mean it's a big deal. Hank is a coward at heart, like all bullies. He's not the sort to pal around with anyone but other insignificant bullies."

Rio touched a hand to his battered face, his expression troubled. He hesitated on the words, but finally said, "He's your *brother*."

She knew what he meant, knew he couldn't understand how she could walk away without knowing for sure. After a moment and a glance at Owen, she said, "I'll give him a call. I honestly don't see him as being involved in anything heavy and I don't think our Pittsburgh goonboys expected anything near the resistance they've encountered."

Owen gave her one of those tight smiles. "I'm absolutely certain of that. However, I do think there are enough inconsistencies that we should follow through. We need to catch these guys if they're still in the area, and we need to know we've gotten to the bottom of whatever's happening."

"If only so we can stop looking over our shoulders," Kimmer agreed.

Owen cleared his throat. "About Shara Ingleswood—"

Kimmer shook her head, wishing she could be entirely dismissive. "Not about to see the big picture. I rattled her cage a little, but I'm not sure it was enough."

Rio said, "She still has to get her story past her producer

and the station manager. And she doesn't have anything other than the initial film—already old news."

"We won't assume," Owen said dryly. He flipped the folder closed, glancing at Kimmer. "You've got your copy of this. I'll keep you updated. Frankly, I think we can best make use of you at this point by dangling you out as bait."

Rio's voice turned flat and disapproving. "You're going to turn her into a stalking goat."

A what? This from Mr. Crossword Lover? Kimmer giggled, breaking the tension of the moment. At Rio's startled look, she clapped a hand over her mouth. From behind it, she said, "Stalking horse. Or scapegoat. Take your pick."

"If it gets a giggle out of you, I think I'll stick with stalking goat." He looked at her as though Owen weren't right there, amusement in his almond eyes.

Kimmer wrinkled her nose. "Baa-aaa."

"That's a sheep," Rio observed as he pulled his feet back and stood up. "It's more like *beh-ehh.*"

"And you know this because you've been around so many goats?"

"No." He looked down at her, and his expression went from lighthearted to serious in a heartbeat. "I know this because I'm usually the stalking goat."

And now Kimmer was the stalking goat. Rio just wished she'd take it more seriously. He wished she'd take it *all* more seriously, including the potential danger to her brother. She wanted to believe the latest round of threats and goonboys weren't as much trouble as they thought they were. She wanted to believe her brother too shallow and ineffective to have gotten caught up in anything serious.

To believe otherwise was to face too many hard things.

How she felt about her family. How she felt about herself for feeling that way.

At least she'd taken the lead in searching the house when they returned to it, checking both exterior and interior for signs of incursion before putting her SIG away to hunt up Hank's phone number while Rio pestered OldCat in the kitchen. The house itself hadn't even been locked, a decision Rio couldn't disagree with. The old house had nothing but deadbolts that Kimmer rarely used in this neighborly rural area. If the BGs wanted in, they'd get in. There was no point in forcing them to break a window or a doorjamb. Now that they were home, those deadbolts were slammed home. The BGs could still get in—but by the time they did, they'd have a welcoming committee.

Odd how things worked out. Here he was, sliding into the old CIA frame of mind—working out contingencies on a moment-to-moment basis, trying to think one step ahead of the BGs without having a handle on their precise motive, trusting no one. Behind that casual conversation in Owen Hunter's office, the CIA part of Rio had been eyeing Kimmer's boss with perfectly hidden distrust, wondering what he wasn't telling Kimmer and just how high he'd dangle Chimera in front of the BGs.

Okay, he hadn't previously thought of them as BGs. That was Kimmer's doing, one of her smart-ass all-purpose nicknames for the bad guys.

But other than that, it didn't seem like much had changed. He hadn't planned to be back in the case-officer frame of mind—ever—but with Kimmer in his life, the change had been worth it. The thing was…

He wasn't sure just how much Kimmer was in his life after all. He wasn't sure she was ready, no matter how she tried.

Gah. He needed to do a crossword puzzle.

After this phone call.

Rio turned OldCat upside down and patted his pouchy old cat belly—quickly, so the animal wouldn't have the time to consider his dignity—and then put him gently on the floor as Kimmer's phone call went through to Hank's household, a number she'd no doubt never expected to use. With poise he thought remarkable given how tightly her white-knuckled fingers gripped the phone, she identified herself and asked for Hank, putting her spine against the kitchen counter.

Earlier she'd offered Rio the extension. He'd declined, figuring he could follow the conversation from the outside in. It didn't turn out to be hard.

"When do you expect him back?" A mild eye roll for his benefit, to indicate the person on the other end of the phone didn't know. "Is this Susan?" Hank's wife, seldom mentioned during his time here other than the moments he had tried to trowel guilt on Kimmer for her complete absence from their lives. "Yes, this is Kimmer. Hank's sister. I just wanted to make sure…everything's okay there? No, no reason it shouldn't be. I just thought…Hank seemed worried about some things when he was visiting this last week and I thought…no? Nothing?" A long pause. "No…no, I'm not try-ing to poke my nose in—" She'd forgotten Rio was there, now, her voice growing hard in spite of her obvious effort to remain light. "I just wanted to be sure…yes, I'm sure you have plenty to worry about already…no, no message." An-other brief moment passed. Her hand tightened another notch around the phone and Rio began to fear for it. "You do as you choose. I can't imagine why he came up to visit me, either." And for a sign-off she used a rude phrase in Japanese that she'd somehow picked up from Rio.

Hmm. He thought he'd been careful about that one.

Carefully, so very carefully, she thumbed the off button and set the phone on the kitchen counter. She picked up her bottled Frappuccino, took a long gulp and deliberately returned it to the counter. "Well," she said, her voice remarkably even, "my knack doesn't work so well over the phone, but I'd say that woman is more worried about protecting her happy little family from my influence than any trouble Hank might be in."

Rio made a cage of his arms, a hand on the counter on either side of her. Not that he'd ever consider Kimmer truly caged…but she let him, and she sighed as he put his cheek next to hers, a touch she leaned in to. "I'm sorry," he said, even as he greedily inhaled whatever spicy, luxurious thing she'd used to tame her hair this time. And there was her ear. So close. Such a perfect little curve.

But Kimmer's mind was on other things altogether. "No surprise that Hank married someone as unpleasant as he is." She took a deep breath. "But we know what we needed to know. He's not missing, he's not hiding in the basement, and whatever's going on up here doesn't seem to have any ripple effect down there. Nothing makes any more sense than it did, but I don't see any reason to change our plans."

Very close to her ear, Rio murmured, "Beh-ehh."

In the next few days Kimmer and Rio managed to dine out at least once a day. They went to Geneva and took in a movie, and then they hung around in the video rental store having long discussions about which movie to rent. They kept an eye out for any sign of Shara Ingleswood's story, and they toured the Fox Run and Torrey Ridge vineyards and tasted good wine. They made sure Kimmer was visible and apparently carefree. They also made sure her S&W snub nose, her war club and a variety of knives were always at hand, and always undetectable.

No one came after them as they walked the vineyards. No one accosted them outside the various eating establishments they chose. No one chased after Kimmer on her early morning run and no one followed them into the drugstore—although that, Kimmer told Rio, was perfectly understandable. No self-respecting goonboy would hang out by the tampons.

Her house was searched not once but twice. Kimmer took advantage of the mess to weed out some underwear that no longer suited her and to donate books to the library. Rio bought a new puzzle book to replace the one the intruders had ripped to pieces.

No one bothered OldCat.

And now they sat outside the ice-cream shop on a spring day that had started beautifully but had dull, hazy clouds piling up, contemplating the situation and their next steps. Kimmer sat at the bench of the picnic table provided there and Rio plunked his butt down on the tabletop, his feet resting on the bench beside her.

"Maybe," Rio said, licking wildly colored sherbet from the side of his waffle cone with enough of a gaze directed her way to let her know he'd seen her watching, "you should head down to—"

"No!" Kimmer startled even herself with her vehement reaction. She nibbled a careful bite of cold pralines 'n' cream and pressed it up to the roof of her mouth, letting the ice cream melt while the praline chunks remained behind. Once she'd chewed them, she turned back to Rio. "I checked, remember? Everything's fine down there."

Rio's response was mild, as he might well keep it given

the smudge of bright green sherbet along his bottom lip. Yeah, kissable. She wondered if he did that on purpose. The breeze stirred his startlingly fair hair, threatening to whisk their napkins away from the picnic table. Rio snatched them, weighing them down with his wallet. "It's worth a try. You might see something that Hank and his wife don't. Or you might stir things up, push them into making some sort of move."

And if she hadn't wanted to avoid that area so badly, it might even have made good sense. But…

She didn't.

"It's been quiet for days," she told him. "They've given up. I'm beginning to think we were right all along. We didn't underestimate these guys. We *overestimated* them. That Hank is still alive and kicking pretty much proves the point. It's obvious there are more than just the two dead guys involved, but if they were truly bad-ass BGs, Hank would have been gone the minute his SUV waddled back home."

"There's one way to make sure," Rio suggested, not bothering to be subtle about it.

"There are plenty of ways to make sure," Kimmer shot back at him. She bit off more of the ice cream than she'd meant to, and struggled with a surge of brain freeze. Dammit. "I'm tired of the whole goat role, that's for sure. It's gotten boring, and boring is dangerous. How's Wolchoski doing in county, anyway? Might be it's time for another visit. He might be bored, too. Might feel like talking." It was time to stir the pot…or walk away from it and put herself in the roster for another assignment. She often had periods of inactivity—Owen tended to hold her aside for those times when her knack of reading people would be truly crucial—but the circumstances of this one had made her antsy.

But when Rio nodded, his expression had grown more distant. She couldn't tell what he was thinking…didn't have a clue. Only that it made her uneasy. It finally occurred to her to ask. "What?"

And he looked at her with that heartbreakingly honest matter-of-fact way he had and said, "I'm having a hard time with the intensely ironic juxtaposition of your reluctance to connect with your family when it's killing me to stay away from mine."

Pow. Kimmer's gut flinched from those words, feeling them like a physical blow. She fought to swallow the dab of ice cream in her mouth and somehow managed. Finally managed, too, a few paltry words of understanding. "I'm sorry."

Not that she felt guilty over how she'd handled Hank. Not that she intended to do anything differently. But she understood, looking at his face, how truly different it was for him. Couldn't imagine it, but understood that somehow it could be different. Rio looked back at her, his brows drawn enough to shadow troubled eyes.

"Why don't you call them?" Kimmer said. "It's been days."

"Too many days," Rio said, and finally noticed that a splotch of bright green sherbet had landed on the knee of his jeans. He scrubbed briefly at it with a finger and let it go. "They must be overwhelmed."

"They'd have called if there was more trouble?" Kimmer asked, uncertain. Nothing on which to base her guess but secondhand acquaintance and that brief glimpse of another way of life.

Rio nodded. "I'd have heard. Caro again, probably. Dammit, I'll bet they're trying to protect me. Since I got back—"

Kimmer looked askance at the thought of anyone feeling the need to protect Rio. Tall beyond tall, sturdy with his Danish genes, tempered by years in the CIA. He looked down from his perch on the table and saw her, gave a wry smile of acknowledgment. "They're my parents," he said. "And it hasn't been so very long since they wondered if I wasn't going to be anything more than a black star on the wall at Langley."

CIA officers killed in the line of duty and a wall of anonymous stars. Kimmer had been there once, with Owen. Briefly, as a visitor. But the wall had made an impression.

"Even once they knew I'd live...I think it shook them up, seeing me like that." Rio looked away from her, a rarity. "Rehab took a while. I wasn't a pretty sight."

She snorted, unable to keep her natural irreverent humor from coming through. "I find that hard to believe."

That got him. He looked down at her with a flash of a grin. "Flattery will get you lots of places," he said. "But you'll just have to take my word for it."

"So call them," she repeated.

"Actually," he said, watching her carefully enough so she knew he was waiting for her reaction, "I'm thinking about going home."

Chapter 8

I think you should, she'd said. Never mind the fear that trickled through her at the thought. What if they decided they needed him? What if *he* decided they needed him? Or maybe he'd even find the contrast between his loving family and his loner girlfriend with her twisted sense of humor to be too great.

What if he doesn't come back?

Not that he'd said any such thing. Not that he'd even earned that kind of distrust.

But Kimmer had learned not to make assumptions.

She heard the zip of his weekender bag. The flicker of relief that he'd packed such a small bag was short-lived; half his things were still in storage with his brother. Before she knew it she lingered in the doorway to the bedroom, watching him stuff a few last things into the side pocket of the carry-on. He glanced up, saw her and straightened. "Hey," he said, full of reassurance. "They said she's doing fine. They've just been so busy…they can use another hand to get the household changes sorted out. And since my brother's still trying to run a business…" He shrugged. "If nothing else I can get a few boats into the water while he handles family stuff."

Kimmer stiffened her spine. She hadn't meant for him to see that wistful look, but then, she'd never truly been able to hide herself from him. "Your grandmother lives with your parents," she said, in the manner of someone repeating what they've been told but not truly believing it.

Rio grinned. "Oh, yeah. For as long as I can remember. She's got her own little section of the house and to us kids it was like an inner sanctum." He finished stuffing something into his bag that probably shouldn't have been stuffed at all and stopped again, this time his look more serious. "I wouldn't be going if Owen didn't agree with you. Whatever was happening here, it's not happening anymore. The BGs convinced themselves that the keychain stick doesn't exist."

"Either that or they decided I wasn't going to do anything with it anyway." Kimmer realized she'd crossed her arms over her stomach. Good God. The next step would be going fetal. None of that around here.

With much determination she unfolded her arms and compromised by leaning on the doorjamb and crossing one ankle over the other. "He's in agreement. Another discreet visit to Wolchoski, and Hunter is done with this. We know these guys are from Pittsburgh—no surprise since Hank is the connection—and we know they want a keychain stick that doesn't exist. We don't know to whom the damn recording was supposed to be a threat, and we'll probably never find out." She shrugged. "Well, we *could* find out, but Hunter's not going to waste man hours on something that no longer poses a threat. They already sent all our info to Pittsburgh. Let them deal with their own dirt."

"And Hank?"

Kimmer had that one ready. "I'll call him this evening, after I see Wolchoski. His wife will blow me off again, but if things are still in the clear down there, I think we're safe to walk away." Hank might end up in trouble with the law, but he'd earned it. "Owen's already got something else in mind for me." *And for you.* But she didn't say the words. She wanted him back down here on his own, not prodded into obligation.

"Sounds like a plan." He pulled the crammed weekender upright on the bed, zipper pulls tinking against each other.

Kimmer regarded it with skepticism. "It might explode."

"Hasn't yet," Rio said, and gave her that look, the one that meant he'd seen beneath her words and the face she'd put on. "I'm coming back, you know. As soon as they don't need the help."

Whenever that might be. But out loud she said simply, "Okay."

He watched her, a long, searching look. He opened his mouth, closed it...and opened it again. "Kimmer," he said, oh-so-carefully, "how I deal with my family...how you deal with your family...it's not about them. It's about you. Whatever you do or don't do about this thing with Hank, it's about *you*."

She heard him. She heard the unspoken parts, too—that it was about the two of them, as well. About Kimmer and Rio. She nodded, unaccepting but understanding. And when she went to kiss him goodbye, she made it one for him to remember.

Albert Wolchoski spent the time awaiting his trial in the Schuyler County jail in Watkins Glen, but there'd be no chatting with him there in a way that Owen—or Kimmer—considered discreet. He was still an oddity among the prisoners, an actual big-city goonboy among the drunks and petty criminals and wife-beating scumbags, and his every move and every conversation was of note.

So Kimmer planned to have her little chat when Wolchoski went on his field trip to the Primary Care Center beside the hospital in Montour Falls. All on the up-and-up, as Chief Harrison knew what she was up to and had no problem with it as long as his transporting officer stayed in the room. Rather than make herself another visible oddity at county by joining them at the front end of the trip, she pulled over to the shoulder just south of Watkins Glen and waited. Roger Conners, the transporting officer, expected her.

But sitting there gave her time to think. Too much time. Too many events whirling around the core of her life, sharp-edged and slicing into what she thought she knew. Rio…gone. Leaving a void bigger than she'd imagined possible after only a handful of much-interrupted months together. Her home…invaded. Tossed and turned, and even though she'd expected it to happen, she'd also thought she could deal with it. She'd thought expecting it would prevent the lingering feelings of anger and violation.

Wrong.

And after all these years, she'd made herself vulnerable to her family. She'd let Hank stay in her *home*—almost as big a violation as the break-ins. She'd even phoned him not once but twice.

The second time hadn't gone any better than the first. Worse, in fact. Hank's wife Susan had accused her of making trouble, had told her to stay out of their lives. Had hung up on her.

And alone in the violated house, Kimmer had found herself staring at the phone with no better understanding of family than she'd ever had. For all she knew, this was simply part of it. The rudeness, the hanging up.

Then Rio can keep it.

That wasn't fair. He'd never hung up on Carolyne; she'd never hung up on him. They played their word games, they teased each other, they got upset with one another...but they didn't batter at one another.

Fairy tale. That's all it was. Rio was wrong. Dealing with family was all about them. It was about what they did to you, and how you managed it.

Kimmer kept her eyes on the rearview mirror, watching for the squad car. She practiced some deep breathing. Her thumbs beat a tattoo on the steering wheel until she realized what she was doing and then went back to the deep breathing. She stared at the cell phone, tempted to call and confirm Wolchoski's follow-up surgical appointment. And then she glanced in the rearview mirror and froze, astonished by the look of her own face. A haunted look, one she'd so often seen as a young woman but thought she'd long grown out of. She might as well still have that long, unmanageable mane of curls; she might as well still have the port wine stain splashed across the side of her face. Her eyes glinted back at her with the clear deep blue they'd always had, and yet they suddenly struck her as young and frightened and powerless.

She wasn't that person anymore. She was Chimera as much as Kimmer. Hank's reappearance into her life, Rio's departure, her house in a shambles...none of it mattered. She had all the strength of the girl who'd run away to find her own fate. The girl who'd taken her mother's rules to heart and built herself into the resourceful young woman who'd once caught Owen Hunter's eye at a dark bus stop.

And boy, was Wolchoski going to regret he'd been any part of this.

She refocused her attention on the road, ignoring her own reflection in the mirror. And there, finally, came the city squad car. Kimmer started her Miata and rolled along the shoulder until the car passed, then pulled smoothly out to the pavement. Finally. She'd already double-checked on Hank, and after she talked to Wolchoski she could report to Owen and Chief Harrison and throw herself back into her work. She'd leave loose ends behind, but nothing she couldn't live with. After all, there was no keychain memory stick. No reason the damn goonboys couldn't eventually figure that out. And Hank had said the two toasted goonboys were the only ones involved in the murder. Whatever else these current goonboys wanted, Hank's hide was apparently not included. Time to wipe her hands of the whole thing and reclaim the life she'd built for herself.

Even if some very small, very tentative little voice said it all didn't quite make sense.

The squad car traveled out ahead of her; there was no need to ride its tail on this road. Fifty-five miles an hour, light traffic. But when something even farther out moved across the road, she couldn't suss out the details, only knew that it raised her hackles.

Here we go.

She leaned on the accelerator, making up ground.

Not enough. The squad car slewed badly over the road, brakes squealing; it lifted off one set of wheels and flirted with flipping before settling to a hard, rocking stop.

By then she could see the figure rise from the shoulder,

could see the Chevy Malibu at the other side of the road cutting across asphalt to angle to a squealing stop in front of the squad car. The figure ran up to the squad car, smashed a crowbar against the window, and tossed an object inside. Smoke instantly poured from the broken window, and by then Kimmer had the Miata up past eighty, swerving around the road debris of the spiked stop stick, shredded tire and crippled squad car to target the back corner fender of the Malibu. And who knew, dammit, that the Malibu's driver would choose that moment to back up slightly. Just enough so she hit it hard, but not so much that it stopped her cold. The Malibu spun out of her way as her air bag blew, a stunning explosion that knocked her hands off the wheel and left her blinded and dazed.

When she blinked she'd come to a stop and the air bag was slowly collapsing into her lap. A quick, if still blurry, glance to the left showed she'd ended up halfway on the shoulder, clear of oncoming traffic. A quick and blurry glance to the right showed the Malibu turned around to face directly against traffic in the middle of her former lane. And smoke still poured from the squad car with a dark silhouette hunched over the wheel coughing and fumbling in a way that told Kimmer Officer Roger Conners was too stunned or injured or otherwise incapacitated to get his seat belt undone.

And coming back up on the squad car from the shoulder, the same figure she'd seen once before. Hammy Hands.

The goonboys were back on the job.

Kimmer didn't wait to see if this was a jailbreak or an execution. She fumbled for her own seat belt, grabbing the SIG Sauer holstered at her side, and then surprised herself by tumbling right out of the car when she opened the door. *Get it together!* Half stumbling, half running, she skidded into place behind the driver's side front wheel and took another accounting of the scene—the Malibu still where it had been, the driver stunned behind the wheel. Hammy Hands on his way to the back door of the smoke-filled squad car in a crouch that was far from friendly, and Roger Conners still all but passed out at the wheel.

If she was a cop she might have given him warning. She might have tried the old *freeze, sucker!* line that always worked so well in the old cop shows. But she wasn't, and when she discovered her hands still unsteady from the impact she'd just taken, she merely braced her two-handed grip against the edge of the car before she pulled the trigger.

Hammy Hands spun away from the car, discharging his own gun through the back window with such timeliness that his finger must have already started its pull before Kimmer's bullet even struck him.

Not a jailbreak. Execution.

Hammy Hands rolled away from the car and into a desperate crawl away from the vehicle, gun still in hand and with any luck quickly clogging with debris as it jammed into the ground along the way. Kimmer pushed away from the Miata, one eye on Hammy Hands and one on the anonymous figure silhouetted behind the wheel of the Malibu. Pigeon Man, no doubt. His hands moved on the wheel, cranking the tires around; roadside gravel and bits of scattered glass spat back at Kimmer as Pigeon Man hit the gas, the tires squealing until they took solid hold.

For an instant Kimmer was impressed with herself, that her very approach would scare him into leaving a colleague behind. And then she realized there were people on the other side of the road—Good Samaritans, stopping to help a cop in a traffic accident without even thinking the accident wasn't an accident at all. Hadn't they even heard the gunfire? Kimmer made sure they would, firing off a round into the hard ground of the shoulder and not waiting for their reaction as she turned her complete attention back to Hammy Hands, certain by now he'd think to turn back on her and catching him just as he torqued his body around to swing his sights on her while the rest of him still lay in the dirt.

No time to brace on anything, hardly time to bring the gun up into a Weaver stance, both hands supporting the grip, body centered and balanced and *blam!* the 9 mm round drilled Hammy Hands in the chest. He fell back and she wasted no time darting up to grab his gun, her eyes watering at the smoke curling out of the squad car windows to dissipate on the light breeze.

Please be calling for help, people. Please don't just be gawking.

They'd crossed out of Watkins Glen…surely there was a sheriff's deputy around here somewhere. Or a state trooper. Or even the nearest EMTs…

Kimmer wrenched the gun from Hammy Hands's weak grip and hesitated long enough to realize his gurgling noises were a plea for help. She gave him a hard look. His big hand wrapped around her ankle, changing the plea to a demand, his fingers digging into thin skin over bone, painful enough to feel like he'd cratered her flesh. She deciphered his first guttural words even as he repeated them, "Get help."

"I *am* help," she said, twisting her leg free. "But I'm busy." And she left him on his back, his hands scrabbling ever more weakly against the ground.

She had a very bad feeling about Wolchoski. She made it to the squad car and tried to yank the back door open; damned if it wasn't still locked. Finally steadier on her feet, she ran around to Conners's door and yanked that, too, until Conners managed to unlock it. Kimmer held her breath, tears already streaming down her face from the gas, and leaned in to fumble at Conners's seat belt. It finally clicked free and she retreated, smacking the door lock controls on the way.

When she pulled the back door open, Wolchoski fell out. Kimmer ducked to catch him, crouched up against the car door and awkwardly shoving back at him with her shoulder while she tucked her gun away. It was like shoving toothpaste back in the tube. Beside her, Conners staggered out of the front seat and fell to crawl away, choking and half-conscious.

It was just about time to start laughing at the absurdity of it all. Kimmer's eyes watered; her nose ran fiercely and she swiped a hand across her face, regaining just enough clear vision to see that Wolchoski's eyes were still open. Still seeing.

"Tell me," she said, her voice ragged but her words hard. "What the hell is this all about? Who sent you? What does Hank Reed have to do with any of it?"

Pounding footsteps came up beside her—a man's tread, heavy and work-boot hard. Kimmer got a glimpse of him bending to help the officer and kept her attention on Wolchoski, who might be alive for the moment, but judging by the hole in his chest and the bloody froth at his lips, might well not make it until help arrived. She'd come to question him…she damned well intended to follow through. She fumbled for the short, stout toothpick blade in her back pocket and pulled it out to rest the blade at his ear, hidden from anyone who might come up on them. She pricked him with it; his eyes widened. "Talk to me," she said. "Or we can make your last moments the worst you've ever had."

"You…can't—"

"No?" She smiled at him. No doubt a truly fearsome sight, with airbag marks on her face, eyes red and nose running from the tear gas. "You don't get it. I'm not a cop. I live by my own rules. Now get chatty." *And do it quickly, before you die on me.*

He looked down at the blood-rimmed hole in his shirt, a wound that made the brace on his leg seem an absurd precaution. There was very little blood; Kimmer knew it meant he was bleeding on the inside. He passed his hand over the wound in what might have been disbelief, losing focus. Kimmer got it back again, raising a spot of blood on the soft skin beneath his ear. "Who sent you? And what about Hank?"

"In over his head," Wolchoski said, and gave a little laugh—but stopped short, startled, at the blood that came up with it. "He thought he could save himself…he just put things off."

"Save himself from who?" Kimmer demanded, feeling that first trickle of desperation as Wolchoski's face suddenly turned an odd shade of gray. "Save himself *how?*"

Wolchoski gave another little laugh. "You should know, Kimmer Reed. But he was only ever marking time. So were you. After *this*—"

The same footsteps came up behind Kimmer. She wanted to turn and glare, but knew that would make no sense whatsoever to this stranger who thought he was helping. And when he put a hand on her shoulder, she wanted very much to whirl and sink the little knife into his arm for taking such liberties—but he wouldn't understand that, either. *That* was an impulse she thought long buried, carried out of Munroville with her after serving her so well for so long. He said, "Miss? Can I help?"

Yes. Go away so I can prod this dying man with my knife.

On the other hand, she had plenty already, didn't she? This mess was about Hank, and it wasn't over after all. Maybe it was really just beginning. She glanced over her shoulder and discovered a wiry man in his fifties, signs of construction work—probably a contractor—written all over him. A man used to taking charge. Good. Let him. "I can't hold him up any longer," she said, palming the little knife. "If you can help me get him out of the car…"

"We probably shouldn't move him." The man looked down the road as though an EMT might suddenly appear.

And Kimmer looked down at Wolchoski's half-closed eyes. "Oh," she said dryly, "I don't think it'll make much difference to him." Probably she should have put a quaver in her voice—to judge by the man's startled look, that would have been best. But Chimera didn't have to answer to this man. She had to take her information to Owen—and she had to get out of here before the cops arrived or she'd be tied up with them for hours. She couldn't afford that. And it didn't sound like her damned brother could afford it, either.

The man beside her didn't make any profound comment about Wolchoski's death. He simply moved in to take the goonboy's not inconsiderable weight, easing him out of the car as Kimmer casually returned her knife to its sheath in her pocket and backed away, just as casually turning on her heel to head smartly for her car. By the time the man realized she'd left, he had other people moving in. A second bunch had gathered around the cop, offering water, and a teenage girl had gone around the squad car to discover the gruesomely dead Hammy Hands. The fuss she made covered Kimmer's tracks long enough for a quick check under her car—no copiously leaking fluids—and by the time she heard the faint siren in the background, she'd slipped behind the wheel and shifted into gear, heading back toward Watkins Glen. Belated shouting followed her; no doubt someone would get her license plate. She didn't care. She fully intended to report to Chief Harrison.

But not until after she spoke to Owen.

Owen's office door was closed. Kimmer knocked hard once in warning and walked in anyway, unrepentant under a laser gaze of deep disapproval tinged with anger. Standing beside the visitor's chair in an unsettled way that meant he'd just leaped up, Owen's younger brother Dave regarded them both with a certain wariness. No doubt he'd often felt the sting of Owen's glare, black sheep of the family that he was. Why Owen would offer Kimmer such a reaction momentarily escaped her.

Then she put a hand to her face. Airbag abrasions. Reddened nose and eyes. Streaks of who-knows-what on her skin.

"I'm busy," Owen said.

Dave Hunter—much leaner than his older brother, his face more aesthetic and his bright blue eyes every bit as commanding as Owen's—backed away a step. "Not on my account."

"We're not done here," Owen reminded him.

"I suspect we probably are." Dave hitched up a shoulder. "I'm fine as I am, Owen. And I'm always happy to help out when you need an extra hand. But my work…it's important, too."

Kimmer gave him a sharp look, momentarily diverted, fascinated by the unspokens between these two men and by the depth of the determination in Dave's expression. He meant it, more than Owen had any idea. She raised an eyebrow at Owen. "You're wasting your time."

Owen stiffened in quick resentment. Dave looked at her in open surprise. Then he grinned. "You're the one."

"Yes," Kimmer said. "I must be. And since I've never walked in on this office uninvited before, and since I look like—" she indicated herself with some disgust, gave up on finding a word and finished "—this, then there must be a pretty good reason I'm here, don't you think?"

Owen raised his hands in surrender. "All right, then. For the record," he pointed at Dave, "this is not the end of the conversation. For the record," he shot a dark look at Kimmer, "this is not okay. But for now we'll move forward."

"Good," Kimmer said, moving right along into brusqueness.

Dave held up a hand, excusing himself. "I've got an appointment in Virginia," he said. "And since we've already established how this conversation will end, I think I'll just go keep it." He raised his chin fractionally, another acknowledgment of sorts to Owen. "I'll stop by next time I'm in the area."

"You'd better," Owen responded, and watched with a gaze that turned worried as soon as Dave's back was turned.

"What's the deal?" Kimmer said. "He likes what he's doing."

"Not up for discussion." Owen, too, could be brusque.

"So it's only my personal life we talk about?"

He looked back at her, his gaze even and unrelenting. "That's right."

She made a disgusted noise and slid down into the chair, one leg over the arm and her body protesting as hard as it had the last time she'd been here. She'd had about enough of being kicked around for Hank.

Except she thought she was probably only getting started.

Owen raised an eyebrow. Kimmer said bluntly, "Wolchoski is dead. Hammy Hands is dead, too. Officer Conners will be okay."

"And of those things, for which are you responsible?" Only Owen could maintain that dry tone in the face of such startling news.

Kimmer pretended to give it some thought. "Well, technically...two-thirds of them. Hammy Hands shot Wolchoski. I killed Hammy Hands. And since Hammy Hands was going back for seconds before I stopped him, I'll take Conners, too."

Owen gave himself a moment to rub his hands over his face. Then he said, "From the top?"

"Ambush on the way to Montour Falls. Pigeon Man got away—he was in a maroon Malibu, but I don't know how long he'll stay in it. I didn't get the plate—it was Pennsylvania, though. They must have expected to handle this and go." Which didn't quite make sense, because Kimmer had been a loose end, too. She spoke over her own reservations. "I took care of Hammy Hands and exchanged a few words with Wolchoski and left before backup got there. I wanted to get to you first."

"Considering that current modern convenience called the cell phone—"

"Batteries," Kimmer said vaguely. It was convincing enough. She had somewhat of a reputation.

Owen's brow raised slightly higher. "You wanted to be here when the chief calls."

"Could be the sheriff," Kimmer said helpfully. "It was county turf."

"You left the scene of a crime."

"Only so I could come make a full report before making myself available to the police." But Kimmer quickly grew more serious. "I can't afford to get tangled up in this, Owen. I didn't cause it, and if I hadn't been there things would've been a lot worse."

"Witnesses?"

"Yes. And Conners knows I was behind him, even if he doesn't remember the seat belt thing."

"You're going to have to make a statement."

"And I will. But listen." She took a breath, hunting for thoughtfulness, finding mostly resentment and anger. "I thought this thing was over. I thought I could leave Hank out of it. Just a few hours ago I spoke to his wife, and she told me to get lost. But things have changed. Wolchoski had enough air left to let me know it's *not* over. Whatever double dumb-ass thing Hank's done, it's still following him around. It's still following *me*."

"It's not doing a lot for our quiet presence in Schuyler County, either," Owen said, back to being dry again. "You've got to make a statement. I'll have a lawyer meet you there. She'll keep it as quick and painless as possible."

Through a sudden swell of impatience, Kimmer said, "Pigeon Man is still out there. I'm tired of being the hunted. It's time to do something about him."

"Without an ID? Without any other plan besides waiting at the state line and hoping he'll drive by on the way to home?" Owen shook his head. "We underestimated these men. Now two of them are dead and the other is at large. We'll go after him, all right, but with a plan. That means knowing more. And that means talking to your brother."

Kimmer gave a soundless snarl. "I'd rather wait at the highway for a week."

Owen pushed the phone across the desk. "Call Hank."

"He'll lie."

"Probably. But his lies might tell us something."

This was Owen the Boss. Owen giving her the bottom line.

Kimmer picked up the phone and punched out the numbers vigorously enough that Owen should have winced. He didn't. He waited, apparently unaffected by Kimmer's seething resentment. The phone rang several times and then a machine picked up, and Hank's voice, awkward and stilted, told her to leave a message.

She hung up.

Owen didn't need to be told what had happened. "Then go make your statement. And then get back here. I've made some preliminary contacts with the Pittsburgh police, and by the time you get back I should have access to some mug shots. You can try to reach Hank again then."

She wanted to protest. She'd given him a photo. Surely the Pittsburgh cops could work from that. Surely anyone in the agency office could work from that. But she was the one who'd seen Pigeon Man in person. No photograph could replace that advantage, only augment it. And Owen had a bottom-line look on his face that she'd never seen before. For all the years she'd pushed and prodded and lobbied to do things her own way, he'd never responded like this. Implacable. Unmoveable. As taciturn as ever…only more so. Things going unsaid.

Because this time the Hunter Agency was on its home turf—and this time Kimmer had spent the past several weeks giving the local law reason to regret instead of appreciate the agency's usually discreet presence.

In the past, she'd threatened to walk away once or twice. Now Owen was drawing that line. *This is what you'll do if you want to stay with us.*

She heard him. She knew it wasn't a bluff. And she wasn't

ready to let it happen—not when this job was suddenly the only stable thing in her life.

And so she spent the afternoon at the modest Watkins Glen police station on North Franklin, describing the ambush, turning over her SIG Sauer for ballistics testing and carefully omitting her conversation with Wolchoski. She squelched her constant impulse to go out and find Pigeon Man, as if she could simply sniff him out. If Chief Harrison had any information about Pigeon Man's location—or if Hammy Hands had been in possession of a convenient hotel key or a nice PalmPilot full of contact info—he wasn't letting on. The only bright point of the afternoon came when Officer Conners made his way back into the station house, his eyes still red, his voice hoarse and his handshake full of gratitude.

Maybe it wasn't coincidence that Harrison let her go shortly afterward.

Back to Hunter, as required. But first…she reeked of sweat and the lingering stink of the tear gas, and she had a whole bottle of eye drops waiting for her at home. Not to mention she ached to talk to—

Rio.

Who wasn't there.

Who might not come back.

Get used to it. Rules were rules, and she knew better than to forget the most important. *The only one who'll take care of you is you.*

Chapter 9

Rio picked his mother right up off her feet just as he'd always done since that year he'd grown four inches. And as always, she hugged him back just as hard even as she remonstrated him. She used to say, "Have some respect!" Now she said, "You'll hurt your back, Ryobe!" And of course he only held her more tightly for an instant before gently touching her to the ground.

Kimmer didn't do that, he suddenly realized. She understood his injury; she adjusted to it in many unspoken ways. But she trusted that he knew what he could and couldn't do, and left him to make those decisions without second-guessing or fuss.

Meiko Carlsen took a step back to inspect him, her black eyes sharp. Next to Rio, or his brother Ari or his father Lars, she barely cast a shadow. But she still ruled the household, and Rio warmed to her smile. "See?" he said. "I didn't starve to death. I haven't even been existing entirely on fast food."

His mother gently poked his side. "You could use some padding."

"I'm fine," Rio told her, just as gently. "I'm here because I'm concerned about you, so don't try to distract me."

Now she said it. "Have some respect."

Rio gave her the slightest of bows. "Always." He picked up his bags and stepped into the familiar living room, leaving his sneakers behind in the mudroom. He'd come prepared; he pulled a pair of thong sandals from the weekender bag and dropped them to the floor, forcing his socks to stretch around the thong itself. From the other bag, a fancy mall bag, he pulled a beautifully wrapped box of his mother's favorite English toffee, and presented it to her with a small bow.

"Ryobe!" she said. "You're family, not a guest." But she took the package, pleasure and anticipation lighting her face—a face with angles more severe than his, slightly flattened Asian features barely affected by her paternal Danish heritage. "Such a beautiful wrapping."

"It's not much," he said. "I hope it pleases you."

"Domo," she murmured, and set the package aside on the small, gleaming wood table in the corner of the room that always seemed to hold some special object—a careful flower arrangement, a casual pile of perfectly arranged rocks and a feather or, as today, a small blown-glass decorative vase. She'd open it later, so as not to seem too eager. "I have a room ready for you."

He let her lead him through the living room with its sparse, precisely chosen furniture—most of it in clean, organic Danish lines—and to the guest room, a place he'd never again thought he'd stay. He'd had his own house here not so long ago. A rental, to be sure, but near enough to being his.

Rio dropped his bags on the bed and sat down, putting his

mother closer to eye level. "Tell me," he said. "How is she? How are you?"

The direct questioning caught his mother by surprise. She twisted her hands together, realized she'd done it and stopped. Always poised, that was Meiko Carlsen. Always well dressed—as she was today in a flowing tunic and pant combination. Always well coiffed. Her drop earrings matched her outfit and her minimal makeup brought out her beautifully almond eyes and her small rosebud mouth.

Except today he caught a hint of tremble in those earrings. And her black hair held more gray than he thought he'd remembered from even half a year earlier. The strain of Sobo's illness showed in her face…and in the way she once more twisted her hands. "I'm well," she said, and he supposed that to be the truth. *Well—under the circumstances.* "Your sobo…" She hesitated, shaking her head. "She is a most determined person, as she ever was. The doctors believe she should be in assisted living."

Rio offered up a skeptical expression. She laughed, a light sound. "Exactly so. Your father and I have been investigating those places, but I don't think anything will come of it. I think—" and she stopped, suddenly, biting her lip and continuing only with the same determination she'd attributed to her mother, "I think she would rather be here when she goes, even if it means she goes sooner."

Quick panic flashed through him. "Is that a worry? Now?"

His mother waved away the question with a graceful hand. "No. Not like that. But perhaps…soon."

"I would have come," Rio said. "I've *wanted* to come."

Meiko straightened slightly at that. "We've handled things in the way we thought best," she said. "We have a social worker from the hospital also working on Sobo's behalf."

"I wasn't questioning your decisions," Rio said, his voice quiet with understanding. But he also shook his head, knowing this wasn't a conversation he wanted to have right now, not the first thing he did upon arriving home. "Anyway, I'm here. And I can pick up some of the extras for a while."

"That would be helpful," his mother allowed, and that alone was enough to tell Rio how strained they'd been. "Perhaps you'd like to see her? She's usually awake at this hour and she knows we're expecting you."

"Of course I want to see her. And after we've visited a while—" he glanced at his watch "—I'll fix her some tea. Unless she's no longer into her late afternoon tea, but if that were the case I'm pretty sure the shock waves would have reached me even down at the Finger Lakes."

"Come, then." His mother held out a hand to him in invitation. "But Rio…be prepared for some changes."

Changes. No kidding. Rio's fingers tightened on the gift he'd brought his grandmother—her very favorite See's chocolates, elaborately wrapped. Sobo had called for them to enter her little domain instead of coming to the half-open door on which his mother had knocked. Now she regarded him from her small recliner, a tiny old woman with her eyes almost hidden in their wrinkled folds but her face lit from within nonetheless. "Ryobe!"

Rio bowed, more deeply than he offered anyone else, more deliberate than the quick acknowledgments he sprinkled through his life without even thinking about it. He glanced at his mother; Meiko nodded, and, with her own little bow, wordlessly retreated. "I'm sorry I wasn't here sooner." He crossed the room in a few long strides, finding it pretty much as he'd last seen it—sparsely furnished with lacquered fur-

niture once brought from her homeland with great care, along
with several hand-painted watercolors. The recliner he knelt
by…pure Furniture City. The quilt over her lap made by a
cousin, and the pillow behind her head a truly childish con-
coction, definitely not square. Carolyne had made it in her
Brownie days. Rio presented her with the chocolates, and
smiled at Sobo's only partially concealed delight. She knew
as well as he did what lay beneath that silvered wrapping
paper and the many-tiered bow.

She was, of course, much too proper to open the gift immediately. She murmured *Domo* and set it aside for later, then
gathered his hands up in her gnarled fingers. "There was no
need to disrupt your new life."

"*I* had a need to disrupt my new life," Rio said. "Only out
of respect for your wishes did I stay away." Then he cocked
his head and admitted, "Well…until I couldn't stand it any
longer."

"And your Kimmer Reed…does she understand?"

Damn. Sobo had always been able to do that. And Rio
wanted to be able to say *yes, of course she does*—but he
wasn't sure. All he knew for sure was what he'd told Sobo.
"She tries." He sat back on his heels, leaving his hands under
her warm, papery touch. "Kimmer…her life has been so different from ours."

"Her family." Sobo nodded. Rio had told her of Kimmer,
of what he'd known before he left. Now he knew more.

"I met her brother," he said, and shook his head. "I think
I understand a lot better now. And at the same time, I'm not
sure I can ever truly understand at all."

And when Sobo nodded again, Rio thought he caught a
glimmer of wistfulness on her face. *What an idiot I am.* Of
course Sobo would grasp Kimmer's situation, perhaps much

better than anyone else in the family, even without knowing what Rio knew. Without ever having seen that look on Kimmer's face when the past caught up to her, sometimes struck out through her. His grandmother, too, had once been caught between two worlds.

"Do you think," Rio asked, hesitating on the border of becoming more personal than would be polite, "it will ever be easier for her?"

Sobo was silent a long moment, long enough that Rio took a breath, ready to apologize for the question. But he closed his mouth quickly enough when she spoke. And he wasn't expecting her to say, "That depends on you, Rio-san." She smiled at the look on his face, a quiet smile, and she nodded ever so slightly in his direction. The faintest hint of a bow. "Your grandfather is the one who made my life possible, in so many ways. Certainly I could not have made the transition between our worlds without him. I loved my own too dearly, and would have returned to it at the first opportunity."

"I wouldn't say Kimmer loves her past." Rio's words came out more dryly than he meant them to.

"But she is tied to it nonetheless. She needs a strong present if she is to pull away from what she knows." Sobo patted his hands. "She will never be as you're used to, Rio-san. But look around this room. Do you think I was without these things when your grandfather was still alive?"

Rio didn't have to look. "I think you've always had them."

She nodded. "And he loved me for what I was." Then she pulled her hands back and rested them in her lap.

Rio was quite certain she had more to say than that, and just as certain she'd leave him to think about it himself. "Thank you, Sobo."

"You're a good boy, Rio. You'll be fine. Now come back later, and I might have a chocolate to share with you."

Rio grinned. "It's a deal." He leaned over to kiss her wrinkled cheek as he rose to his feet, and left the room with a vivid image of Sobo unwrapping the chocolates so carefully, so precisely. He was still smiling when he reached the living room, where his mother put him to work setting the table.

Home again, all right.

Returning home felt different. Hollow. It didn't matter how many times Kimmer reminded herself that she'd very happily lived this way for quite a long time, or that she'd always known better than to count on someone else. It was what it was. And it didn't matter that she expected to spend only a few moments at home—a quick shower, a quick sandwich— before heading back to Hunter and to the Pittsburgh mug shots.

She turned down her street at early dusk, her mind on that sandwich and most determinedly not on the empty house. So, okay, there was a cat there. Rio's cat, if anyone could be said to own a cat. Kimmer was doing litterbox duty and if she neglected it she'd sure enough know the house wasn't empty.

And a glance down the street showed her she might well not be alone this evening after all. Upon spotting the sedan parked at the curb, Kimmer eased off the accelerator, taking an instant to narrow her eyes and sort through the possibilities. Not Rio's. Not Owen's antique pickup truck. Not a squad car. In fact...it looked surprisingly like a certain Malibu, its color gone black in the poor light.

If Pigeon Man came to visit, would he leave his car at the curb?

But the closer she got, the more certain she became. And

when she was only one yard away, she spotted Pigeon Man on the porch steps before her partially open door. He stood, sent a nasty leer in her direction, and thumbed a lighter, the little flame flickering clearly in the dusk. He held it to several indistinct objects tucked between his fingers, and just before the flicker bloomed into true glaring fire, Kimmer understood.

Molotov cocktail.

She stomped the accelerator, burning rubber and building speed before she hit the brake just as hard, cranking the Miata around to block Pigeon Man's escape. By then he'd stepped onto the porch and flung the first of the cocktails into the house, creating an instant glare of fire. Another through the window as Kimmer leaped from the car, and then he smashed the last bottle on the porch itself, oil and gas spreading over the wood boards to block entry to the house. At that he ran off to the side, hovering, and while Kimmer first assumed that he waited for her to run to the house and clear his way to the sedan, she quickly saw it was a taunt. A choice. *Are you coming after me, or will you try to save your house?*

Kimmer wouldn't think about the house.

She wouldn't.

She dove back in the car for the S&W in the glove box, grabbed the quick reloader that went with it, and snatched up her war club from the front seat. A few quick strides and she'd jammed the gun up against the Malibu's front tire and pulled the trigger; the explosive decompression of the tire was as loud as the gun shot. With her eyes on Pigeon Man, she jumped up on the hood. Ooh, she'd made him mad.

Good.

The door to the Morrows' house opened. Kimmer pointed the revolver straight down and emptied it into the Malibu's engine. Steam hissed from the holes. The door slammed again. *Bring it on, 911.* Nothing more she could do—the house had been beyond her scope by the time that first Molotov cocktail landed in her hallway.

Later. Think about it later.

In the failing light, Kimmer pinned Pigeon Man with her gaze, replacing the revolver load without looking. *What now, goonboy?*

Pigeon Man backed a few steps. He'd expected her to go for the house, to try to beat out the flames, to rush in and grab her most cherished belongings—or perhaps to call 911 herself and sit in her car and cry until they came. He hadn't expected Kimmer defiant, destroying his car and glaring at him from the steaming hood.

He backed a step...then another. Then he turned on his heel and ran.

Gotcha.

He hadn't been expecting to run. He wasn't dressed for anything more than a short sprint. He truly didn't have anywhere to go—no back alleys into which he could duck, no twisty streets.

Kimmer leaped from the hood and hit the ground running. He gained good ground initially, darting along the front lawns of her street, but she'd expected that. She slid into her miler's pace—good, strong, smooth strides. One hand curled around the S&W in a safe grip—around the trigger guard, so there'd be no accidental discharge should she stumble in the dusk—and the other around her war club.

After a handful of yards Pigeon Man neared the end of the street. He glanced back and faltered slightly upon seeing Kimmer—not on his heels, but running easily, running well. Drawing on all those days of uphill runs to maintain her pace.

He hesitated another moment, bringing up his own gun, but evidently—and wisely—deciding to draw her farther away before slinging bullets.

In fact, he took the same left turn Kimmer had taken in Hank's Suburban, the slight uphill on the road that would soon turn steep and rutted and interrupted by switchbacks. The same road she often ran herself, and knew just how to pace herself to make it to the top with steam to spare. She notched back on her speed as she took the turn. Pigeon Man already had the slight lack of coordination in his movement that meant he'd blown his anaerobic capacity and floundered to find a new stride he could maintain—if he was even that fit. She'd have to hold the right combination of distance between them to keep him moving, yet not so close he was inspired to take a shot at her. If he wore out too soon, he'd simply stop and stand his ground.

She could deal with that. But she'd rather do it her way.

It would have made for a boring chase scene in a movie. She could see his hesitations, his realization that she wasn't going to quit, his hovering decision to end things. But he also knew she'd killed the first two goonboys who'd given chase; he knew she'd evaded his first attempts to nab her, and that Wolchoski had ended up in jail for his own efforts. She'd taken out Hammy Hands during the ambush on Wolchoski, and she hadn't fallen apart at the sight of flames in her home.

She and Owen may have underestimated the visiting goonboys, but they'd underestimated her in return. Every step along the way.

If he was smart, he'd keep running. He'd try to ditch her in the brushy roadside or make it to the woods. He might even try his own extemporaneous ambush from the top of the hill.

Too bad for him that she planned to beat him to it.

As Pigeon Man approached the first switchback, Kimmer pushed him, deliberately edging up on him, the first touch of burn creeping into her thighs. And as soon as he was out of sight around the sharp curve, she plunged into the brush to take the tiny, tangled footpath straight up the slope to intercept the road.

Now she felt the burn, all right. Now she set her legs to pumping, ignoring their increasing heaviness, knowing where to set her feet even in this growing darkness. She'd run this trail in the dark before. And he might hear her noisy progress or he might not, not above his own rasping breath. Or above the sound of fire engine sirens closing in on her house from the tiny Glenora station.

She topped out at the edge of the road and stopped short, her own breath noisy in her ears. She gulped a big lungful and then held herself still and quiet, not breathing, until she heard his approach. Practically walking to judge by the sound of it, slogging along in a way that told her he'd never taken advantage of the Pittsburgh hills to train. At the most, a nice flat treadmill in an air-conditioned gym….

She let herself breathe again. Panting but quiet, recovering quickly as she positioned herself at the road edge, waiting.

Waiting…

Now!

She took him from the side in a tackle that hit his tired legs at the knee, dropping the war club to dangle from its thong while she sought his gun hand. Sought it, found it, didn't try to control it other than closing her hand around his on the grip so she'd know where it was pointed. Then she jammed her revolver into the closest convenient soft spot—his belly. "Gut wound," she growled at him. "You'll never be the same."

She hadn't expected much fight. She certainly didn't expect him to snarl, "Fuck you, bitch!" and to fire his gun off into the night as he exploded beneath her. The gun was for the effect, the flash and noise and pure physical impact of the discharge so close to her head.

And it worked, dammit—ears ringing, disoriented for even that instant in the darkness—Kimmer hung on to his gun hand by dint of pure determination while he landed a few hard blows to her ribs, lifting her slightly, giving him more room to move…dislodging her gun from its secure little spot in his belly.

She couldn't see, couldn't hear, couldn't breathe as he landed a lucky blow just below her diaphragm, one she hadn't been ready for. In the next instant he found her wrist and twisted, grinding bone and ligament until she cried out.

But she didn't let go. She had just enough control left of her fingers to pull the trigger, with only a general idea of its aim. She was ready for the noise and she followed it up by turning into a wild thing, kicking and finding the trigger again and even sinking her teeth into his arm, releasing it swiftly so she didn't receive a severe jerk when he pulled away—leaving her gun hand free, if numb. She didn't even try for fine control or aim. She bashed the pistol in the general direction of his head and scraped her knuckles against hard-packed dirt when the road was closer than she'd thought. He cried out at the impact and his resistance faded. She drew back and landed another blow, a harder one.

He went limp beneath her.

"Asshole," she hissed at him, just for good measure. Then she wrenched his gun away, tossing it carefully to the side— not too far, but far enough. Panting, she quickly patted him down—and glory be, he had a pair of cuffs and the key. Also a long-bladed knife, a switchblade and a backup gun on the outside of one ankle. She relieved him of them all, along with his wallet, as he started to stir again, then she pushed the gun up against the bottom of his jaw. "I've got four bullets left," she told him. "How many do you think it would take to turn your brain to mush?"

She allowed him the brief, feeble burst of profanity he aimed her way and then gave the gun a shove. The front sight would be digging effectively into his jaw with that one. "Very nice," she said. "Points for creativity. But I'm in a hurry." Indeed, the sirens had come to an abrupt stop, and a glance toward her neighborhood showed a night alive with red and blue flashers. "So let's cut to the chase. Chase, get it? Very punny. You may now laugh."

He didn't believe her until she gave the gun a nudge, a sharp and painful nudge. He offered an effortful, "Ha, ha," and she had to allow him a handicap because she was kneeling on his chest.

"Very good. Now here's the situation. Thing one…you've pissed me off so thoroughly that I won't regret it if you startle me into pulling this trigger. And I feel very delicate right now, if you get my drift. If you understand that, you may grunt."

Obediently, he grunted. She kept her free hand on his biceps, alert for tension there, alert for tension anywhere in his body. "Now, thing two…you've screwed up big. One way or another, you've lost all your goonboy pals. You've made a big fuss, and you've got every law officer in this area hunting you down and then some. If you hadn't interrupted my evening, I'd be off identifying your mug shot right now, fresh from the Pittsburgh law. In short, you can't ever make this mess right with your boss. You're safest in prison…and you'll get to prison safest if you make me inclined to care. You following me so far? You may grunt."

Pigeon Man grunted.

"You might live through this yet. Now, I'm going to take my hand off your arm, and I'm going to cuff your wrist to your ankle. You should know that I'm going to do this without removing my gun from your head. Can you guess what will happen if you're anything but noodle-limp? I should probably remind you of all the grief you've put me through, and the fact that you've just torched my house." *Don't think about that. Focus.*

He didn't need the prompting this time. He grunted all on his own.

"Good for you." Slowly, Kimmer removed her hand from his arm. She'd left the cuffs sitting on his chest and had no trouble snapping them around his wrist. The ankle took some ingenuity; she tugged on his pants leg just below the knee until she could crank the ankle up. At one point he tensed and she gave him a reminder bump against the inside of his jaw. He stifled a response and she finished wrapping him up. Then she sat cross-legged on his stomach, gave him a moment to figure out how he might possibly breathe, and said, "The sooner you talk to me, the sooner I go away. I'll take your weapons and I'll leave you at the side of the road. I wouldn't thrash around much trying to get away—if you fall over the shoulder, you could be there all night before the cops find you. And there are briars."

"Bitch," he said, but his voice was low and sullen.

"That's right," she said, giving him her cheerful voice even when she felt anything but. "Now. All those things I need to know. Tell me."

"Get this straight," Pigeon Man said, released from his silence, his voice hoarse. "I'm not giving up my people. That's a death warrant, jail or no jail."

"Hmm. Well, that's okay. When I get down there I'll just put it out that you told me. Think they'll believe me?"

"Doesn't matter. I'm not doing it." And he meant it, too. Whoever he worked for had enough clout, enough reputation…

Great.

She didn't get hung up on the matter. Not yet. It would depend on what else he had to say. Not that she'd hesitate to make him hurt. Her throat and chest ached with the hard, hot knot of anger Pigeon Man had put there. He and his goon-boy friends and even her brother. She was done playing their games. From here on out, it would be *her* game. She let him hear the threat in her voice. "Then tell me something else I want to hear."

"Your brother…" Pigeon Man said, and hesitated, but this time it wasn't because he wouldn't talk. This time he was concerned about her reaction.

"That little woods weasel?" Kimmer said, opening the door wide for anything Pigeon Man cared to say.

He relaxed slightly beneath her, as much as he could and still draw a breath. "In way over his head. Stupid fucker, he thought he could kill Jerry and—"

Whoa. She leaned on the war club—not tapping him, no real pain—but enough to get his attention. "Say that again?"

"Hank. Has a woman on the side. Jerry took to her. Hank caught them together, killed Jerry. Lit out for your place. Got followed."

Hank killed the man. Didn't witness the murder. *Did* the murder.

Super.

Kimmer dropped a deliberate tidbit, just for the reaction. "When I toasted them—that was an accident, by the way—Hank told me I ended his trouble."

Pigeon Man gave a jerky little snort of a laugh, which she took to mean *no way.* He said, "When Reed came back, he came straight to deal. Said he'd give you up to even the score. Said he'd give up that recording, even though he made it to cover his ass."

Kimmer's mind gave a little blink. That hot knot of anger swelled, spreading out to encompass her, to stiffen her. Pigeon Man must have felt it. He, too, froze, stopping his labored attempt to breathe, waiting to see if she would—literally—shoot the messenger.

Hank. He'd thought to trade her off after she'd saved his life. Hell, maybe he'd come up to see her hoping the goon-boys would at least find themselves caught and jailed. Maybe he'd counted on her to cause enough trouble for the goonboy gang that trading her off had been his intent all along. He'd certainly known that their search for a nonexistent keychain drive with a nonexistent recording on it would keep them busy…and quite probably tear her life to little pieces.

Has it?

Owen was on the borderline of allowing her to stay with Hunter, or at the least of allowing her to stay in this beautiful area she'd come to love as home. Rio was gone…and though he'd had plenty of good reason to go, she'd known there was more to it. After seeing Hank, after seeing her reaction to Hank, he had to be wondering if he'd made the right decision after all. If Kimmer Reed was simply too different, too scarred, to fit into his life.

Pigeon Man ran out of air; he sucked in as deep a breath as he could manage, rocking Kimmer on his stomach just like he'd rocked her world. And then, cautiously, he said, "Dumbass thinks he's bought his life. Gets to go back to the way things were. He's lost his little sputzie, thinks his wife don't even know about her. That ain't the way it is. Soon as we wrap up with you, he's done."

"Not caring," she said.

Except he had kids. And a wife.

Losing Hank could be the best thing for them.

Having Hank out of their lives might not be so bad. Losing him like this…

Might not be so good.

Not something to decide this moment, either. Time to wrap this up, get back to her home—and hope there was something left of it. And let Harrison know this little bundle of badness was waiting by the side of the road.

She leaned close to Pigeon Man, rocking forward on her crossed legs. "I want two things. I want your name—we'll get that regardless. Don't even try to tell me your prints aren't on file somewhere."

He hesitated, and realized she was waiting for an answer before continuing. "Jarvis Slowicki."

"Jaar-vis," she said, playing with him a little, letting some of her own tension ease out. "So distinctly unpleasant to have made your acquaintance. Now here's the other thing. You tell the chief I said you could have two phone calls. And after you call your lawyer, you call someone from your Pittsburgh crew, and you tell them this…. There. Is. No. Recording."

He made a noncommittal noise and she bounced slightly on his chest, inspiring an *oof!* "Practice," she suggested. "Say it like you mean it. Because I do."

"There is no recording," he said quickly, if not convincingly.

"Jarvis," Kimmer said, as patiently as she could, "let me put it this way. Hank says there's a recording. I say there's not. You've had a chance to get to know each of us. So you tell me…who's actually telling the truth?"

She gave him a thoughtful pause in the darkness, and just before she would have nudged him, he offered up a begrudging, "Truth could bite Hank in the ass and he wouldn't know it."

"That's my brother," Kimmer said with patently false affection. "Alrighty then. I've got things to do. Reports to fill out, other bad guys to catch." *A house to check.* Except if they hadn't put the fire out by now, there'd be no house left at all. She climbed off him, keeping the war club against his chest as a pivot point—and the S&W still close at hand, although he'd have no way of knowing that for sure. If he was smart, he'd guess. She did briefly tuck it away in her back pocket as she bent to tug him closer to the side of the road. "Don't forget the briars," she told him, recovering the weapons she'd left there and then straightening to assess herself. Nothing more than the aches and pains a minor tussle usually engendered, even if there'd been a few moments when minor verged on major.

"I can't believe—" Slowicki cut himself short.

Kimmer grinned in what by now was full dark. "Can't believe I'm leaving you here? Suck it up, Jarvis. I told you I was gonna do this, and I am. You see? I am the one who tells the truth." She took a few long-strided steps to warm up, ignored his profane muttering, and jogged down the road with somewhat less intensity than she'd come up it.

The flashers still lit the sky, blue and red localized auroras that might have been pretty had it not been for the implication of their very existence. Two engines parked along the street behind the Malibu, an unnecessary ambulance stood by just down the street and a state car blocked the road. Made sense; Glenora was well outside the Watkins Glen city limits. And just as well—the state troopers hadn't interacted directly with Kimmer before now.

Although the neighbors had been kept back to huddle on the front lawn of the house across the street from Kimmer's, she didn't join them. She jog-walked right past the engines and to the Malibu, which hadn't been locked. Hadn't even had the keys removed. She grabbed the rental agreement from the glove box, found a proper gun case to fit the Glock stuffed in her back waistband. It held extra magazines, and she took the whole thing. She found a photo of herself at Lafayette Park, big surprise.

Nothing that would tie the goonboys to their boss—to whoever and whatever drove the car theft ring Hank had thought to use for easy money. Not unless the rental agreement held some hidden treasure, and Kimmer didn't expect it.

What she did expect was for someone to notice her, to call out with demands that she get out of the Malibu, to get away from the scene altogether. Instead the shouting was all to and fro, accompanied by staticky bursts of the fire chief's big hand radio, and the flashing lights painted the lawns and houses with such surrealistic strobing shadows that no one noticed a petite figure taking the spoils from one car—one badly shot-up car, or had they even realized that yet?—to another. She tossed the goods behind the Miata's driver's seat and closed the door as quietly as possible.

And then, finally, she let herself look. *This was my home. Was.*

The charred porch made a cavernous entryway to a blacked interior. Though no flames remained, the fire crew continued to douse the hallway with a wide spray of water.

At least there hadn't been family photos on those walls. Photos and scrapbooks…that's what seemed to hit people first. That they'd lost their memory-makers.

Kimmer didn't want photos to commemorate the things she remembered.

Heavy-duty flashlights strobed through the rooms, hunting flames. The air stank of diesel fumes and throbbed with the *hrum-hrum-hrum* of the emergency vehicle engines. Under it all was the stink of spilled gas and oil, the accelerants Jarvis Slowicki had flung into her house with such sadistic glee. He'd been so sure she'd rush to save the house—fumbling for her cell phone, panicked at her loss. He hadn't done his homework very well.

Although looking at the house, she wondered if she'd made a mistake after all. For now she had to live with the results. With the sudden, clenching realization that *oh my God* Rio's cat had been in that house.

But it hadn't all burned. Flashlights shone through the upstairs window; it must be safe to walk up there. Surely that savvy old creature had found himself a safe nook in the house somewhere….

Kimmer headed for the house. She stepped so quietly, so neatly, that she'd reached the house without being spotted; the fire crew was absorbed in their task. And she wasn't heading for the strobe-lit charred front porch, but rather around back, to the basement entry. Down a set of concrete steps into the door well and she was in.

God, it stinks. Heavy smoke, wet charred wood, sharp searing chemicals from burnt carpet and household synthet-

ics…a thick, wet combination of smells. Water dripped freely
from the ceiling, splashing over the weight set and soaking
the boxes neatly stacked away on her storage shelves. The
other shelves…not quite storage. Kimmer grabbed up a
small, tough red Cordura gym bag and swept the shelf contents within—cartridge boxes, several braces of knives, iron
knuckles, a folding baton, a regular officer's baton, a handful of esoteric war darts and specialized blades. She zipped
up the suddenly heavy bag and slung it over her shoulder. The
contents clanked in a muffled way. Dripping water spilled
over from her hair and down the side of her face. "You'll get
your chance," she told those contents. "Soon."

From there she moved quietly up the stairs. She had nothing to lose if they caught her now, and she couldn't leave
without at least trying. Trying to see what was left—if any
of the furniture had survived, if she could grab cold cuts from
the fridge, if she'd be doing repairs or rebuilding from the
ground up. She slipped out into the kitchen, waited for the
pair of firefighters to pass from the interior to the front door,
and then moved out to the stairs, her footsteps careful and her
sneakers crunching on charred wood. *I made love to Rio on
these stairs.* That was a memory. That was a memory that
surged up so strongly as to bring her first sense of loss. She
bit down on it—literally clamping her teeth together—and
moved on, her eyes on her footing and her ears tuned to those
also moving through this house. It wasn't hard to catch the
remarks. *What a mess. Don't know if this can be saved. Watch
your step, the floor won't hold you there.*

They had no clue she was here. But then again, her early
life had made her the best, hadn't it? The best at staying out
of the way.

In the bedroom, she found what she was looking for. The

room itself was barely touched; it reeked of smoke but had been spared most of the damage. Rio's family album sat on the windowsill. And there, in the very middle of the bed with his feet tucked beneath his chest in his imperturbable cat mode, OldCat waited. He looked so normal, so natural, that Kimmer instantly felt an absurd flare of hope—hope that turned just as quickly to pain when OldCat didn't move, and when she realized, here in the darkness with only the unnatural aurora of flashing light reflecting through the window, that OldCat's head had drooped forward until his nose touched the bedspread.

No doubt he'd heard the ruckus. No doubt he'd chalked it up to one of those strange things that humans do. The old dock cat had seen plenty of it in his day. No doubt he'd come up here to wait out the disturbance, confident in his ability to do so.

Kimmer rested her forehead against the door frame and took a deep breath. She remembered quite suddenly why she'd never chosen to get a pet of her own—not after a series of dogs and clever little goats and even a pig had paid the price for being loved by gawky young Kimmer Reed. She remembered how it had hurt.

The house, it seemed, held more by way of memories than she'd ever expected.

She heard someone come up the steps behind her. A flashlight beam bounced into the room, settled briefly on OldCat, and then mercifully moved away. From right behind her, a woman's voice said, "Smoke inhalation. Looks like he went pretty peacefully, if that's any comfort. Just passed out from the smoke."

Kimmer said roughly, "He was an old cat."

The firefighter gave her another moment and then said, "You shouldn't be here."

The story of my life. And no reason to change it now. But Kimmer glanced back at her and nodded. She gathered up the afghan at the head of the bed and carefully bundled up Rio's dock warrior companion, holding him as carefully as if he were still alive. With all apparent meekness, followed the firefighter down the stairs and out the front door, even accepting direction across the unstable front porch and assistance in descending without the stairs. The firefighter escorted her to her car, although not without some confusion over how the car came to be where it was given Kimmer's absence until this point.

Wait till the morning, when the bullet holes in the Malibu became obvious. Then people would have something to puzzle about. Kimmer dumped her clanking gym bag behind the driver's seat, shoving the Glock case aside. In the dark, no one had noticed the pistol at her back; the .38 had already made it into the gym bag, trigger resting on an empty chamber in the absence of a holster to protect the trigger. She added the Glock on top of its case and then—upon glancing up to find a state trooper headed her way—carefully settled the bundle of OldCat into place on top of the case instead of in the front seat as she'd meant to.

"Kimmer Reed?" the trooper asked. In the background, one of the fire crews finished buttoning up its engine and the huge vehicle rumbled into gear and away. The ambulance followed. One engine crew batting cleanup, the state cop car and the big crowd across the street remained, but even the crowd was thinning, as it became evident the fire was considered to be out.

"That's me," Kimmer said.

"Trooper Zack McMillan. I doubt you've heard of me, but I've heard your name before. Somewhat recently, in fact."

"This does not come as a huge surprise to me," Kimmer said, and sighed. Playing it matter-of-fact…and just waiting for the chance to get out of here. To call Owen out from the winery function he was hosting this evening and let him know the stakes had changed. Again. She added to the trooper, "Things have been exciting around here lately."

"Haven't they, though." He flipped through the little note-pad he'd been holding, aiming his small, bright Maglite at the page. "Witness heard gunfire," he read out loud, then looked up at her. "Quite a few shots, it would seem. I don't suppose you know anything about that? Or maybe you know some-thing about the incident near Montour Falls late this morn-ing?"

"I've been pretty busy," Kimmer said. "I haven't kept up with the news. So I'm not sure what incident you might be talking about." She hesitated, and decided against revealing Jarvis Slowicki's plight at the side of the little no-name road. Owen could handle that situation.

The trooper let it pass, but the set of his shoulders told Kimmer it was only for the moment. That, in fact, this man expected to detain her before the night was over, but that he planned to stay low-key. He gestured at the house with his flashlight. "This fire was set. But then I suppose you know that. Though I'm surprised you're not more upset about it."

Just shows what little you actually know. Kimmer cleared her throat and gathered her fraying temper and tumultuous build of emotion. "I'm alive," she said, not addressing the na-ture of the fire at all. "But my boyfriend's cat isn't. I guess I've got plenty on my mind. In fact, if you don't mind, I've got to call him. I don't want this—" she, too, gestured at the house, and she let her hand tremble visibly in the flashlight beam McMillan had again used to spotlight her, a barely polite distance from her eyes "—to come as a surprise when he gets home."

Never mind that he had no immediate plans to return.

McMillan's voice softened, if only marginally. "You have a cell phone?"

Kimmer indicated the car interior, where the cell phone sat plugged into its cigarette lighter charger. McMillan shone the flashlight throughout the interior, leaned in to snag her keys, and then nodded for her to sit. "Call him," he said. "I'll wait."

Yeah, you'll wait all right.

Kimmer slid behind the wheel, leaving the driver's door open to keep McMillan feeling in control. He backed off slightly to stand with much patience by the Miata's fender. She flipped her cell phone open with her shaking hands, fumbled it and let it slip between her fingers to fall at her feet. Ducking to get it took only an instant—and yanking wires to start the car only a moment more. Kimmer didn't bother with the door; she put the car into reverse, slung it around in a sharp backward turn that put her on her own lawn and then floored it in first gear as McMillan ran for the door. It slipped from between his fingers and slammed shut with the car's movement as the wheels dug up sod and propelled the Miata out onto the street.

McMillan didn't waste time chasing her on foot. Her quick glance in the rearview showed him already speaking into his shoulder mike, and she could only hope there weren't any troopers—or locals, for that matter—in a position to intercept her on the way to Full Cry.

On second thought, she'd better count on it. She'd go a roundabout way, ditch the car and come in on foot. And she'd hope—hope hard—that Owen would be in a receptive mood.

At the first chance, Kimmer headed north, leaving the wreckage of what had been a perfectly good life behind her.

Chapter 10

*T*he night hung dark around her, the moon at a gibbous two-thirds and waning. Not a night for a young woman to be out on her own, hanging at the edges of a cemetery, making her way to the fresh grave near the back. No headstone yet, no marker other than the slightly raised aspect of the replaced sod.

She didn't need a headstone to find this grave. Her mother's grave. She'd been here before. She'd found the spot before her mother was buried, she'd marked it in her mind's eye, and she'd come back every evening since the burial.

Pneumonia, they'd said. This mother's daughter knew differently. Pneumonia might have been the end of her, but it hadn't been the death of her. Her family had played that role—years of abuse, sons who'd grown up not to protect her, but to scorn her weakness.

As a mother, she'd given all her strength to her daughter.

Protecting her. Teaching her. Setting an example to be avoided.

And yet the loss was unfathomable.

Here, crouched not beside the grave where she could be easily seen but behind a nearby tree, she wrapped her arms around her knees to crush them to herself. Maybe the pressure against her chest would keep her from flying apart from the vast swell of emotion in her throat. Maybe not.

She forced back the sob, knowing if she let it slip past, there'd be no stopping the explosion. Knowing she'd never survive it.

She was alone, now. Just as her mother had said. She was the only one left to take care of herself...just as her mother had said. And she found it to be a role she gladly would have accepted had it not come at such a price.

The night hung dark around her, the half-moon just rising. Kimmer sat in the car at the end of a service road on the backside of Full Cry Winery, rows and rows of freshly leafed vines stretching out before her, and fought a sudden sense of loss. More than just her house, more than just a cat she told herself she hadn't known for all that long anyway. More than her awareness that deep down, Rio might well not be able to accept what her life had made her. And more than that brief glimpse she'd seen in Owen's eyes, the regretful one that meant he was coming up to a line he wouldn't cross for her.

All together, they took what she'd made her life and turned it inside out.

I started over once. I can do it again, if I have to.

And she could. But it would still hurt. It would still mean the loss of who she was, the Kimmer Reed she'd built for herself...and been happy with.

It struck her then, that perhaps she hadn't realized it before. That she'd not only gotten away from her past, but that she'd finally found a way to be happy with her present.

So for a long while, while the moon rose and the OldCat lay in silent vigil beside her, Kimmer sat in her car, struggling with what lay in front of her. All of it. Facing Owen. What she'd learned from Pigeon Man, aka Jarvis Slowicki.

And what she was going to do about it.

But first, she had a phone call to make.

Z-D-P-L-U-R-T.

"Plurt," Rio said, frowning at the Scrabble letter tiles arranged before his crossed legs. "It must be a word. As in when someone plurts out bad news."

"Yeah, nice try." His brother Ari—stockier than Rio, browner of hair and broader of cheek and currently carrying enough stubble to be on the way to a beard—displayed no sympathy at all.

"Plurt," Rio repeated, in the manner of one reciting a memorized phrase. "The sound of Scrabble tiles bouncing off your head."

Ari shook his head. "All that CIA training and that's the best response you can manage?"

And their father, his blond hair gone slyly gray and his face newly worn, lowered his paper from his spot on the couch and gave their mother a meaningful eye. "I thought you said they'd outgrow this stage."

"Did I?" she murmured, quietly tending paperwork—insurance stuff, Rio was given to understand—at the sleek secretary desk against the wall. She'd recently escorted Sobo to her rooms so that frail lady could putter slowly around them and make them just so before she retired. Not that they ever weren't.

"Ten years ago. Or so."

"I must have been mistaken."

Lars Carlsen shuffled his papers back into place with a har-umphing sort of sound, and Ari looked over to give Rio a wink. Rio got the message quick enough—that things had not been this relaxed around here for a while, that his brother was relieved to see their parents joining in the banter.

There hadn't been much discussion this evening. Rio hadn't been out of touch; between the phone and the grow-ing necessity of e-mail, he knew that Ari had broken up with the woman he'd been dating—no big deal, since it had never been serious. His dock and repair business was in the seasonal boom, just as fall would keep him busy with storage duties. He thought it would be good if Rio decided what to do with the stuff still cluttering Ari's garage but didn't truly mind hav-ing it. Not yet, anyway. And he'd done what he could to make things easier for their parents, but they weren't asking as much as they should because of the busy season factor.

In fact, right up until Carolyne had called Rio to let him know about Sobo, Rio hadn't felt particularly distant from them at all. And then they'd gone into crisis, and they'd been doing the hospital juggle, and suddenly he'd felt a million miles away. And here, now that he was home…

This place had always been home, even during his CIA years, but now it suddenly felt like something he'd left be-hind and simply come back to visit. But it was not quite, somehow, where he belonged anymore. No matter how im-portant it was to be here at this moment.

Much to his disgust, Ari displayed zero respect for Rio's interlude of thoughtfulness and played a killer *Q* word. Rio said, "Oh, *right,*" and was plenty happy that his cell phone chose that moment to ring.

"CIA," Ari murmured. "I know you arranged for that call to save your ass."

"Of course." Rio flipped the phone open, discovered Kimmer's cell number on the caller ID and greeted her, "Hey there! You kept it charged."

Her hesitation was all it took. No smart response, no flippant comment. Just that hesitation. He straightened; it was enough to catch Ari's eye. "Kimmer?"

"Rio." And another hesitation. "Things got busy here today. Hank's goonboy friends weren't as gone as we thought."

He couldn't figure out her tone of voice. Kimmer didn't hesitate over goonboys. She got mad. And then she did something about it. "You're okay?"

His father's paper lowered again, and his mother turned sideways in her chair, her ankles neatly crossed and her posture quietly attentive.

"I'm okay," she said, and Rio gave the faintest of nods, automatically including his family in on the conversation. "I won't need to work out for a few days, but I'm okay." The phone crackled; wherever she was, she didn't have a great connection. But he heard her take a breath, and knew she would finally say what she hadn't been saying. "Pigeon Man torched the house."

Rio blinked, felt a strange kick in the chest and realized he'd stopped breathing. Breathing was good. Breathing would let oxygen flow to his brain. Would give him something to say. Some distant part of him realized she'd said *the house* instead of *my house,* as though she couldn't yet face the loss. And just as he was about to ask again if she was okay, she rushed through another set of words. "Not the whole house. Molotov cocktails, but the firefighters got there pretty fast. The hallway's a loss, and the porch, and the den. Basement's flooded, the kitchen, too. But Rio..." and she ran out of words again.

He suddenly understood. "Oh, God," he said. "OldCat."

"In the bedroom." Kimmer's voice came through strained and he didn't think it was just their bad connection. "Untouched, but...the windows were closed. The smoke..."

Rio closed his eyes. Tough old cat. He'd thought he'd done the right thing by taking him off the docks. He'd thought the old fellow deserved a posh retirement.

Kimmer said, "I'm sorry," and behind the usual steel in her voice Rio heard the misery.

"You didn't do it," he said, finding his voice at last. "Pigeon Man did it."

Ari raised his eyebrows at "Pigeon Man." And though there was no way he could have followed the details of the conversation, the dark look on his face said he'd understood about OldCat's passing.

Kimmer's voice got hard again. "I misjudged him. I misjudged the whole situation. I didn't take Hank seriously so I didn't take the rest of it seriously, either." But then she regained some of her offhand flippancy. "On the other hand, Pigeon Man, otherwise known as Jarvis Slowicki, made the same mistake about me. And he'll have plenty of time in jail to think about it—unless they kill him like they did Wolchoski."

"Wolchoski's dead?" He'd definitely lost his grip on this conversation.

"And Hammy Hands. Also underestimated me. You'd think he wouldn't make that mistake twice."

"You'd think," Rio said. But he got his conversational feet back under himself and said, "What now?"

He really hadn't expected more hesitation. But after a loud crackle of static she said, "I'm not sure. I'm about to pull Owen out of some wine thing he's got going on tonight. The sheriff's department is looking for me…things got a little dramatic with Pigeon Man on my street. I don't think the fact that I left him gift-wrapped is going to make much difference. I've got to avoid them or I'll never—" She broke off. Stayed silent.

"You there?" Rio asked. His brother and parents watched him quite openly, and for the first time since his awkward teenage dating days, Rio wished they weren't. He wished he was down in Glenora—or wherever Kimmer now sat—having this conversation in person.

"Yeah," Kimmer said. "Here's the deal, or at least what I know of it. Hank killed one of the goonboys, because said goonboy was making time with Hank's woman-on-the-side. I think maybe…dammit, I think he came to me for help not just because he thought I could handle things for him, but because once I had, he could divert goonboy attention from him to me. Buy his way to safety by giving them the one who'd really caused all the trouble up here. I think that's why he made up that bit about the recording, to make me more enticing to the goonboys."

You're plenty enticing, Rio thought, but he didn't say it. He said what Kimmer didn't seem to be able to, even though she'd never doubted her brother's nature. "That son of a bitch set you up."

She seemed relieved to hear him say it. Relieved, no doubt, that he could see it in spite of Hank's family status. "Probably. Whether he intended it that way or whether he made it up as he went along…he thinks he's safe now."

"As if."

"Exactly. As soon as they're satisfied they don't need more information from him, they'll get rid of him. And my guess would be that they've just about reached that point. They've lost five men now. Jarvis seems to be a new believer as far as the recording is concerned. And I bet when the goonboss hears that, he'll cut his losses. It's not like he has to kill me to save face. He's got no reputation to preserve here, and no one to contradict him if he says he's taken care of the situation. All he's got to do first is kill Hank."

"I can be there in a day." A very long day of excessive driving for which his back would make him pay, but he could still make it.

"You went up there for a reason," Kimmer reminded him.

"And guess what? They don't really need me. They're tolerating my help so I can feel useful." Rio ignored Ari's surprised look. "I've picked up a prescription and cased out some assisted-living situations. But Sobo is feeling better. Her medications are working, and life here has changed…but it's settling in."

"No," Kimmer said. "It's bad enough I don't get the whole family thing when it's so important to you. I'm not going to get in the way of what you need to do for yours."

"Kimmer—"

"No!" she said, and hung up.

Rio stared at the phone, and looked up to find his family watching him with concern. "She's frightened," he told them. And he knew it for the truth. Not frightened of the goonboys…

He closed his eyes, put himself in her place. Owen had drawn the line about maintaining Hunter's local reputation. Rio had openly struggled with Kimmer's attitude toward family, and then he'd left to return to his own. She'd never assume he would return for good, not even with OldCat and many of his clothes left behind. Except now OldCat was gone…along with her home.

She must think she'd lost everything. Or was about to.

But now Rio understood the depth of Hank's betrayal. He just hoped he hadn't understood it too late.

Kimmer hadn't seen herself in a mirror. She didn't know what she looked like. She knew her jeans were torn; she knew she smelled like smoke. Her legs and arms ached from the day, and she was tired enough that maintaining her balance with the very heavy gym bag swinging off her shoulder and her arms full of one very special afghan proved to be a challenge.

As soon as Owen looked up and glimpsed her in the doorway of Full Cry's wine tasting room, his eyes flashed a peculiar combination of concern and anger. No one else noticed—or would have recognized it had they seen it, as quickly as Owen covered his reaction. She faded away from the doorway, knowing he'd make polite excuses for his impending absence. The old barn, as refurbished and spiffed up as it was, still held the same kinds of nooks and crannies that had served her so well in her childhood. She found one, propped herself up in it, and waited.

For the moment.

Until she'd talked to Rio, she hadn't known what she intended to do. She'd known Owen would want to keep her under wraps and pull in Hunter agents to clean up whatever trouble remained here locally. She'd known she would resist such a course, that she wanted to follow up on her own. To look through those mug shots Owen had obtained for her. To take herself down to Pittsburgh and find the big goonboy behind Hank's chop shop and put a complete and final stop to this mess.

And then she'd talked to Rio. Rio who'd gone up to see his beloved ailing grandmother and the family he missed. Who'd offered to drive back in a day, when his back had forced him to take two days on the trip up into Michigan. And who'd done all those things because of what he'd so recently said to her: *it's not about the other person. It's about you and who you are.*

Or maybe who she wanted to be.

In her heart she'd known just as Rio had so quickly realized—once the big goonboy thought she was out of the picture, he'd move on to Hank. Possibly Hank's family. His children. Hank…Hank probably deserved whatever he got. But the kids? Two little girls, he'd said, though he hadn't had any photos in his wallet. They wouldn't deserve it if the situation slopped over on to them.

And dammit, in order to live with herself, she had to make sure that didn't happen. Hank wasn't likely to come out ahead no matter what, but she had to make sure the situation didn't affect the girls.

She at least had to try.

That meant not heading out to Pittsburgh to deal with the goonboss as she so badly wanted, but heading for Hank's place. Doing what she had to, and then trying to wrap things up in the city—preferably with a nice neat bow—to make this mess right with Owen.

Not that Hank had told her where he lived. But she wouldn't have to prowl the Internet hunting for phone listings, because she'd taken it off his license while he was here.

Gee, if I'd known I was headed your way, I'd have saved your underwear instead of trashing it.

Or maybe not.

But first she had to get back on the road. And that meant getting past Owen without, somehow, severing her ties to the agency.

If it was even possible.

Fifteen minutes passed before Owen walked by. Kimmer made a clicking noise with her tongue. Quiet. Subdued. As was she.

Owen gave her a hard look. "I don't know what the hell's going on, and I should. But we've obviously got to get you out of sight while I figure it out. Let's go." As an afterthought he held out his hands to accept part of her load—from the way he held them he obviously expected the bundle, but Kimmer slid the heavy weapons cache off her shoulder and held it out, resisting her arm's impulse to tremble under the awkward, extended weight. Surprised or not, Owen took the bag.

He led the way out of the barn, a back way known only to longtime employees and otherwise blocked by a door that looked sealed shut. They exited at the back corner and Kimmer struggled to keep up with him, annoyed by her fatigue and his impatience. He quickly triggered the security protocols at the viniculture building, adding the code that would allow them both to pass without creating a lockdown. They made their way to his office in silence. Once there, Owen settled the gym bag to the floor with every indication he had discerned the contents, and sat behind his desk. "Now," he said. "What the hell is going on?"

Kimmer kept it short. "Hank was in a lot deeper than we thought. Still is. And he sold me out to try to save his ass. Hell, I think he probably set me *up* to save his ass. I believe you're familiar with the weasel factor in my family."

Owen took it in with narrowed eyes, then gestured at her. "That's the big picture. I need the details."

So she told him about finding Pigeon Man on her lawn. She told him Pigeon Man's name. She told him the locals needed a heads-up about Pigeon Man's location. She told him about the house. She told him about leaving Trooper McMillan in midgape on her front lawn. And she carefully placed OldCat's bundle on Owen's desk. "This is Rio's cat. He didn't survive the fire. I don't think I'll be in a position to take care of him."

Owen looked at the bundle in surprise, and then quite gently removed it, placing it on the worktable behind him. "We cremate the winery cats and spread their ashes over the vineyard," he said. "I can arrange for that, if it suits you."

Kimmer felt relieved of a tension she hadn't known she'd carried along with her fatigue and anger and grief. "Please," she said. "Rio always said the cat deserved respect after the life he'd survived."

"Then consider it done. And you?"

"Not quite ready for cremation," Kimmer said dryly. "Though we should talk about the fact that McMillan and his friends will be looking for me."

He raised an eyebrow at her, but the thinning of his lips revealed more about his true response. "That's a given. They'll call—any moment, I expect. Suppose you answer my question anyway."

Kimmer took him seriously enough to close her eyes and assess herself. "A shower. Something to eat. A good night's rest. I'm bruised but not broken. And I want to look at those mug shots. We still haven't identified Hammy Hands…he might be the final piece of the puzzle leading us to the goon-boss."

Owen's eyes narrowed. He knew her well enough to expect that she'd want to follow up any leads they found. "You should know I'm inclined to give you to the locals."

Kimmer gaped at him. She knew she gaped at him, and she couldn't stop herself.

But Owen had obviously been thinking about the matter even before this latest development. "As far as I can tell, you've got a good case for self-defense with everything you've done—even Harrison has acknowledged you saved his officer. You've discharged another weapon within a residential area…that's about it. Even then our legal firm will probably get those charges dismissed. But this situation has gone beyond a rueful shrug and an apology, Kimmer, especially if Ingleswood breaks her story—and she just might, after this evening. Harrison and the staties have to believe that we'll play by the rules. I believe you understand the necessity of rules."

She shot him a glare of pure ire. That wasn't a fair blow, and he knew it. Not even when she actually understood his position.

Except it was the position she'd most feared. The one that put her in a no-win situation. She rubbed her hand over an itchy cheek; it came away smudged with soot and she scowled at it in lieu of scowling at Owen. "Do that, and I'll be tied up for ages."

He nodded. "Possibly."

She shook her head, sharp and defiant. "I need to get to Hank's place. We all know that whatever he thought would save his ass, it wasn't good enough. I probably don't have much more than a day or two before they send someone to take care of him, now that Hammy Hands is dead and Pigeon Man is in custody."

"I don't think that's best right now. I'll send someone else—"

His phone rang. The extra line, the number that Owen put on his business cards for anyone outside Hunter and that had its own separate phone. The Bat Phone. He reached for it and said, "Get out."

She hesitated only an instant, but when he confirmed his words with a jerk of his chin at the door, she saw the weary duplicity in his eyes and understood. She left her gym bag and stepped out into the hall—just far enough so he couldn't see her. And indeed, when he answered the phone, the murmured conversation quickly got to the point. Owen didn't try to hide his concern as he informed his caller that he had no idea where exactly, Kimmer might be located. Okay, points to him for splitting hairs into microscopic sections.

She didn't mistake it for the notion that she'd won her argument. Owen simply wasn't ready to turn her over in the middle of the discussion.

And indeed, when she heard him hang up and came back around the corner to linger in the doorway, he shook his head. "I've only put them off. They have every reason to believe you'll be in touch with me. The only reason they believed me now is because they've stationed a trooper at the winery entrance and they know you haven't gone past them. This was more of a heads-up notice than a demand. Next time it'll be a demand."

Not to mention that come daylight, they'd probably find her car.

Kimmer dove right back into her argument. "Look, I know how to blend in down there. It's why you sent me down there last fall in the first place. And in case you hadn't noticed, *this* is exactly the reason I asked you not to. I didn't want those miserable people who call themselves my brothers to screw up my life again. And, oh!" She mimed slapping her forehead in dramatic discovery. "Look! One of them *has*."

That shook him. He slowly sat back in the spiffy comfort of his office chair, and he didn't look comfortable at all. He rubbed a hand over his face, eyes closed in thought. Eyes still closed, he said, "Tell me you understand the position this situation has created for the agency."

She wanted to say *give me a break.* She wasn't stupid. Though he probably thought that under the circumstances, she was likely blind. So she took a deep breath of her own and she recited, "I understand the position this has created for the agency. Hell, Owen, I went back there today, didn't I? I let them grill me, didn't I? Just because I was in the wrong place at the wrong time and I was willing to step in and help their deputy?"

"Yes," he said. "You did that."

Kimmer crossed her arms over her chest, a deliberately defiant gesture. "If I hadn't, I would have been home when Pigeon Man pulled up in front of my house. I would have stopped him."

"Maybe," Owen agreed. "Maybe not."

"Another Hunter operative could go to Hank's," Kimmer said. "But he'd lose time getting Hank's family to trust him."

Owen made a gentle snort of a noise. "And you think he'll trust you?"

"I think he knows me. I think he'll work with me. I can report back once I get a better understanding of the situation, but right now someone needs to keep that family alive, even Hank. And I need to quit having this stupid argument when you know I'm right. I need to spend my time in the shower and stuffing my face and looking at mug shots."

Owen nodded, but then added with reluctance, "You know I can't give you a different car. You'll have to take your own. Assuming you didn't shoot it full of holes, too."

"My car is fine." Well, once she dug out her spare keys and

put certain wires back where they belonged. "Except for the highly recognizable problem."

He shook his head. "If you do this, it has to look like you've done it on your own." He added a dry twist to his tone as he said, "I'm sure I'll have my hands full keeping this story off the air." As Kimmer winced, he added more matter-of-factly, "You'll need to be out of here before daylight—and to go unseen in between."

"I can do that," Kimmer said. "I'll take one of the overnighter rooms. Grab me some food from the reception and those Pittsburgh mug shots, and I'll still have time for four to five hours of sleep."

"There's food in the overnighter," Owen said, giving her the look that said she should know that.

"I know that," Kimmer said. "I just want some of that skanky cheese you're serving up tonight."

Kimmer got her cheese. She got her shower, her mug shots, a replacement SIG, a can of soup marketed as gourmet and her cheese. No coffee, no tea, not even Raspberry Reaction—but an uncola washed the cheese down just as well as the wine she didn't dare have without a full night's sleep ahead and miles to drive the next day.

Rio couldn't have come. He couldn't have driven back here in one shot and then turned around to drive several hours west and south. And she'd told him not to come. She'd hung up on him, for Pete's sake.

She could do this alone. Chimera in action. It wasn't any different because of the circumstances.

Right. The dead cat, the destroyed home, the absent boy-friend, the boss who might end up sacrificing you to the cause...

No different at all.

Chapter 11

"Here," Kimmer had said, presenting the mug shot to Owen shortly before her departure. He'd found the time to change into casual flannel and jeans, and she suspected he'd grabbed his own nap. Kimmer still wore her torn, smoky jeans, but she'd grabbed a dark jersey top from the limited offerings in the overnighter closet, and a dark taupe lightweight jacket—too big—to go over that. She had her bag o' goodies, and a supply of cash courtesy of Owen. And though on her first time through she hadn't identified anyone in the mug book, there was one picture that caught her attention. After a few hours of sleep and a second look, she'd realized it was Hammy Hands with a totally different nose—unbroken, and set over a thick, trimmed beard and mustache. Different nose, obscured jawline…but it was him, all right. "Call me if it leads to anything," she'd told Owen, and then she'd left, easing back through the vineyards to pick up her car and take a roundabout back-roads route toward Erie, Pennsylvania.

At Erie she grabbed breakfast, eating more than she really wanted against possible scarcity in the days to come. She double-checked that the phone charger was actually functioning; she had only the one battery. The one battery, the bag of hastily gathered weapons…otherwise not so much as a change of underwear, no intel…nothing but Hank's address.

Talk about going in unprepared.

She wished Owen would call with the news that Hammy Hands had been the last piece to the goonboy puzzle, and that they knew who the goonboss was. That they could turn it all over to the authorities and let them gather evidence about this goonboss who'd covered his tracks so well—and who'd been so ruthless in the process. If she'd been only Kimmer Reed instead of the trained operative Chimera, she'd have been killed with his first attempt on Hank—or in his first follow-up attack. Kimmer would have gone to Lafayette Park and never returned, and no one would have understood why or how.

How many others had the goonboss destroyed? *You need to be stopped. Now.*

Starting with the chop shop at Hank's farm. Starting with the goonboys who would come after Hank in the wake of Kimmer's escape and Pigeon Man's capture, and then…

Then they'd see. If she turned up enough evidence to send the Pittsburgh police after the goonboss, all the better. She could go back home and rebuild her life. See if she still had a job. A home. A lover.

A sudden blitz of doubt washed over her—doubt akin to terror. What was she doing on the road, haring off to rescue the weasel brother who'd gotten her into this mess with his conniving betrayal? Even if he hadn't planned it from the start, he knew well enough what he'd done when he'd put the goonboys on her trail, muttering about nonexistent recordings. *What the hell am I doing?* Racing back toward Munroville, and in the process endangering everything that meant anything in her life? Endangering her life itself, as well?

She almost pulled over to the shoulder, her hands shaking on the wheel and her jaw aching from where she'd clenched hard without even realizing. Almost.

And then she realized what her subconscious already knew—that she'd reached the county line. That the next exit would take her to Munroville, and a few winding roads before that she'd find Hank's small farm. That as much as anything, she was simply frightened of where she was.

She pushed her foot down on the accelerator.

A flashing light bar appeared in Kimmer's rearview mirror just inside the county line and just before her exit. She checked her speed…too fast. Dammit. A deep breath brought perspective. She'd take the ticket, she'd apologize to the nice officer and she'd drive on. In the grand scheme of things, it wasn't a big deal. A fifteen-minute delay.

She flipped her blinker on and pulled over to the shoulder, then sat quietly in the car with her window down and her license ready while the state trooper approached her with rather more care than necessary. Wary tension tightened Kimmer's back. Either this was no regular traffic stop, or her knack had been skewed by her arrival in this area.

But Kimmer didn't think her knack was skewed. Not when the officer's gun hand hovered a little closer to his holster than it had any reason. She hadn't been going that fast.

Play the game, she told herself, and smiled at the man. An average man in his late thirties, a little thick around the middle but still plenty fit, a man with enough years under his trooper utility belt to know how to do the job right. "Hi," she said, and handed over her license with carefully slow movement. "I'm sorry. I should have put it on cruise control."

He took her license without comment, comparing the picture to her own ruefully smiling face. He didn't return it to her; he tucked it in his front shirt pocket.

And he didn't even have his ticket book with him.

Uh-oh.

"Would you step out of the car, please?"

"I'm sorry?" Kimmer said, pumping up her confused and harmless act. "Why—?"

And he should have said, "Just get out of the car, ma'am," but instead his nerves overrode his years of experience and he said, "I've got an outstanding warrant for your arrest. You'll have to come with me."

I don't think so. Even if he'd had some kind of bench warrant, the situation was still well within the bounds of a normal traffic stop experience. This was more than that. The trooper was on edge, believed he had a lot riding on the success of this arrest, knew he was dealing with someone who was more than she seemed.

The goonboss, it seemed, had connections.

Of course he has connections. He'd be in jail by now if he didn't.

And the trooper's gun hand moved slightly, and Kimmer, still offering him puzzled compliance—the slow movements of a woman who didn't understand what was going on as she unlatched her seat belt and opened the door. He'd done well to move just behind her door; she couldn't see him except in the side view mirror and she sure couldn't slam the door into him as she opened it.

Didn't stop her from slipping on the brass knuckles from her jacket pocket or groping for her war club. *Gotta be careful.* The statie could be directly connected to the goonboss, or just a regular guy doing his job as best he could.

Up till now.

Kimmer turned in the seat, kicked the door open, rolling out in a pivot to end up at his feet. *On* his feet. She slammed the brass knuckles into his shin, hitting the sensitive nerves there. His leg buckled. She pivoted around to sweep behind the other leg and he fell right on his ass, still scrabbling for his gun with one hand, the other heading for his pepper spray.

Sorry. She would have said it out loud had she the breath for it, but she lunged for the gun, tapping his wrist with the war club and wincing as he cried out. She yanked the gun and tossed it carefully away, far too aware that it didn't have a safety. He had the pepper spray out by then and she lunged to land on his hand with her knee, wrenching the spray away as well and knowing she had only an instant more of this advantage. He was bigger, he was stronger, and if she didn't get control now she was going to lose this one.

Reluctantly, precisely, she knocked the side of his head with the war club. Not enough to put him out, only enough to daze him.

How many cars had passed them by? How many had noticed the scuffle?

She didn't even bother to get to her feet. She scrambled around behind him, slid her hands under his arms, and yanked. He slid roughly across the gravel of the shoulder. "Sorry, sorry," she muttered, gathering herself for another tug, and another, then rolling him over behind the Miata to snag his handcuffs and *damn*—

She hadn't hit him quite hard enough.

She'd held back, not really wanting to hurt him at all and only making it harder for both of them. She had only one wrist cuffed when he rolled around to swing out at her, connecting without any real strength but enough impact to knock her out of her crouch and back to the gravel.

She struck out with her foot, a double-tap into his ribs. He doubled over with a grunt of pain and it bought her the time to throw herself on him and try, in desperation, the thing that had worked with Brown Suit on their first encounter. She reversed her grip on the war club and jammed it into his ribs, making sure he felt it before he could even consider how lightweight she was on top of him. "Freeze, dammit!"

He froze.

"Good," she panted, hesitating just long enough to make sure he'd truly stopped fighting. "Now listen up. Have you got it figured out that I'm not your average traffic stop? Has it occurred to you that I could have blown you away with your own gun and instead I threw it away?"

The cop said nothing. Panting. Thinking. Probably hurting. Probably planning his next move, just as she would do in his place.

"The warrant's a fix," Kimmer told him. "Not that I expect you to believe me. It comes courtesy of someone I'm chasing down in Pittsburgh."

"Don't be stupid," the cop finally grunted. "You're only making it harder on yourself. You won't get away—"

"With this? Yes, actually, I will. I'm pretty good at getting away, and I'm pretty good at bringing in whoever I'm after.

So here's the deal. Bring your other hand behind your back and I'll cuff you and then I'll go away."

The back of his neck turned red. "Fuck you," he spat.

"Can't. Busy right now. Take a breath, get your temper back and give me your other hand. I've still got the brass knuckles, and I've got the little club you're still trying to figure out. Next time I hit you, I'll have to do it harder. And I really don't want to leave you by the side of the road with a brain bleed."

His shoulder radio crackled something fuzzy and obscured by his body pressing it into the ground; he stiffened slightly. Hoping. Kimmer made a disgusted noise and jerked the cord loose. "They'll find you eventually, but I'm not going to make it all that easy," she said. "Now give me your damn hand." She prodded him with the end of the club. Hard.

Very slowly, he moved his hand into her reach. She grabbed it, cuffed it and then pushed herself away from him, letting him warily work himself into an awkward sitting position to regard her with subdued resentment. He tried to regain his professional composure. "If the warrant's a fix, we can straighten this out," he said. "If you walk away from me, there's no turning back." He eyed her, hunting for a strategy to talk himself out of the situation. "Even a bounty hunter can't get away with assaulting an officer."

"Think of me as freelance rather than a bounty hunter," she said. "And you're perfectly right. Too bad I don't have any choice. I've got someone's life to save. His whole family, in fact. Even if he is a weasel-creep." She climbed to her feet, keeping an eye on him as she tested the patrol car's front passenger door and found it open. She considered smashing up the communications panel in the center of the dash and decided against it. She was in enough trouble already, and he wouldn't be able to do anything with it with his hands cuffed behind his back. By then his gaze had turned wary along with the puzzled undertones. He couldn't figure her out.

She couldn't blame him. She couldn't figure herself out, either.

She returned to his spot behind the Miata, crouching down out of reach. "Here's the deal," she said. "I'm going to walk you over to your car and tuck you inside. Sooner or later, someone will find you. Sooner, if any of these drivers turn out to be Good Samaritans." There was no telling who'd seen what, who had a cell phone and who didn't. She had to get out of here. Now. "And here's a freebie clue for you: someone in the system is dirty. If you already know that, then you're dirty, too, and I take back my sorries for what happened here today. If it's coming as a big surprise, then it's time to keep your eyes open. Someone in Pittsburgh is calling shots they shouldn't be calling."

"Don't do this," he said, displaying a mixture of dawning awareness and concern that told Kimmer clearly enough he wasn't involved.

"Gotta," she said. "It's a lose-lose situation, no doubt about it. But still…gotta." Too much of her life was already on the line to get squeamish now. "Now come on. Into the car."

Another flash of resistance crossed his face, and Kimmer growled, "Do it!" at just the right moment to cut it short. Didn't hurt to heft the war club.

And so he let her help him to his feet, and he cursed silently but quite obviously when she buckled him safely into place and then wound duct tape—damned straight the Miata had duct tape stashed in the back—around the seat belt latch just in case he turned into Houdini. He couldn't reach the radio, he couldn't reach the car horn even with his head, and she finished up by scooting the seat forward so his legs were trapped against the dash.

And then she calmly pulled the Miata out into traffic and took the next exit off I-79.

Gotta ditch the car. Cops across two states were looking for it now. Maybe Hank would have a junker; maybe she could lift something from a neighbor.

Hell, maybe she could find something in the little chop shop Hank had invited to his home.

But for now Kimmer pulled off the road onto a gravel service lane for the power line, hoping she wasn't so close that her cell phone—fully charged!—wouldn't function. She called Owen's Bat Phone, knowing that if he wasn't in the office, it would reach his cell with a customized ring. He'd never not answered that phone.

Nor did he let it trip to voice mail this time, either. But when he answered it, his voice held a false tone, and the single word was clipped. "Hunter."

"Not alone?" she asked. Dammit.

"Not right now," he told her.

"Friends of mine?"

"So to speak."

"Then I'll make this quick." She had no fear of traces or eavesdropping, not with the souped-up phone Hunter had provided, but she also had no desire to make things harder for Owen. "The goonboss has an in with the cops—the staties, anyway. Got stopped and there's some kind of warrant out for me. You'll note I'm not in custody."

"Clearly," he said, and his droll tone let her know he immediately understood the implications.

"I'm heading toward Hank's place. Nothing new other

than that…but I wanted you to know. Don't trust the Pennsylvania cops."

"I've got someone I can go to," he told her.

"And Ingleswood?" she asked, shorthand he'd understand.
Have you stopped that damned reporter yet?

"Still working on that. I think we'll be able to cover the
situation, but it's going to be costly."

Great. More anti-Kimmer points, adding up in the big
tally she'd started.

On the other hand, it couldn't get too much worse, could
it? Almost a cheering thought. "Gotta keep moving," she told
him. "I'll stay in touch."

"Do that." And then, for the sake of his company, "Sorry
you're already scheduled. I'll try you again next time."

But when Kimmer hung up, she closed her eyes and
bumped the phone against her forehead and fervently hoped
there would even be a next time.

With Ari taking turns in the driver's seat on an all-night
drive, Rio hit the south end of the lake at midmorning. He
dropped Ari off in Watkins Glen to yawn through the day and
drive a rental home the day after, and then headed for Full
Cry Winery. *That,* he told Kimmer in his mind, *is what family is supposed to be about.* As if he could have stopped Ari
from pitching in to get Rio back here in a way that left him
rested enough to drive safely onward to Erie—and would
leave his back functional once he got there.

As if it would have stopped me even if he hadn't. No matter what Kimmer had said. Because she clearly didn't get it:
she, too, was family. And though he'd needed to go home and
reassure himself that things were under control, he needed
just as badly to get back here and be with Kimmer. Not so

much the white knight—Kimmer had her own suit of armor—as just making sure that for once in her life, she wasn't alone in her trouble.

Okay, so it might take years for her to believe it. First step was making sure they had those years.

On the way to Hunter he detoured north to Glenora, winding the side streets long enough to hit Kimmer's street. No traffic. He took the luxury of easing down the street, hesitating in front of the house without actually pulling over.

Forlorn, it was. The blackened porch, the broken front windows, streaks of soot climbing up the siding, curtains gone. The warped door didn't quite close. The sharp scent of wet, charred wood reached him through the Element's fresh air vents and the tickle of it in his sinuses triggered protective anger. All this over a nonexistent recording. All this for a man who'd come up here to use Kimmer, and who'd left knowing he would then betray her.

It suddenly made perfect sense to him.

Not family at all.

Not that man. Not the others she'd left behind.

Kimmer wasn't the only one who had a different world to learn.

Rio headed for Hunter. He drove just over the limit and passed the slow cars where he could, and when he unfolded himself from the driver's seat, an innocent winery employee took one look at his expression and skittered to the other side of the small parking lot. He snapped his cell phone open and dialed Owen's regular line. His secretary answered. "Rio Carlsen," Rio said. "Here to see Owen. Now."

"He's—" The voice held denial. Rio didn't let him finish. "—going to see me or I'll be standing outside that viniculture development door making all sorts of noise," Rio said. "He'll know what it's about."

"So do I," the secretary said with some aspersion in his deep tenor. "He's at the winery office. I'll let them know you're coming."

And by the time Rio made it to the winery barn, Owen was stepping out the front door. He didn't even hesitate, but put a friendly hand of steel on Rio's shoulder and steered him away from the entrance to walk the pine-bark path along the outside of the barn. "I've sent for Dave," he said. "Everyone else is considerably farther away. He'll work from within the Pittsburgh police department. He knows who to trust."

"I'm going, too," Rio said. "I need Hank's address. Don't tell me you don't have it." And then he stopped short. "What do you mean, 'who to trust'?"

Owen glanced back at the winery entrance and relaxed slightly; they were out of earshot. Only if someone else came meandering around the path to enjoy the spring flowers blooming up against the barn would they need to move on. "It seems the system isn't entirely free from corruption. There's a bogus warrant out for Kimmer."

"They didn't get her?"

Owen's mouth quirked in a brief, wry smile. "They did," he said. "But not for very long."

Great. She'd be on everyone's radar if she'd had an encounter with a cop. "Then I need that address," he said, "because she needs help."

But when Owen merely looked at him in response, measuring his words, Rio's hackles went up. He wanted a shave, he wanted sleep, he wanted a meal and a good Twinkies fix, but more than any of that he wanted—needed—to be headed straight for Kimmer. "I can get the information on the Web," he said bluntly. "I can stop at Erie and find an Internet café…I bet it'll only take a white pages search."

"And I'd prefer you didn't," Owen said. "This thing has spun entirely out of control. I've barely kept it out of the headline news. I'm sending Dave as a Hunter rep and we can't afford to muddy the waters—"

"You mean the agency can't afford it," Rio said. "That's what this is about, isn't it? You want your brother down there because you know he'll watch out for Hunter interests, and Hank Reed has already caused enough trouble. Notice I said Hank and not Kimmer."

Owen raised a single imperturbable eyebrow, damn him. "If you knew my brother Dave, you'd know what an absurd statement that is."

"Yeah, yeah," Rio said. "He left the family business to do his own thing. So what. If he's working for you, he's working *for you.* I'm going. I'll be working with Kimmer's interests in mind."

Owen stiffened slightly. Good, at least he was paying attention. "And should I ask if you're still considering the offer to sign on with us?"

Yeah, the man was good. Rio got it. Rio got it quite clearly. But if Owen thought he could control Rio with that threat, he had another think coming. "That depends," he said evenly. "I'm still assessing your field support."

"Kimmer's not on a Hunter assignment. In fact, she crossed state lines in express defiance of my wishes."

"To clean up a mess that started because of an assignment she took against her wishes," Rio snapped, quite suddenly aware of the inches he had on Owen, if not the weight.

And to his surprise, Owen merely sighed. "She said the same." He shrugged. "And she was right, too."

Rio's eyes narrowed. He could have floundered for words, but kept his silence and his demanding stare in place.

"Don't take me wrong." Owen started them walking again, veering off the path to walk the soft green grounds on approach to the back of the viniculture development building. "My concerns about Hunter's situation are significant. But I won't leave Kimmer out to hang in the wind, either. That should be obvious enough, given that Dave is already on his way."

"Don't," Rio said, hearing the dangerous edge to his own words, "*don't* tell me that was some sort of test."

"Test?" Owen glanced at him. "Not so to speak. Feeling you out...yes. If you'd been that easy to deter, you're not the sort I want working with Hunter. And I'd want someone else at Kimmer's back."

"I thought you said there was no one else close enough." Owen raised that eyebrow again. "*I'm* here."

Rio didn't sputter. Not quite.

"Now," Owen said, swinging wide around the building to reach the entrance. "Let's get that address."

She slipped through the trees between the barn and the pasture, feet assured. She knew just when to duck to avoid low branches in the darkness. She knew just when to hesitate to hear if anyone else might be out here. And she knew just where to bend back the best long, springy branches, releasing them to whip in the faces of those who might follow—but who seldom did since she'd already proven her timing and accuracy with those natural weapons.

No. Not here, not now. It just seemed that way. The trees were the right mix of secondary growth hardwoods, the poison ivy scattered just thickly enough, the back of the barn the same weathered wood of a building not quite kept up but still serviceable…and the partitioned goat shelter in which Kimmer crouched the same rain-softened mucky ground that would suck her sneakers right off if she didn't step carefully.

And the smell, of course. That, too, was the same. A small herd of dairy cows, a yearly litter of pigs, the goats for milk and weed control. The one still in the pen with her had a big bell around its neck. She would bet there was another one out wandering the property, eating around the edges of the cleared areas but never too far from the leafy green alfalfa dinner serving.

Beh-eh-eh. That was Rio's voice in her head where it had no right to be. Kimmer scowled and pushed away the large brown goat currently nibbling on the edge of her borrowed jacket. "Stupid," she muttered at it, and couldn't have said which of them she was talking to. But she kept her voice low, for not so long ago a goonboy in garage coveralls and greasy hands had wandered out here to relieve himself and to walk what must have been a habitual perimeter, judging by the worn scuff of a path he followed. A multipurpose goonboy.

She looked beyond the barn to that which made this property utterly unlike the small farm on which she'd grown up. The huge Quonset building, shiny metal through the leaves. Ugly in shape, ugly in color…a big human blotch upon the land. As was the junk lining the sides. Hank's scrap and scrounge business must have been going strong even before the BGs spotted him as a likely mark for their chop shop location.

She doubted they'd realized that Hank's world was so entirely about *Hank* that he'd kill one of them and then convince himself he could get away with it by waving his troublesome sister in front of their eyes. But she'd played the part of distraction long enough. It was time to put an end to this thing. If that meant putting an end to the goonboss, all the better.

Especially since she doubted she could dig her own way out of this trouble—with the cops, with Owen—without that big payoff.

Against her hip, something vibrated. Cell phone. Normally in a pocket, but she'd loaded every pocket she had with every weapon she could fit and had resorted to her belt clip for the phone. SmartCarry holding the .38, the trooper's Glock in a back pocket and good only for the remaining bullets, her club and toothpick knife and brass knuckles, a small stun gun and a larger knife strapped to her jeans at the outside of her calf. Loaded for goonboy. Kimmer pushed the goat's questing nose away from her back and retrieved the phone, flipping it open to check the caller ID and more than a little smug at the full charge the battery carried.

Rio.

For once she wished the phone wasn't enhanced, so technologically spiffy. It told her quite bluntly that Rio was at Full Cry Winery. She couldn't even pretend that he might be on his way. That she wouldn't be alone in this.

Not a chance. For one thing, she'd told him not to come—to stay with his family. For another, there was no way he could get back down this far unless he'd suddenly taken up piloting his own small plane. He'd taken two days to get up there, being careful of his back so he could still be of some good to them when he got there. Under most circumstances he was the same strong, deceptively capable man she'd thought him when she'd first seen him at the little roadside gas station last fall. Taller than most who considered themselves tall, striking of feature and build…and yet he'd carried himself so casually, so relaxed. He'd taken her by surprise when he'd easily handled one of the men sent after his cousin Carolyne. Quick and decisive and effective…and then, when he'd taken his cousin in hand, right back to easygoing. But soon enough Kimmer had learned he paid a price for those moments of chivalry. That he'd always pay that price, as little fuss as he made about it.

And quite suddenly she missed him—fiercely, as she seemed to feel everything these recent days. She wished he were here.

But she couldn't talk to him. She couldn't let it mess with her head…and she couldn't risk being overheard. She'd let voice mail pick up—which it did even as she made the decision, telling her just how long she'd been lost in thought. *Stupid*. Not alert to her surroundings, not even aware of the—

Goat.

She snatched her hand back too late. The goat targeted the phone, all grab and no finesse, knocking Kimmer back a step in the muck. It lifted its head to that cocky angle goats seemed born to assume, staring at her with its eerie light brown eyes, rectangular pupils distinct…phone clenched in its jaws.

"Give that back!" she snarled at it, a phrase most goats heard from kidhood. Still staring at her with its accusing, indignant gaze, the goat gave a quick sideways chew, determined the phone to be of no interest and dropped it in the muck. Kimmer waved her hands in its face and it bounded away, lifting its tail to drop a few fresh pellets in its wake.

Gingerly, Kimmer plucked the phone from the nastiness in which it resided. No need to worry if the muck had wrecked it; the goat had done that for her. Cracked and nonresponsive, the phone display flickered once and went out for good.

No phone.

She felt the urge to close her eyes and mutter a few good strong anti-goat invectives, but resigned herself to the situation, bouncing back as she ever had. If she had to retreat and find a pay phone, she would—supposing it didn't rain and bog her Miata down in the back pasture where she'd stashed it. *Doesn't matter. I'll make it work. I won't give up.* Giving up was a luxury she'd never had.

Kimmer lured the goat back over with a few greens plucked from beyond the pen, and wiped the phone off on its coat. She couldn't leave the phone here to be found, but didn't want any residual smell to give away her presence. Once she left the pen, she'd rub her shoes off with grass. For now, she tucked the phone away on its clip and sighed.

Well. The battery was still charged.

Chapter 12

When she'd watched long enough from the barn area to assure herself there was currently only one man hanging out at the Quonset hut, Kimmer moved in to take a closer look. One goonboy...didn't make sense. If such limited manpower was SOP, then no one could have witnessed Hank's crime; he could have dumped the body elsewhere and avoided direct suspicion. And if this chop shop handled the kind of volume that would attract a goonboss like the one who'd had five men to spare first on Hank and then Kimmer, then one man couldn't handle the load.

She needed to know more.

A careful inspection of the Quonset interior through one of several small, dirty windows showed her lots of empty space, and a tiny corner office area that was much neater than she'd expected. She managed to confirm the single goonboy theory—as well as the supposition that it wasn't always like

this. Not given the equipment inside, given the gear. He probably just handled cleanup and small jobs in between larger
shipments. Caddy Escalade, Dodge Stratus, Jeep Wran-
gler…the popular targets.

She'd have to come back later. Or not. It depended on what
it took to extricate Hank from this situation—or whether he
was truly in the danger she thought he was in. It depended
on whether she had the opportunity to follow through, to find
the goonboss and redeem herself.

If redemption was even possible.

It won't be the end of the world. Just because her life with
Hunter was the only thing she'd known since leaving home.
She'd been valuable to them as a precocious fifteen-year-old,
valuable enough to mentor and train. Now she had that training, and she still had the knack that had drawn Hunter to her
in the first place.

She'd find another situation if she had to.

But for now she took one last look around the building, as
much as could be had through the dirty window. Paint tents,
a whole row of work bays, slick rolling tool caddies, a parking area, a solidly graveled approach drive not quite big
enough for a truck. That meant they had goonboy-wannabe
drivers, grabbing a hundred bucks or so to deliver the cars to
their distribution points. Possibly even the same people who
stole the cars in the first place.

It meant any number of people might descend on this place
at any given time, and Kimmer had no idea when that might be.

Hank's wife might know.

Hank's wife was the next step in any event.

The house sat closer to the road, at the end of a curving,
rutted drive that made this property an excellent choice for
the goonboss. How had they approached Hank? Posing as

door-to-door evangelists, scoping out the options? Maybe in a bar—no doubt Hank was a known fixture in several. It was even possible that the conniving weasel-boy had gone out looking for connections.

Doesn't matter. Kimmer had to clean it up, no matter how it had gotten dirty in the first place.

The house had an abandoned look, and Kimmer glanced at her watch. The kids wouldn't be home from school yet, not quite. She'd expected a dog—something scruffy and ill-tempered, chained where it could give good warning of her approach—but found only an empty scrap-built doghouse and an upside-down food bowl.

He'd had a dog, and they'd made him get rid of it. Too much noise, Kimmer guessed. Too much declaration of their presence, their comings and goings. Now they probably made do with the goat.

Rural detritus littered the area around the house. An old torn screen, bent T-posts, a headless doll…Kimmer watched where she put her feet. No one popped out of the front door or the back to challenge her, and the wraparound porch kept her from gaining a clear idea of the interior. Once she had a decent understanding of the interior layout, and once her presence failed to scare up any goonboys, she hesitated in the overgrown landscaping long enough to be certain no one was inconveniently turning up the driveway, and then she went and knocked on the front door. A nice, firm, no-nonsense knock. No skulking for her.

Almost immediately she heard movement from within the house—but the door wasn't as quick to open. She repeated the knock before the footsteps approached the front door, and then she stood back so the occupant—Hank or his wife, she hoped—could open the door. With fingers crossed against

goonboys Kimmer had both her war club and the recently acquired Glock at the ready within the roomy pockets of her borrowed REI jacket. She loved REI. They made the best pockets.

When the door opened, she found herself face-to-face with
a woman taller than her—taller than Hank, for that matter,
and clothed in a worn cutesy country sweatshirt that didn't
at all suit her demeanor. A woman with lank hair that caught
a deep chestnut glint in the light of the early afternoon sun,
and a face with features that looked as though they'd thick-
ened instead of refined themselves over the years. A face with
a belligerent, mistrusting undertone to its expression, and
eyes that weren't improved by their narrowed suspicion. A
face that looked...

Kimmer squinted back. The name, the features...they fell
into place. "Susan Goldman!"

The narrowed eyes widened, blinked. "Holy shit," Susan
said. "What the hell happened to that mess on your face?"

Laser surgery. A wonderful thing. But Susan didn't actually leave any room for Kimmer to respond before she added,
"Hank wasn't kidding when he said you'd changed."

Same to you, Kimmer thought. This woman had been in
Hank's high school class, and at that age had been an attrac-
tive girl—always a little coarse, but always carrying herself
well. With pride.

Being married to Hank had probably taken care of that.

Although...this woman had nothing of the downtrodden
about her. Chronically frustrated, yes. And with frown lines
between her brows that seemed pretty well entrenched for her
age of just past thirty. But she had no cower in her. No lurking flinch. And she was still talking. "What the hell are you
doing here? Haven't you caused enough trouble?"

Okay, Kimmer hadn't been expecting that. But she shot

back, "Not nearly enough. I need to talk to you." And her hand only tightened a little around the war club handle.

Susan glanced over Kimmer's head to the driveway, and in the direction of the barely visible Quonset. She concluded with obvious reluctance that it wasn't in her best interest to be caught with Kimmer on her front porch, and stepped aside so Kimmer could enter. She didn't take a closer look at Kimmer herself, and showed no awareness that Kimmer's jacket pockets were full of more than her hands. When Kimmer stepped into the house, Susan closed the door abruptly behind her and didn't invite her in any farther. The bright afternoon sunshine streamed in through the south facing windows of the house, dimmed by the screen of dirt but leaving plenty of light to display Susan's accusatory flare of nostril and the slight twitch of her cheek—not quite a sneer.

No, not what Kimmer had expected of Hank's wife. She delved through her memories to hunt those few she had of Susan Goldman, remembering only the sturdy young woman who seemed to have plenty of friends in tow.

That's how it had been. They'd been in tow. She'd been the one in charge.

"How," Kimmer said bluntly, "did you ever come to marry Hank?" She'd been so sure Hank would choose a mousy woman. Someone he could bully, continuing family tradition.

Susan's mouth tightened. "He got me pregnant. He wanted to get rid of the baby. That's not the way we do things in my family. My daddy let him know what was expected."

Kimmer remembered Susan's father as one of the largest men in Munroville and quite suddenly wished she'd been there for that conversation.

But not so much that she regretted running away.

Susan didn't wait for Kimmer to work it through. "The

only reason we're talking is because I can't afford to have you hanging around on my porch. You didn't answer my question. What the hell are you doing here?"

"It's not obvious?" Kimmer was pretty sure Susan would miss the dry tone of her voice, and didn't much care. "I'm here to save Hank's scrawny ass."

"Save it?" Susan snorted, leaning forward to use her height as intimidation. "It's your fault we're in this fix in the first place!"

Kimmer took a slow, deep breath, carefully unclenching her jaw. She swept away thoughts of her burned home, of her jeopardized job, of the recent goonboy encounters in her own backyard. "Really?" she asked, eyeing Susan with her best predatory expression. "And how is that?"

She didn't really want to know what Susan thought. She didn't really care. Except that her understanding of this situation had taken a sudden detour, and if letting the woman spew acrimony made things more clear, well then, let Susan spew.

Susan jabbed a finger at her. "You should have let him die!"

Kimmer blinked in surprise. It didn't even slow Susan down. "You haven't been here in over ten years. What do you care about Hank Reed? What do you care about any of them? I bet you don't even know your father's dead. But *no*, you had to play hero! You not only saved his scrawny ass, you killed the wrong men to do it! Now they've got Hank working a delivery and they've grabbed my kids to keep him in line. This was supposed to make my life better—it would have made my kids' lives better—if you'd only done your part!"

"Then maybe you should have sent me a little heads-up," Kimmer said, waiting to be hit with some sort of shocked reaction to the news of her father's death.

Nothing. Just faint regret that he'd never known of her success in spite of him. Just a little spot within her that had always been hollow now knowing with final certainty that it would always be that way.

"You're a Reed," Susan spat. "I counted on you to act like one."

"Your mistake." Kimmer couldn't believe her voice came out so calmly. She couldn't believe she stood here in Hank's entryway and listened to this angry woman spit out her cruel and angry words, and yet she felt nothing. Nothing but the hollowness at losses old and new. *Dissociation.* She knew the terms, the words to use. They seemed meaningless just at the moment.

Susan pounced on the quiet response, mistaking it for true hesitation. "You should have stayed out of the way. You've ruined everything!"

Anger finally pushed away the shock of Susan's earlier words. Kimmer gave her a mean little grin. "You think I've been trouble? I haven't even started. My life is upside-down because of you, and I'm here to straighten it out." She pulled her hands from her pockets, forewarned by Susan's shift of weight. "Whatever you've started, it's way out of your control. Whether you like it or not, what happens to your ass next is my decision."

"You dare!" Susan drew back to deliver a powerful slap, and Kimmer's hand shot up to block it. Just as fast, Susan went after her with the other hand. When Kimmer blocked it she wrapped her hand around Susan's wrist, slid to her thumb and twisted. With a cry, Susan went down to her knees. Kimmer didn't break the thumb because…

To be honest, she'd provoked the woman on purpose. She didn't have time to argue. She certainly didn't have time to convince someone who saw the world through Susan's conniving eyes. She leaned over Susan and said, "I killed those men, you bitch. I killed them because of you. You brought me into this mess. Now you've got to deal with me. So start talking. I want *everything*." She twisted the thumb a little harder.

Susan's face drained of blood. "It's not my fault! None of it is my fault! They came here—"

Kimmer used her free hand to gently tuck a strand of lank hair behind Susan's ear. "Susan, dear," she said, her voice no louder than a gentle whisper, "Did Hank ever mention how I know when people tell the truth? He ever mention my knack, how his weird little sister seemed to know things she shouldn't? It's true. It's very, very, true. Should I add another 'very' to make sure you get it?"

Dumbly, Susan shook her head.

Kimmer leaned closer. "I killed those men, Susan. It wasn't hard. And I feel like hurting someone right now, so I think you should talk fast. Really fast."

"You—!" Susan gasped, but it was in disbelieving comprehension more than protest, so Kimmer let it pass.

"I'm going to let go of your hand," she told her erstwhile sister-in-law. "But you should notice that I'm between you and the door, and that I'm faster than you, and also that I'm currently armed in more ways than you can even imagine. And do I have to mention there'll be no screaming? Even if there's a nice goonboy or two close enough to hear you, I don't think he's going to worry very much about hitting you in the inevitable crossfire." She waited until she saw the understanding in Susan's eyes, and then slowly released the woman's abused thumb. Susan instantly shifted away from her, ungainly on the floor. Kimmer crouched to look her in the eye. "Talk," she said. "Talk now."

"My father knew…" Susan started, and then stopped to look away. "I wanted to save for the kids, in case they made it to college. I wanted something nicer to drive. I wanted to fix this place up. And Hank…he started out pretty well, working in Dad's garage. But then he got this idea he could do better on his own."

Kimmer filled in the blank. *He'd been wrong.*

"Dad was approached by this guy from Pittsburgh, but they decided the garage was too visible. So Dad thought of this place, and he asked me, and I put it to Hank. He wasn't hard to convince." Susan got a hard, triumphant little look on her face. "Give me a night or two, and I can convince that man to do anything I put my mind to."

Kimmer wrinkled her nose. "That," she said, "is too much sharing. Just stick to the whole goonboy thing. Do you know who's behind it? Who's sitting pretty in good old Pixburg?"

But Susan was telling the story her way. "I know about Hank's little affair. It's not like he doesn't get enough at home. He's just a jerk." She gave an indignant little toss of her head, seeming to forget her own precarious situation and her undignified slump on the floor. "I've had enough of it. With the money this car thing brings in, I don't need Hank. God, what a moron. So the girl came around a little too often, and caught a city boy's eye. What did Hank expect? What did he think would happen if he killed the guy? That no one would find out?"

Yes, there was a little gleam of triumph hiding in her eye, all right. Kimmer said, "You told them. *You* ratted him out."

Susan didn't even bother to nod. "I didn't want things getting messy around here. And I thought about what Leo had said when he drove over to drink himself into a stupor during the Superbowl with Hank. He kept talking about Hank's little sister, about that girl who'd run out on the family, how she'd made him a hero to even the score." She slanted a look at Kimmer, a devious expression. "Some kind of superspy, he called you."

"Aw, shucks," Kimmer said, flat of tone. The woman thought she could change her tune and start throwing around compliments? Call on the notion of sisterhood? *Not gonna happen.* "So you didn't really believe it, but you thought you'd send Hank my way to get the action out of your back-yard. And then you aimed the goonboys at Hank."

"I figured they'd catch up to him before he reached you," Susan said, dropping her gaze.

"Yeah, yeah. Don't be stupid, Susan. I'm not." Kimmer drummed her fingers against her knee. "Hank thought of trying to shift their attention to me," she guessed. "That wasn't your game plan. You wanted Hank feeling the heat. And Hank thought of selling me out for some nonexistent recording."

Susan glanced at her, long enough to openly assess her chances of lying, of denying any knowledge of that aspect of things. She'd no doubt be horrified if she knew how easily Kimmer could read even that much. Finally she nodded, a tiny jerk of a thing.

"So here we are," Kimmer said. "Your life's a shambles and so is mine. I don't have a lot to lose at this point, in case you didn't get the implication there. In case you haven't fig-ured out that you made a huge mistake when you brought me into this." *When you put my boss on the spot with the locals. When you destroyed my home. When you showed Rio just how different we really are.* "And in spite of the fact that you're a heartless, conniving bitch, I suspect you don't want to see anything happen to your kids."

Susan flinched with the first sign of vulnerability she'd shown. Her voice was barely audible. "No."

"Then talk to me about what will happen here next. Where's Hank, exactly? Where are the kids? How old are they? What are they like, how do they react to scary crap? And Susan," Kimmer lowered her voice into meaningful territory, leaning close again, "have you ever let Hank smack them around?"

Susan's snort was unfeigned. "He'd never dare. He wouldn't touch me again if he so much as raised a hand to them. Or should I say, I'd never touch him."

Hank the sex slave. A new and disturbing thought. Kimmer shook it out of her head. She tilted her head in warning as Susan shifted her weight with the intent to rise, and the woman sullenly settled to the floor. No longer scared, apparently…no longer intimidated beyond her own capacity for craftiness. Kimmer had to give her that much. Whatever Hank had thought he was getting into, he'd met his match.

The thought was strangely satisfying.

"You're fine right there," she told Susan. "Now. Tell me about the kids."

On the road again… Kimmer hummed the Willie Nelson tune soundlessly, just under her breath. Hank was behind the wheel of a stolen car, bringing it in from the city and expected sometime this afternoon. Tomorrow the others would converge on this place, the full crew of deliveries and mechanics, working their magic on stolen cars. Within days those cars would be in someone else's hands, repainted and scrubbed clean of their original identification, some of them broken down for parts with the leftovers hauled off as part of Hank's salvage business.

Susan had described it all openly, her words and tone carrying derision for these criminals she'd decided to use and not nearly enough concern for the girls being held in the Quonset. The girls were fine, Susan assured her. She'd seen them, she'd taken food over. The BGs liked Susan; they knew Hank's bumbling wasn't her fault. They wouldn't hurt her kids.

Kimmer thought, with little kindness in her mental tone, that Susan didn't have a clue.

Whatever else the goonboss was up to, stolen cars was the least of it. He was ruthless, slick and entrenched. He probably had his fingers in every piece of criminal pie the city had to offer.

Kimmer thought she'd see about taking said goonboss down when this was all over. But for now she again crouched outside the giant blight of a hut, waiting for the lone man to come outside and admire the spring flowers or scowl meaningfully across the landscape or even take another stroll around the perimeter. Then she'd deal with him, free the kids, and wait around for Hank. She'd escort the family to a safe house until Hank was suddenly the least of the goonboss's worries. Of course, she still had to contact Owen and arrange for the safe house, but that was the least of her concerns at the moment.

C'mon, c'mon... What was the guy doing in there, watching *Oprah?* Kimmer's jacket wasn't warm enough for lurking in shadows. Her toes were numb with inaction and her body slowly chilling, and she wanted this done before Hank showed on the scene.

She used a few more moments entertaining herself with the image of Hank and Susan, dumped in a safe house and left to deal with one another, Susan's scheming revealed. Not the kids, of course. Once they were cleared of injury, the kids would be sheltered until provisions were made for their care. Two girls, seven and four and described as quiet, obedient girls. Kimmer wondered if they'd had all the life stomped out of them or if they were just savvy.

Oh, enough waiting is enough. Kimmer had children to save. A big BG to bring down. And mostly, a life to salvage. Maybe it was too late, maybe not, but she wouldn't have the chance to find out until she finished up here. She eased up to the corner of the building, over junk Hank had somehow forgotten to salvage and through several seasons of brushy growth—sumac saplings, old mullen stalks and fresh green growth plattered at the ground along with the inevitable poison ivy. A peek through the Virginia Creeper clinging to the corner showed her the door. It was open to the sunshine; more sunshine finally sliced off the corner of the building to warm Kimmer while she watched for signs of movement within and saw nothing.

The rescue thing had to be done before things got busy here again, even if Susan had said Kimmer would have the rest of the day. She hadn't been lying. Kimmer's knack told her that much. But Kimmer still didn't trust her.

She crept away from the building and made her swift way to the goat pen, where she coaxed the wary goat over with a handful of the alfalfa hay under shelter on the other side of the fence. While she was there she kicked aside the spilled bale of alfalfa and yanked the baling twine free, stuffing two of the lengths in her back pocket and twisting the third around the animal's head to create a makeshift halter, unbuckling the bell collar while she was at it. Another handful of the alfalfa, fed in carefully metered portions, and she got the goat through the pen gate and out near the door of the hut.

It wouldn't stay there long—only as long as the alfalfa lasted. Time to get Lazy Boy outside. She tucked herself back in at the side of the building, where she sliced off a slender, freshly leafed box elder branch. Before the goat could get too interested in this potential food, she reached back to tickle the metal side of the building, a random pattern of movement. After a few moments with no response, she pulled it back with her other hand and let it whap the building—and then she stilled, listening.

For a moment, the only sound other than her own breathing and the faint breeze in the trees that encroached upon the back of the building was the goat's happy chomping. Its tail flicked sporadically, happily, as the goat snuffled over the ground in gustatory pleasure—and then it stopped. No flicking, no chewing, head in the air.

Now this *is a stalking goat.*

Lazy Boy sauntered out of the building to stop some distance away from the goat, his hands on his hips and a rough upholstery pattern imprinted on one side of his face. *Sleeping, were we?* Kimmer eyed his rumpled coveralls for signs of a gun. If he had one, it was well hidden—and he had no reason to keep it hidden at all.

Which didn't mean, as Kimmer withdrew the gun and set herself in a solid two-handed stance, that she wasn't going to watch for any signs of a fumble toward a gun. And she didn't want to startle him; she wanted him turning to look, but without alarm. She shifted her foot against an old mullen stalk, making it rattle, and when he glanced behind himself it was a thoughtless, automatic reaction—until he saw her. He stiffened, still twisted around his planted feet.

"Tsk," Kimmer said. "Sleeping on the job. See what happens?"

But his baffled expression said he was still clueless, although he teetered slightly in his altered balance, not daring to move.

Kimmer nodded at the gun. "Glock," she said, and lifted her chin slightly to indicate herself. "Kick-ass babe. Get with it, goonboy. This is a rescue."

"Those girls!" he blurted. His wide-eyed expression sounded the *Oh shit!* he didn't quite say out loud.

"Bingo. You get the Mr. Badwrench award. Now turn around before you fall over, and back up in this direction. You've probably seen it done on *Cops*. Just pretend you're a star." Once he complied, she removed a hand from the gun and fished the twine from her pocket. It cut cruelly into his wrists when she looped them together, and he whined a protest.

"Aren't you the tough guy? Jeez, they really weren't expecting any trouble here, were they? You the only one here?" She patted him down, hoping for a phone and not finding one. He must have one…he'd set it down somewhere, no doubt. Careless and inconvenient of him.

He gave a sullen shrug that meant he didn't want to admit he was alone. It satisfied Kimmer. She pushed him into the building and over to one of the tool carts, where she pointed to the floor. Once he'd sat on the hard concrete—and he'd be feeling it soon enough, to judge by that skinny ass—she made sure the wheels were locked, secured him to it and gagged him, and then precariously balanced a tray of massive wrenches on the cart directly above his head. "Do I have to explain this to you?"

He shook his head, a stiff and fractional movement.

"Good. Now the children and I are going for a walk. Once I've got them to safety, you and I will have a chat."

And then it's look out, goonboss.

Chapter 13

The children. But not until she'd done a quick sweep of the building, confirming what she'd seen from the window. Nothing much different. The paint tents, the work bays…there was a shelf area right next to the window that she hadn't been able to see, piled with parts from donor cars. No lurking goonboys.

In the office she found her earlier perception of its small size borne out, but now the foreshortened appearance made sense. Now she knew that behind it, there was another small room, the kind of small room that a goonboy crew would want to keep on hand for those private moments of intimidation and pleasure. They'd been clever in constructing it, which merely made it discreet instead of blindingly obvious. Kimmer made a quick survey of the office. These goonboys were organized, all right. Registration paperwork, a book listing those recently deceased for use as faux owners with the bribery-bought paperwork, a list of neighborhoods to avoid because of recent heavy "harvesting." All out in the open. No phone; they probably stuck to cells. She couldn't help but give the computer—currently turned off—a wistful glance. If she could walk out of here with that thing, she was willing to bet she'd have everything she needed not only to find the goon-boss, but to put him away for good.

But she wasn't here for the computer. Not this time. And she was willing to bet once she had the girls and their unde-serving parents away from here, that computer would become scrap in a heartbeat. If only she had someone local she could trust...some cavalry to call.

Then again, if only she had her phone.

No good pining over it. She'd call Owen from the house once she had the girls. She left the desk and the file cabinet and quickly discovered that the heavily shadowed back cor-ner was more than just a corner. It was a slice of space just large enough for a medium-size person to slide in and face the door of the sort-of-hidden room. Kimmer tried the door-knob...locked. Dammit. And not enough room to kick the thing open. Not a sound from within. Either they'd been moved or they'd learned to keep quiet.

She glanced out at her prisoner to make sure he hadn't found some way to circumvent her silly booby trap, and returned to the desk drawers. Those, too, were locked. And while Kimmer was no slouch at lock picking, she hadn't had the time to res-cue her pick set from her smoldering house. Sudden impatience flamed through her. She strode out to the work area, found her-self a tire pry bar, and returned to attack the desk most literally.

The second drawer yielded the keys.

Her hands shook as she unlocked the door. She could only pretend not to notice. *Let them be all right.*

The door opened to a sight she'd pretty much expected—

and at the same time, not. She'd expected the cot bed along the wall, and even the toilet off in the corner. She'd expected the food wrappers and the general odor of the unwashed, even the inoffensive odor of unwashed child and the faint smell of stale urine. Judging by the silence, she'd expected the girls to be huddled on the bed, fearfully waiting to see what this new arrival meant for them.

She hadn't expected the youngest, hardly larger than a toddler, curly hair largely escaped from childishly plaited braids and knobby knees drawn up beneath her chin, to have all the body language of fierceness in hiding. The older girl—brown, dirty hair too short for braids, her jumper torn—looked both frightened and exasperated. Whatever the younger had in mind, the older hadn't gone for it.

Kimmer said, "I know your father. I'm your aunt. I've come to get you out of here."

The younger girl looked at her with narrowed eyes and blurted, "You're That Bitch Kimmer!"

Kimmer snorted in amusement. "No kidding," she said. "And whatever you're holding in that grimy little hand of yours, I want it."

"It's a hair thingy."

"It's not." Kimmer held out her hand. A closer look at the little girl revealed similarities Kimmer hadn't seen at first on those diminutive features. *That's me. Five years old, and that's me.* And perhaps not quite so obedient as Susan thought. "Give it up."

"Karlene," the older girl said, and her bossy tone had tears mixed in. "She knows!"

Karlene gave her sister a supremely disgusted look and held out her hand, slowly uncurling her fingers to reveal a sharp wiry twist of metal that could only have come from somewhere on the bed. Kimmer didn't bother to smother her grin as she took it. "Good thinking," she said. "But we'll use a different strategy." If Hank couldn't see Kimmer in this child, he must be in deep denial.

"What stragedy?" Karlene demanded.

Kimmer smiled at her. "The one where we walk out of here together."

The two exchanged glances, and in this, the oldest—Sandy, Susan had called her—made the final decision, pulling gently on a lock of hair as she nodded. "We'll go see Mommy and Daddy?"

"Not right away." Lying would get her nowhere. "We'll go somewhere safe, so your parents can deal with the bad guys." Sort of. More or less. Especially when "someplace safe" meant the Miata. Until she could make contact with Owen, Kimmer had no one to trust. She felt a wistful fondness for Trooper McMillan, who at least would have seen the little girls to a safety that Kimmer knew would actually be safe.

The girls hesitated at this news, for which she didn't blame them. She said, as gently as someone who didn't get children and had never truly had her own childhood could manage, "It'll make things easier for your mommy. She's worried about you now, and she wants me to make sure you're safe."

That got them. Kimmer held out her hand again, this time in a welcoming gesture, waiting for a smaller hand to fill it. "Let's go."

And just as Sandy reached for her, the ground vibrated slightly beneath Kimmer's feet. The girls both stiffened, exchanging frightened looks. Young Karlene threw herself into her sister's arms with no sign of her previous defiance. Far too close to suit Kimmer, a semi used its engine brake, gear-ing down in a noise that reverberated through air and ground alike. Sandy said, "The mean people are here!"

"How many?" Kimmer said sharply, and modulated her tone with effort. "Are there usually lots of them, or just a few?"

Karlene said, "Lots and lots. Someone always looks at us. They say mean things and tell us to be good."

It's too early! Susan hadn't been lying, Kimmer was certain of it. Something had changed, and the crew had returned early with their latest harvest.

Doesn't matter. These would be mechanics, no tougher than Lazy Boy. They'd be hired hands, with maybe a few real goonboys spread among them. But she couldn't deal with them from in here; she couldn't fight her way out and be certain the girls would stay safe in her wake. She needed them to stay in here—as safe a place as any with action going down—so she could step back and identify the problem goons, pick them off and then take out the others on the way in. By the time the girls came out, the way would be clear.

"Change of plan," she said, dropping her hand. Sandy's face crumpled. Karlene glared at Kimmer through hot, angry tears. "You're leaving us!"

"For now," Kimmer said, her attention divided as she strained to hear the very first sounds of arrival—and knew she had to be away from here before then. "I'll be back."

"Baloney!"

Startled, Kimmer looked back at Karlene and suddenly realized how very lame her reassurance must have sounded. "Listen," she said. "Do you think those mean people want me to come back?"

No, they didn't. Sandy shook her head through her tears, and Karlene finally followed suit.

"When your daddy talks about me, does he say I *ever* did what he wanted?"

Both girls stilled, their attention fixed on her in unwilling hope.

"No, he damn well doesn't." She gave an inward *oops* at her language but didn't let it slow her. "I did what I wanted. And right now I want to get you away from here."

"Why?" Karlene asked, her tone that of habitual suspicion.

I don't have time for this….

Kimmer relied upon an answer as old as the question. "Because." And then she stuck her head out the office, just in time to see a spiffy, gleaming dark blue Escalade pulling up the curving secondary drive. "I've got to go. I'm going to lock and close this door behind me, and then I'll show the mean people what *mean* is all about, and I'll be back to get you. Believe it?"

"No," said Karlene, her little face set in stubborn. But Sandy poked her and she relented. "Maybe. Prove it."

Kimmer grinned at her. "That's fair," she said. "Listen. Don't tell anyone I'm coming back."

"That's lying," Sandy said, most solemnly.

"If they ask directly, it is," Kimmer agreed. "Just don't *offer* it to them."

Karlene pressed her lips tightly together and put her hand over Sandy's mouth. Kimmer refrained from rolling her eyes. They were just little girls.

She'd cross her mental fingers. It'd be best if the goonboys didn't realize she'd been in this vile little room at all, best if they absorbed themselves in the bustle of arrival, and didn't check on the girls until later. Lazy Boy was going to tip them off to her invasion—but he knew only that she'd come to the office, not what she'd done here. Not that she'd found the key and had known to look in the room.

She headed for the door, hoping for escape before Karlene remembered to ask for her little weapon back. She ducked out of the room, pulling the door closed behind her and locking it, heading for the desk....

Oops. She hadn't exactly been subtle in her search for the key. With that in mind she put the key where she'd found it and broke open the remaining desk drawers. Let them think she'd searched in a frenzy and not found what she wanted. Let them think anything, as long as it bought her time to sort things out.

She left the office, sliding along the wall and back toward the single exit door at the other end of the building from the big sliding entry doors, the gravel drive and the accumulating pack of vehicles. They wouldn't be able to see Lazy Boy till they got inside the building; she'd made sure of that. Now she could only hope that the back door would open easily and quietly, and she'd walk right out from under their noses. Already she'd realized that the goonboys would probably be sent out to the woods to water the trees since the toilet was out of commission; perhaps Hank even had an old rickety outhouse around here that had been pressed into service.

An excellent time to pick them off. She thought she could get several before they realized what was going on at all.

She slipped by the gray metal shelves with their incongruously mundane supplies—garbage bags, toilet paper, paper towels, a few tightly rolled sleeping bags. Boy Scout goonboys, always prepared. Finally she crouched by the metal door, glancing over her shoulder as her hand fell on the knob, testing it and finding it loose. No one had come in the front yet, which surprised her but suited her. She stayed down anyway, just a matter of caution, drawing the Glock. She cracked the door open.

It all happened at once—the gunfire, the sharp jerk of pain in her arm yanking her hand from the doorknob, the sullen impact on the metal door frame just behind her. *Whatwhohow?* Kimmer threw herself back and then instantly forward—*get him now, get him fast*—and emptied the gun into the too-soon-triumphant figure moving away from the outside of the building beyond the door. *Blamblamblamblam,* wasting ammo but riding a shocked adrenaline high that peeled her lips back against her teeth and sent her straight to ferocity. And she would have kept right on going had she not glanced down and seen the blood spatter, the drip of bright red off her elbow.

Even city boys could follow the trail she'd leave. But there'd been those shelves….

She rolled back against the half-open door, leaving one foot to hold it open while she dropped the useless Glock and snatched a careless handful of garbage bags from the gray shelves. The goonboys saw her, of course, a wave of men rushing through the front doors as though they'd been lurking just beyond, and Kimmer jammed the bags into her less-than-useful left hand and went for her SIG, managing a single covering shot that sent the mechanics diving for cover but didn't deter the hardcore goonboys at all.

A tremendous crash of metal and heavy tools startled them all, as well as the muffled cry of pain. The hardcore goonboys were close and slowing to draw bead on her and Kimmer was up against the door. Helpless.

Not gonna make it. She should have taken her chances with the blood trail. She should have known Susan would be wrong—except Lazy Boy had thought just the same. But they'd known she was here. How the hell…? They'd set a trap for her, waiting for her front and back. She should have realized.

Nowhere to run. Not this instant, and not if she got through that door. The law was corrupt, and her presence here had been blown in too many ways to count. No safe harbor...no backup.

And they'd kill her if they got their hands on her. They'd play with her first to see if they could extract the truth about Hank's elusive recording, then they'd dump her body in the woods.

Kimmer pressed up against the door in an instant of pre-ternatural self-awareness. The wild thump of her heart, the tingle of her face going pale, the warm blood streaming inside her jacket...the weakness in her knees that was shock, and which would take them right out from under her if she didn't make some kind of move. Face the goonboys and run.

She'd always been on her own. But she quite abruptly couldn't have felt more alone.

A tremendous crash jarred the air; Kimmer found herself too vague to make out the nature of it. Even to guess. But the goonboys startled to a stop, jerking back to look out the front doors and to shout words Kimmer could no longer puzzle out. *Not good, that roaring in my ears...not good—*

But not enough to keep her from taking advantage of the moment—of slipping right out the door. She glanced at the dead goonboy's semiautomatic but didn't bend to scoop it up, not trusting herself to get upright again. Time to run. If you could call this running. She forced herself into a moderate but steady pace, already gasping. Not toward escape, but directly away from the Miata, from Hank's house, from the road... headed into the wooded acreage backing Hank's property. She stopped when she figured she had enough of a lead to catch her breath. Kimmer pulled a trash bag from her gunky hand, thrusting her fingers through the bottom and using teeth and her free hand to tie a cuff from the bottom corners, then slicing two wide ribbons of plastic from a second bag to tie directly over both entrance and exit wound. *Deep breathing.* Get her body through the shocky moments and hope for a second wind, hope she hadn't lost so much blood she couldn't find her legs again at all.

Her arm burned as she tightened the second tie. *Whatever,* she told it. Just stop bleeding. There'd been no spurting, but there'd been enough of a flow to let her know something important had been nicked. She flexed her hand, testing—nerves intact.

By then her heart had slowed from an explosive rate to something merely frantic, and her vision only grayed around the edges. She stuffed the remaining garbage bag and remnants in her back pocket and prepared to move on, this time with as much stealth as possible.

At some point in the last few moments she'd gone down on her knees. Now she used her good hand to haul herself up the nearest stout sapling. She altered direction and pushed herself into a forced pace—four steps jogging, four steps walking. Her world became all about moving forward and listening backward, and her vision was just some vaguely useful tool that let her avoid the biggest trees. The sweat she'd worked up grew clammy as the afternoon cooled, and she hesitated long enough to slice head and armholes in the remaining garbage bag, cutting an extra hole through which to tuck her wrist and rest her injured arm. The all-purpose garbage bag. She giggled and clapped a hand over her mouth.

That couldn't be good.

Suck it up, Kimmer. She'd find the Miata and use it to orient on the dairy farm to which the pasture belonged. All she needed was a barn with a loft—no one would know she was there, nor even think to look. She'd get warm, she'd see about stealing an egg or two to supplement the snacks she'd left in the Miata. And then she'd arm herself to the teeth and go back to where two little girls waited.

If they're even still there.

The thought snatched away her energy; a stumble turned into a fall, and she had just enough wherewithal to turn her good shoulder into it and roll away the impact. From there she blinked up into the spring canopy of the woods, unaffected by the disgusted voice in her head that urged, *Get up, you fool!*

Instead what started out as a small conflicting voice quickly grew loud. *I can't do this alone.*

Which was absurd, because she always did it alone. She might be part of a team, she might have Hunter at her back, but she never counted on them, not deep down. Deep down, she was always going it alone because she never gave anyone else the opportunity to be in it along with her. Not Hunter…not Rio.

Did I drive him away?

Foolish, foolish, to lie here on the cool ground and ponder such things.

But I hurt. And I've lost blood. Determination can't always be enough. Sometimes the world was just bigger and harder than any one person could overcome.

Wasn't it?

Kimmer didn't know. For the first time in her life, she honestly didn't know. She gave up and wallowed in it all—the pain of her arm, the shakiness of a body fighting off shock and the big gaping spot in her chest that had been there since childhood, waxing and waning with the events of her life and now torn wide open by fresh betrayals and losses. Quite abruptly she thought *that poor old cat* and found a few big fat tears leaking out the corners of her eyes to roll down toward her ears.

Just as abruptly, anger blossomed. Yeah, she was alone in this. Yeah, she was fighting betrayals on all sides—the police were compromised, Hank had set her up and somehow Susan had given the goonboys a heads-up about Kimmer's presence when the goonboys had arrived hours earlier than planned. How fair was that?

It wasn't. So what else was new? Besides, the odds were so stacked against her that it didn't much matter what she did now, so she might as well do what she could live with on the offhand chance that she would have a life to get on with after this.

It was, she realized, the same thing Rio had said to her. About not making her choices based on who Hank was to her, but making decisions that spoke about Kimmer herself. "Are you listening?" she asked the BGs out loud, still squinting up at the trees. "Because here's the truth about me…I'm *That Bitch Kimmer.*"

Kimmer rolled slowly up to sit on one hip, waited for the whirlies to clear, and then carefully climbed to her feet. She headed for the Miata, where she ruined the resale value of the car by slumping into the driver's seat to bleed all over the interior—and was grateful to see it was more a blood transfer from the existing collection within her clothing than fresh bleeding. She started the car, fumbling through the grocery bags in the footwell of the passenger side for a handful of protein bars and pop-top containers filled with thick, barely tolerable nourishment intended for invalids and the elderly. Her stomach nearly rebelled several times, but she deep-breathed her way through it.

After a few luxurious moments of warmth from the heater, she fumbled her way around to the trunk and pulled out the first aid kit and the blanket from the emergency winter road kit she hadn't bothered to remove from the car. She left the car running so she could return to its blast of warmth, and knelt by the side of the car in the sharp late-afternoon light. As much as she'd prefer not to disturb her arm until she was sure it had stopped significant bleeding, her hand had gotten clumsy and tingly. No choice.

With care, she removed the garbage bag—she intended to make a sling of it when she was done, something she could use or shove aside as needed. Beneath it, the jacket was a mess. "Sorry, Hunter Agency budget people," she muttered, easing the jacket off and then slipping it back over her back and good arm—she was all too vulnerable to chill even sitting here in the spring sunshine. The shirtsleeve had to go— soaked and cold and clammy, it wasn't doing her any good, anyway.

And after that she just moved as quickly as she could, revealing the elongated oval of an entry wound from an angle, lifting her arm to find the messier exit. Not a large caliber from the looks of it. Could be worse. With plenty of hissing and cursing and a little kicking of the ground for emphasis when the antiseptic bit in, she tore freely into the first aid kit to swab and mop and firmly rebandage, using a whole pile of gauze pads at the still-dripping exit wound, glad for the sharpness of her knife and the additional tool of her teeth. One-handed, she shook the jacket out, snapping it into the afternoon's light breeze and then sluicing off the sleeve with a carefully metered portion of her bottled water—although she had plenty to spare. She snapped the material free of extra liquid and spread the jacket on her trunk to dry while she pulled the blanket over her shoulders and hopped into the driver's seat again, her jaw aching from clenching she hadn't realized she'd done and goose bumps of pain raising the hair on her arms.

And then she fell asleep.

Not for long. Long enough for the car to grow stifling and the warmth to reach her bones. Long enough so the jacket sleeve was merely damp. Long enough to fall into a weird haze of flashbacks, *running through the night, running through the woods, running to the barn—*

And that's exactly where she'd go. She opened her eyes to the incongruous daylight and blinked across the field. Not to the barn that went with this property, but back to Hank's barn. If they were hunting her, they might well bring the hunt out this far. They weren't likely to check Hank's barn. They weren't likely to believe she'd be back. They had no idea what drove her.

Life. My life. What it needs to be.

Not to mention a damn good dollop of revenge. These goonboys were going down. If she had anything to say about it, they'd go down hard.

She put the jacket back on, made a poncho of the blanket and tied it in place with a garbage bag tie, making sure she had free access to her pockets. She reloaded her pockets so her favorite weapons were accessible from the right. Her stomach only quailed slightly at the thought of the electrolyte drink in the front seat, so she drank half the bottle in measured gulps and loaded the lefthand pockets of the jacket with trail mix bars and a package of Twinkies she'd gotten only because they made her think of Rio. She slung a couple water bottles over her shoulder on garbage bag belts—she thought she'd find water in the barn, but she wasn't taking any chances.

Before, she'd been on a mission to infiltrate and extract the kids.

Now she was on a search and destroy and rescue. And she was well aware that Susan or Hank might get caught in the crossfire. Not her intent, but they had made the decisions that brought themselves to this place. Hell, they'd worked hard to get themselves here, manipulating and lying and finagling. But the girls…the girls didn't deserve this. While the goon-boys…

Deserved everything they got and more.

And she'd do it alone if she had to.

Chapter 14

From the barn loft, perched upon what was left of the previous season's hay and peering out the loading doors, Kimmer could see most of the Quonset hut, the trees crowding the back of the building from which she'd so recently escaped, the vent pipe for the toilet in the girls' prison. She could certainly hear the activity within it—torque wrenches and compressors and men shouting to each other above it all. More trees obscured most of the approaching drive and the front of the building—not the perfect observation perch after all—but she thought if she climbed the final ladder up to the tiny window at the peak of the barn, she'd be able to see nearly all of it. But the ladder, normally used to reach the top level of fully stacked hay, now loomed above mostly empty space. Kimmer had no particular issue with heights, but it'd be a damn shame if she got shaky up there and took a header onto the loft floorboards.

So she watched from where she was, knowing the light would fail her all too soon—or that Hank might return home, or that her own interference in the chop shop might change their plans entirely.

Those girls could already be dead.

Get real, Kimmer. The girls are fine until they're of no further use. And right now the BGs still need this property. They still need Susan to keep up the front of family normalcy.

As if this family had ever been normal.

Kimmer rifled through her weapons gymbag, coming up with a handful of clips for the SIG—fifteen 9 mm rounds each—and distributed them around her various pockets. Easy to reach. Once she started using the gun, she'd have no more need to be subtle. No need to keep the noise down. She made sure she knew where she'd stashed her knives, her brass knuckles and of course the war club, her hand going from one to the other until she no longer fumbled or guessed. She checked that the SIG was in single-action mode, cocked and locked. All the while she watched across the long shadows of the late afternoon, until she finally spotted what she'd been looking for.

The slanted roof of an outhouse, peeking out from beneath immature second-growth trees. Not far from the glorified chop shop at that. She could just make out the movement that had drawn her eye that way, a man on his way to the building. And there…the swing of the door.

That's where she needed to be. She figured she could get a couple of them on the outhouse path before someone came looking, and probably at least one of the searchers before they got savvy and sent real firepower. Thanks to the unlimited hay twine down in the barn and the gags she could make with the rest of the garbage bag partials, she could avoid as much bloodshed as possible.

Though she'd do what she had to.

Great, kid. Don't get cocky. Good advice, once given to Luke Skywalker. She was hurt, for one thing. Under control so far, but definitely weakened. The numb tingling down her arm and the clumsiness of her hand hadn't receded; it'd gotten worse. She closed her mind on the thought that there could be nerve damage. Internal swelling, maybe. That would go away. Meanwhile, these men knew she was here. She could only hope that they counted her out of the action, running as far and as fast as she could go before she collapsed from blood loss, the rate of which would have been obvious from those few moments she'd spent in the Quonset before escaping. But they'd be on guard. They'd be idiots if they weren't, and while Kimmer had any number of opinions about these goonboys, they'd accomplished too much to be idiots. And their goonboss had accomplished too much—infiltrating the police, managing to maintain operations so slyly that even identifying three of the goonboys hadn't flushed out a name—to have hired idiots.

Kimmer stiffened, her hand on the SIG in her jacket as the outhouse door opened—just a glimpse of straight-edge movement in the foliage—then the man's head reappeared...and promptly disappeared again.

He'd stumbled. He'd decided to tie his shoe. He'd found a pretty bird egg.

But he didn't come back up for air.

Kimmer scowled at the place where he'd been and considered the options. He'd either taken a different way back to the hut and disappeared into the foliage, or...*I've fallen and I can't get up.*

How likely was that?

Time to go check it out up close and personal. She'd been about to head that way, anyway.

When she stood, she discovered that short of body fluids or not, some of the recently gulped liquid had gone right through her kidneys. No matter. Not in a barn with plenty of open feed areas for Hank's few beef cattle, who certainly never bothered to go outside when the urge struck. She took care of business and resettled her gear around her, intending to cache the awkwardly swinging water bottles as soon as she closed in on the hut. A cautious glance at the house showed no sign of Susan. Kimmer squelched the urge to go slap the woman silly. *I don't know how you betrayed me, but you did it.*

Later.

Kimmer headed for the goonboys, skirting the edge of the woods. Old survival skills had never seemed so close to the surface, here on a farm so much like the one on which she'd grown up, surrounded by family betrayals. At every step she expected the trees to morph into familiar territory; at every step she was slightly surprised when they didn't.

I've definitely lost too much blood.

She stopped short at the sight that greeted her through the trees—the gravel driveway and its lineup of cars and several flatbed tow trucks, a semi parked off to the side. How they'd gotten a shipment this large out of the city without being spotted…

Maybe they had been.

Not that she'd seen any sign of it. She'd assume they hadn't been spotted; she'd assume there was no backup coming. But what—? In the middle of the lineup, two sweet little Corvettes had tangled with one another. In fact, if she followed the disturbed gravel, it seemed very much like one of them had come from the back of the line, gathered speed and swooped in upon the other.

Nothing but parts, now.

She recalled the commotion that had led to her escape. Between this incident and Kimmer's presence, the goonboys must be beside themselves. She doubted their goonboss would be understanding about the loss of the vehicle and the compromised situation. If she were the goonboys, she'd want to deal with this whole delivery as quickly as possible—and clean up after their mess as thoroughly as possible—before the goonboss ever heard about it.

She contemplated the difficulties the damaged Corvettes would cause for the goonboys and allowed herself a smile. And then she moved on, circling wide and around the Quonset, crossing over her own early brush-crashing trail and the significant disturbance added by those who had followed, and finally approached the outhouse from the back.

The little building was barely in sight—although evident to her nose—when she heard a rustling. She froze, pinpointing the sporadic noise down low. On the ground. Spooked by a chipmunk.

Or not. That had been a distinctly human grunt she'd just heard added to the latest rustle.

Kimmer found her war club, made sure the SIG was within easy access and eased up on the noise, keeping the stoutest of the available tree trunks as cover.

And found herself staring at a red-faced goonboy in mechanic's coveralls, squirming on the cool ground with duct tape over his mouth, around his ankles, and his bound wrists taped to a sapling.

She leaned against her tree, crouching to take in the sight and ignoring the man's alarmed reaction at her intrusion. *What in this picture doesn't belong?*

The carboy didn't seem much reassured by the wave she

gave him, a casual dismissal meant to let him know she didn't care about him, at least not personally. He finally quieted somewhat when she murmured, "Be still. You're surrounded by poison ivy." And then she simply stared at him a moment, and rubbed her forehead with the back of her wrist. Maybe that slight pounding in her head meant she was already feverish. Maybe it meant she was just plain losing it.

Make sense of this. The timely collision in the driveway, allowing for her earlier escape. Somebody already going after the goonboys.

I'm not alone after all.

The quiet knock of knuckles on wood behind her made her freeze up again. She dropped the war club to hang by its thong, her hand poised to dive for the SIG.

And then she remembered not so very long ago when she'd once introduced herself to someone with that very same sound, and she whirled around to find Rio leaning against a tree, that big grin slapped across his face and the sun shining through the trees to dapple his bright wheat-blond hair.

She stuttered over words and finally settled on "Sonuvabitch!" which more or less wrapped up her astonishment at the fact that he was somehow here, that he'd been here, that he'd been working with her even as she'd felt so terribly alone—a realization that left her at once completely baffled and somehow warmed to the core.

By then the grin had fallen away and she thought maybe he'd noticed that she'd taken advantage of her movement in facing him to dip her hand into her pocket, intuiting that the SIG's grip filled her hand and she'd already thumbed off the safety.

She quietly thumbed it back on, even as he said, "God, I had no idea you were hurt. I thought you made it away clean...I would have come after you. I thought—"

She gave a quick shake of her head. He'd thought she was lying low, letting things settle. Scoping things out. He'd had every expectation she'd be back…and he'd quietly started working the very plan she herself had formulated. "You saved my life. And you crashed their profit into little Corvette bits. Doesn't get any better than that. What the hell are you doing here? How did you—"

"Ari," Rio interrupted, doing a quick check of the area before pushing off from his tree and coming to kneel by her, taking her cold hand where it emerged from the makeshift sling and eyeing the blanket-poncho arrangement to plan the best approach to her arm. "He overheard us talking. Wouldn't take no for an answer. I would have done it alone if I'd had to, but we both knew I'd be of more use to you if I hadn't just done all that driving."

"No," she murmured, trying to comprehend that Rio's brother had dropped his life to drive across several states and back again, no doubt in a rental. Trying to comprehend that he'd volunteered to do it, and persisted over objections.

Knowing she was glad of it.

Rio lifted the poncho, found the entrance and exit holes in the jacket, said something angry in Japanese that Kimmer hadn't heard before.

"I like the sound of that," she said, allowing him the examination. "I might have to learn it."

"Chikushou." He gently nudged her shoulder to get a better look at the exit wound. "It means they're beasts. It's pretty stern stuff. Promise you'll never say it in front of my parents. Or, heaven forbid, my grandmother. I'd really like a look at this."

Kimmer shook her head. "It's stopped bleeding. Best if we leave it alone. No broken bones, no spurting. I had a first aid kit in my car and it's as clean as it's going to get out here. And did I mention it's finally stopped bleeding?"

He only scowled at the evidence of how much it had bled in the first place. "Your hand is cold."

"Probably the sling," she told him, and then looked away with annoyance as he kept his gaze steadily on hers. "There might be some swelling getting in the way. It's a little numb, too. Not really useful."

He shook his head, sharply. "Then it's time to go. Owen can clean up here."

"No!" Kimmer said, and rubbed her forehead again at his surprised look. "There's a lot you don't know. Starting with the girls."

Starting with the girls. Rio sat back on his heels and listened—let Kimmer talk in spite of the oh-so-manly way he wanted nothing more than to scoop her up and take her away from here.

Because yeah, that would go over so well with Kimmer.

He heard her words—the girls held hostage, the role Hank and Susan had played to set Kimmer up from the start, Kimmer's supposition that Susan had somehow betrayed her—a guess that fit with what he'd seen from his rearguard position shortly after arrival, when the bad guys had approached the Quonset chop shop with a prepared wariness, even sending one man around the back, chasing off the goat who'd been nibbling choice spring grass at the edges of the gravel.

He heard the words…he just couldn't quite believe them. He thought back at his discomfort at how Kimmer had received Hank in her home, at his sneaking suspicion that she'd been overreacting, even when Hank proved himself to be a number one asshole.

Boy, had he been wrong. Could he have possibly been more wrong?

But he saw the hurt in Kimmer's clear, deep blue eyes, as much as she tried to hide it with the hard edge of her voice. She hadn't expected the betrayal to run this deeply, either.

And then there were the girls.

"No," he said, thinking out loud when she finished. "We can't leave them behind."

"Besides, there's no point in hitting a hospital anywhere within the good old *Pinsivania* line," Kimmer reminded him.

God, she looked awful. Paler than he'd ever seen, revealing freckles on her face he hadn't known about. Shakier than he'd ever seen. And there was enough blood left on the jacket to tell him she didn't have far to go before she hit bottom.

"We'd have to go all the way to Hunter before we could be sure I'd get treatment before I got arrested." She paused, grew more thoughtful. "I wonder what I'm supposed to have done? I should have asked that trooper."

Owen. Rio frowned, resting a hand on Kimmer's knee to keep himself from fussing with her arm. "Why didn't you call for help? Dave is in Pittsburgh trying to track down the Big Bad Guy. He could have been here in less than two hours. Owen himself would have come down here if he'd known the squeeze you ran into."

And here was another new one. He'd never seen her look quite this sheepish before. She cleared her throat. "The goat ate my phone." She looked up at him from a slightly down-tipped brow, a direct dare for him to say anything disparaging.

"Don't tell me," he said. "It's not your fault."

A warning glance. "Right."

"You're worse on phones than *Star Trek* landing parties are on communicators and transporters."

"It's never their fault, either." But she gave him a more intent look, one that said some thought had finally caught up with her. "What do you mean, Dave's in Pittsburgh?"

"Just that. Owen sent him. He's using the names you came up with and a new head shot of Hammy Hands to—"

"I told Owen the cops aren't secure!"

"Tsk," he said, enunciating the word instead of making a clicking noise. "He's working with someone Owen trusts, all quietlike."

Instead of looking relieved, Kimmer's expression came much closer to baffled. Stumped. Faced with something beyond comprehension. "I didn't expect…I mean, I thought—"

And though she interrupted herself, Rio caught that glimpse of little girl hurt that so often lurked beneath the edgy strength of this woman, the dichotomous streak that had caught his attention from the very start. And he knew. "You thought you were alone."

Alone with the loss of her home, the continuing betrayal of her family, Owen's stiff-necked reaction to the impact on Hunter…with a lover who couldn't understand or accept the nature of her early life and her response to the notion of family. Alone, stuck in the woods bleeding from more than a little flesh wound, all the bad guys left to fight and two girls left to rescue. Alone. Of course that's how she'd felt.

Now she looked at him with massive annoyance, never accustomed to his ability to suss her out when their close relationship denied her the use of that amazing skill of reading people. Beneath the annoyance, her eyes shone suspiciously bright. "Dammit," she said, and that was enough to confirm his words.

Rio just grinned at her. "Get used to it."

"Dammit," she said again, this time reacting to this back-assward reassurance that he not only understood, he was sticking around. She'd been worried, all right.

He hadn't meant to do that. To give the impression that their differences were such a struggle. But he thought of Sobo and her quick understanding and he suspected that in this case hindsight was a little blind. That he hadn't really been fair, as much as he thought he'd tried.

Because now, he began to understand. Hank and Susan had set her up for a fall, possibly a fatal one, with less concern than Rio would have felt for a complete stranger.

"Okay," he said, watching her comprehension as his expression hardened, as he came back to the matters at hand. "Let's show these bad guys a thing or two."

"Because it's who we are," she said, and her voice was as strained as her face. Until she blinked and the thought of something else crossed her face, and she began groping in her various pockets until she finally slipped a hand up the black plastic of her sling and pulled out a package of—

"No!" he said, startled on an entirely different level at the crinkly wrapper of the snack food she held. "Since when?"

"I just happen to have them," she said with some dignity, handing him the Twinkies.

He wasted no time, pulling the wrapping apart to hand her one of the cakes. He raised his own in a toast and said, "To beating the bad guys."

Kimmer wasn't slow on the uptake. She tapped her cake against his in the imitation of clinking glasses and said, "To beating the bad guys *together.*"

"Oh, God," he said. "I think I have to kiss you."

He didn't mean to drop the Twinkie on the way, or to get so caught up in the taste of her or the sudden redistribution

of blood flow. He didn't mean to kiss the living daylights out
of the both of them.

But that's the way it was with Kimmer.

Chapter 15

"I can't believe you ate it anyway." Kimmer wrinkled her nose at the thought of Rio brushing the Twinkie clean and taking that first big bite.

"It wasn't on the ground all that long." He slapped a piece of duct tape over their most recent captive and moved on to binding his hands.

The man's look—until now merely stunned—grew trapped and cagey, and Kimmer lifted her chin to get his attention. "Be still," she said. "I might forget I'm set to single-action and think I've got another eight pounds of trigger pull."

"That's much more creative than 'my finger might slip,'" Rio said in approval, but he didn't hesitate to jerk the man's hands around into the twine Kimmer had provided, securing a third goonboy to his own sapling. This one had been as Kimmer expected, someone coming out specifically to check the area. Next time, they'd know something was up; they'd bring more firepower, and they'd be prepared to use it.

"I wonder if that back door is still open." She looked off in the direction of the Quonset. "They'd never hear us."

"There are nine of them." Rio stood and dusted off his hands. "Even if this one's provided me with a nice Browning, it's still nine against one and a half."

And a half? She gave him a sweet smile. "Oh, is your back bothering you?"

He made a face and said nothing, not pushing the point. He'd made it well enough. By tacit consent, they moved away from their small gathering of captives.

"Seven of them are carboys," she said after a moment.

Rio shook his head in a fractional movement. "I feel like being devious. Let's lay us a big clumsy trail back around to the barn, double-back and see who comes along."

"A really clumsy trail," Kimmer said. "If they couldn't follow the one I left when I was on the run from their ambush, they're not going to manage anything short of blazing trees."

"We'll break a few obvious branches," Rio said. "Because you've been hurt and you've collapsed and I'm heroically carrying you to safety."

"We'll break a few obvious branches," Kimmer agreed, "because we'll be herding our little goonboy prisoners along with us. Otherwise they'll be found and we'll end up fighting them all over again. And this time they'll be mad."

Rio winced at that thought. "We've only got ninety minutes of daylight left. If we lose too much time, they won't be able to follow the trail at all."

That made it a decision. They freed the captives from their respective saplings and Kimmer stood watch while Rio tied them together at the ankles. "Don't worry," she told him, as he assessed the remaining supply of twine. "Hank's barn is the repository of old baling twine. We're good." *And these goonboys are so totally transparent.* She stepped in to smack one of them lightly over the ear with the pistol, a smooth efficient movement and then out of range again even as he yelped through taped-closed lips. "I saw you thinking about kicking him. Don't do it. I don't have to make a lot of noise to take you down—I sure won't give us away. You'll just go down, and no one else will be the wiser. Your friends won't have a clue." At the sullen look she got in return, she cocked her head. "Speaking of clues, you have any idea who the big goonboss is?"

At their befuddlement, Rio added, "The top dog. The first banana. Your CEO. Who calls the shots, boys?"

And one of them swore behind his duct tape and the other two exchanged a nervous look and none of them made any attempt to answer the question or even to indicate he wanted the duct tape removed so he could.

Clueless. Kimmer shook her head. "No point," she told Rio. "We probably know more than they do." Which admittedly wasn't much. Only the sense of cold ruthlessness, the efficiency, the organization and manpower involved. The identities of a few deceased goonboys.

How very much she wanted to catch the goonboss and make him pay up.

Kimmer took point, her arm tucked safely away and the SIG secure in her hand, safety off but first two fingers resting securely on the outside of the square trigger guard. Her job was to scout ahead, to be alert for signs of goonboys…to take them by the most secure route. Rio's was to keep the captives in line, stumbling noisily along—too noisily, but nothing to be done about that, not with their ankles tied to one another and their attitudes set to "bad"—and a decent distance back from Kimmer.

It was only after they'd gotten halfway around to the barn that Kimmer realized there'd been no discussion. That they'd just done it, taking up their logical roles and moving on. She bit her lip on the tiniest of smiles and got back to work.

And in spite of the throb of her arm and the growing awareness of the odds they faced—no room for mistakes, not this time—Kimmer hid another smile at the barn. She said, "I told you."

This time Rio caught her, in the midst of his happy discovery of just how much twine they had at their disposal. "Yep," he said, not the least discomfitted. "And now even if these fellows are found right away, it'll still take an hour or so to free them." He grinned with intent and got to work.

Well, maybe not an hour. But the extrication wouldn't be a swift one. Kimmer tucked herself just inside the big main doors and watched the brush, quickly losing the quick flash of humor as her sense of urgency ticking up to wind her tighter and tighter.

Take out the goonboys. Save the girls. Catch the goonboss. Put my life back together. Do it before sunset.

And oh, yeah—don't get killed in the process.

Right.

Kimmer shifted uneasily, reaching the limit of her ability to be still. To wait, when everything about this moment said *run far, run fast.* She barely glanced back as Rio came up behind her. He lifted a hand, caught her changed mood and let it drop away before it landed on her shoulder. Smart man. He said, "Ready to ramble. It'd be good if we call Owen while we have the chance and—" he lifted his cell phone between two fingers, letting it dangle "—a phone."

"Do it, then." She kept her eyes on the foliage. This whole plan would work only if they got back out there to lurk in wait, and that meant getting *out* there.

"Hey," Rio said, no apparent care in the world as he hit the speed dial and put the phone to his ear, "we're good. We've got some of them and they don't have us. We have a plan."

"They have two little girls." Kimmer was surprised at the bitterness in her own voice. "They have my life."

Rio's voice got hard. "No," he said. "They don't." And then, "Hey, Owen. Yeah, found her. This is big…the bad guys have Kimmer's nieces stashed away. We're going in after them, but this place is crawling. What're the chances—"

Owen had anticipated him, cut him off. This time Kimmer did glance back, and Rio made a face at her. After a moment he said, "We need the backup, Owen. There's no way we can handle this quietly without it. Maybe even with it." Kimmer knew just what he meant. With just the two of them, they'd have to take the chances they got, whether it meant taking someone down, or simply tying them up.

And personally, Kimmer thought they'd used up their quota of *easy*. Not to mention *quiet*. Things were going to get messy.

Rio told the phone, "Okay. I hear you. But it's going to get messy."

Kimmer grinned. Oh, yeah.

Behind her, the phone beeped a muted acknowledgment of the severed connection. Rio moved in close and leaned down slightly, putting the side of his face up against the side of hers in a connection that should have and could have led to kisses in tickly places but instead resulted in the quiet matter-of-fact statement, "Dave's tied up in Pittsburgh. The Big Bad Guy is better than expected at obfuscation."

"Say that again," Kimmer murmured back, not taking her eyes from the woods over which she stood sentry.

Rio obliged, not pretending he didn't understand her dark, deadpan humor. He moved his mouth against her ear. "Obfuscation."

"*Szzzt,*" she said, a sizzling noise. "Ooh, baby," as if she wasn't truly absorbing the impact of his original words. That they were on their own.

"He'll come when he can."

"Uh-huh."

"If it helps any, I'm pretty sure the obfuscation involves gunfire and blood. Owen's being cagey, though."

Great. That meant things had really gone to hell for Dave. No wonder the goonboys were unsettled.

Kimmer shifted her arm in the plastic sling, wiggled her fingers to assess their grasping power, and sorted through the interior pockets of the jacket to find the S&W. She tucked it away in the numb fingers, bringing the edge of the plastic up to hide it. She snugged the SIG in there as well, using the sling as a holster. But they wouldn't want gunfire…not until they couldn't help it. So she slipped the thong of the war club over her hand and closed her fingers around the familiar shape of the handle. *Here we go again, you and I.*

She'd found the red oak root tangle, perfect for setting the scrap iron she'd gotten from the local farrier, watching him— bemused but willing—as he shaped it down into a misshapen ball. She soaked the wood and set the ball and wrapped the whole thing in place. Easy enough to drill a few holes in the end and lash a thong through it.

And when it was done, she hefted it against bales of hay, getting the feel for it. She learned to flip it into her hand from the thong around her wrist. She practiced against the make-shift kick-bag until the day the bag burst, raining dirt and moldy straw down around her. Then she moved to wood, tar-geting knotholes. Backhand, forehand, sideways flick. She learned to let the club do the work, trading precision and fi-nesse for brute strength. She carried it with her always, hid-ing it in baggy hand-me-downs, learning the best ways to conceal it while keeping it within reach.

Then she thought she might be ready.

The goonboy came silently along the trail, feeling the lack of a buddy at his back and showing it with nervous glances behind, frequent halts to search through the woods ahead and his gun at the ready.

Not that it would do him any good.

Kimmer lurked in the shadow of a thick white oak, glad for her petite frame and for the dark taupe of her jacket. *Woodsy brown,* the catalog had probably called it. Fanciful but accurate. The goonboy passed her by without looking, then jerked to attention as Rio released a swatch of branches just ahead. Even before the whipping leaves settled to si-lence, she stepped forward and tapped the goonboy on the head, just as he jerked back to look at her. She couldn't pull the blow fast enough. He went down with a grunt and thrashed briefly on the ground, his fingers curled in a spas-tic movement.

Damn, that wasn't good.

Rio stepped out of the woods to look down at the man. Thinning of hair and thickening of paunch…not a kid, but still with the potential of many years ahead. "He's posturing."

"It's not a science, this head-clonking thing." Kimmer scowled down at the man and his jerking hands and feet.

"Might as well leave him there. Maybe someone will find him before it's too late. He's no threat to us, either way."

Rio agreed by way of scooping up the injured man's gun, decocking it and snicking the safety on before he jammed it into his jeans waistband at the hip in a cross-wise draw beneath the drape of his cable sweater. "Move on?"

"I don't think they have many goonboys left, just carboys. Doesn't seem like they'll keep sending them out."

"Smart thing to do is hunker down in their shelter," Rio agreed.

Kimmer looked at the fading goonboy and his gently arching back, making his deathbed on their newly broken trail. "Maybe they're already hunkering," she said. "Or they wouldn't have sent him alone."

"Let's find out."

Kimmer let Rio lead the way this time, hanging back to assess her own condition, deciding that the food and rest and company had given her a second wind. Not a miracle cure—not even fully functional—but ready to bare her teeth at the enemy.

As they neared the back of the Quonset building, Rio let Kimmer take the lead, Kimmer and her hard-learned silent movement. He did nothing more than glance at her for confirmation and then moved in to cover her back, and Kimmer felt a little thrill of satisfaction. *Two. A team. Partners.*

Now let us get through this so we have a chance to prove it. To Owen, to Kimmer herself. *And a chance to live it.*

All the way to the back door they went, and Kimmer's careful silence might as well have been stomp dancing for all the occupants of the Quonset would have heard. Torque wrenches, the compressor…even the spit and sizzle of something being welded. Those inside couldn't possibly hear what was happening on the outside.

Someone shouted from the other side of the door—he had to be close, and he was certainly frightened— "You'ns oughta check it yourself!" he shouted. "I'm just here for the effin' cars, man!"

Kimmer exchanged a quick look with Rio, got raised eyebrows in return, a mutual sense of *aha!* She flattened herself behind the door, while he crouched against the building on the other side, one hand groping for a rock or piece of wood to block the door open. The man coming out that door was also their way in....

And out he came, wary and staring hard into the woods, never suspecting that those he looked for were actually behind him. He clutched a cheap knock-off automatic, but not in a position that would do him any good unless he had a wicked snap-shot. Through the crack at the doorjamb, Kimmer saw Rio give up looking for his solid object and stick his foot in the doorway. When the carboy finally released the door it swung gently closed on that foot and stopped, leaving Kimmer to handle the carboy.

She let the war club swing from her wrist and pulled the SIG from her sling. "Hey," she said quietly, moving a step closer behind him. Close enough. He froze, looked over his shoulder, and found Kimmer—and then found Rio aiming at him from his crouch. He swore in a most heartfelt way. His gaze darted for the door and hope lit his face when he saw he wouldn't even have to turn the knob, but could just grab and fling the thing open. Maybe even just shout loud enough for someone inside to hear. He didn't seem to remember he had the gun.

"Shh," Kimmer told him. "If you call for them, you'll give us away. And if we're already given away, then there's no reason not to make noise with our nice guns. Hell, we'll probably both shoot you just because we'll be pissed off."

"True," Rio agreed. "I'd shoot him, that's for sure."

"I'd shoot him first."

"Look," the carboy said, clear desperation on his grease-smeared face and a twitch jerking his cheek, "this isn't my thing. I'm only here for the cars. They just sent me out to see what Jared had found, that's all."

"They sent you out with a gun," Kimmer noted, the accusation implicit.

"They gave us all guns when we left the city!" He looked down at his, held it out. "I don't even know if it's ready to fire, man."

Kimmer moved another step, never taking his surrender for granted. Just because he meant it at the moment didn't mean he wouldn't change his mind.

But then she quietly twisted the gun from his hand and defeat etched his features, a young man's features with faint petulance softening his chin and mouth. "What about the others? Did you kill them? Will you kill me?"

Kimmer snorted. "What have those goonboys been telling you? They're stashed."

Rio cleared his throat. "Well, except for that one—"

Irritated, Kimmer briefly glared. "Not on purpose. How about you find a rock for that door and truss up this one?"

She turned back to the carboy, finding him bemused and ignoring Rio's muttered, "Touchy, touchy." This one looked more like he'd talk—like he resented being sent up to handle stolen cars and finding himself handling guns and determined good guys. She said, "How many in there came along as muscle? And how many of your friends were eager to get the guns?"

He shrugged, an eye on Rio as Rio found himself the necessary doorstop and pulled tough hay twine from his pocket.

"Some of them. There's only one guard left. They normally only send us up here with one, but—" Oops. He realized he'd been chatty and shut up, offering her a glimmer of defiance.

"Oh, give it up," Kimmer said wearily, shifting her arm within the sling and ready for this to be over. Ready to shut this place down and walk away with the girls. "I can break your kneecap without firing a shot. I don't really feel like playing games. Are you sure you do?"

"Um," he said, and then made a somewhat more gurgly noise as twine settled around his neck.

"Don't mind me." Rio had the damnedest way of sounding casual regardless of circumstances. "Just tying things up." And he was—the man's wrists behind his back, attached to the noose around his neck. "Of course, just *how* I tie things up probably depends on what I hear next." He tightened the arrangement slightly just in case the carboy didn't get his meaning.

The carboy got his meaning.

A moment, a faint disgusted expulsion of breath, and a quiet curse. "Look, we don't normally get the guns. We don't normally get here in broad daylight, either. I don't know what's going on. You think anyone tells me? Work the damned cars, that's all I get told. We weren't even expecting trouble on arrival, but Bruce called that bitch to let her know we were coming early, and she knew you were here. She doesn't even try to come visit those little girls. Bitch!" He nodded to himself, as if pleased to have found someone he could look down upon.

Not entirely useless. He might not know why their schedule had deviated, but he'd confirmed Kimmer's supposition about Susan's betrayal, and how she'd done it without lying. Bruce had called *her.* And as for that schedule...

"Maybe Dave's been more effective than we think," she said to Rio.

"Sounds likely." He finished tying off the last knot, having loosened the length between the neck and wrist ties in reward for the carboy's cooperation. "Go over there and sit down."

Kimmer moved so she could keep an eye on the door and an eye on the carboy. "Bruce is the guard left inside?" If he was the head goonboy, he'd probably have stayed behind and sent out his feckless troops.

Carboy nodded, sitting awkwardly against a tree near the back corner of the building. Rio tied him there, then withdrew his trusty duct tape and stood poised, waiting to slap the gag into place.

"And who bosses Bruce around?" Kimmer lifted her chin a fraction, an indication for Rio to wait.

"Lots of people in the city." The carboy's expression grew sly. "You want me to give up the chief, that's what."

"Yes," Kimmer said. "I want you to give up the chief." And if nothing else, she at least had the nickname for the goonboss.

He shook his head. "No one knows that. I mean, *no one*." Of course not.

"All right," she said, not surprised to see the carboy's relief that she believed him. "Does the chief know what's going on here? Does he know he's lost men?"

The man hesitated, glancing at the noisy building as though someone within would reach out in retribution.

Looming over him, Rio said, "Won't matter if you tell…either they'll go down and won't ever know, or they'll take us down and won't ever know."

"Agency teach you to think that way?" Kimmer asked

him, but didn't wait for an answer. "C'mon, c'mon. I'm in a bad mood. Be smart."

Carboy shrugged, a sudden capitulation. "Bruce hasn't called anyone. He wants us to clean up this mess first. Get the cars done…get rid of you. He wants to be able to say he handled it. He let us all know we'd be the ones to pay if he couldn't."

"Nice guy." At Kimmer's fractional nod, Rio applied the duct tape and left the carboy to return to Kimmer's side. He ducked his head for a sideways sort of glance, one that might have looked coy under other circumstances but this time just highlighted his attempt to remain casual through his concern. "You doing okay?"

"You're kidding, right? The burnt-up house, the mad boss, the big hole in my arm that really, really hurts and leaked all that blood besides?"

Rio looked at his toes in a thoughtful way and added, "Yeah, not counting the whole family crapping on you and the odds against getting those two little girls out of there." He glanced sideways at her again, but couldn't hide his glint of amusement at egging her on, or at the anticipated reaction.

"And that just makes me mad," Kimmer said. "As if you didn't know it. What a brat. Let's just go get 'em."

"I'll take point," Rio said. "I'll play the hero and distract them from you so you can grab up the girls." And when Kimmer hesitated, thinking about the interior of the building and the best way to go in, he said, "You *are* going to let me play the hero, aren't you? A guy needs a little ego booster now and then."

"No problem," Kimmer told him. "Just thinking about the best way to go in, so we don't throw away your heroic gesture for nothing. Dead heroes. Very messy." She shuddered delicately.

Rio straightened with an indignant expression as the carboy made an incredulous, muffled noise. And then they got down to business, and Kimmer sketched him a quick dirt map of the interior—of the available cover, of the work areas, of the office she would be targeting. They discussed drawing the goonboy and his wannabes out to the side, decided it would be too obvious, and settled quickly on barging forward as much as possible to take the action out in front of the office.

"You've got two guns," Kimmer told him. "Use them."

"That's a plan." Rio removed the second gun from his jeans and flicked the safety. "Collecting more guns…also a good plan."

Kimmer held out her SIG, and when Rio started to shake his head, hiked up a warning eyebrow. "I've still got the .38. If things go as planned, I won't even use it. Just don't throw this one away when you're done with it. I want it back."

He took it. He gave her a quick, hard kiss, then took the gun and extra magazines, and he headed for the door and into the thick of the enemy.

Chapter 16

Kimmer slipped into the building in Rio's wake, the periphery of her vision full of welding sparks and busy bee carboys…and of Rio moving stealthily closer, gaining all the ground he could before being noticed. She eased toward the office, striking a balance between casual and an eye-catching slink. Next time she'd find a sling in camo colors. She made it past the painting booth, the jumble of pressure hose, the barrel of rags dirtied and torn beyond redemption, full of grease and just waiting for a careless match. Someone's cigarette smoke drifted her way, cutting through the sharp odors of paint and grease and solvent, the hot metal. Wheels were stacked up in rows along the wall, past the supply shelves that had served her so well earlier in the day.

The first shout rang out. Someone dropped his wrench with a clatter of metal against concrete. Just a single shot and then silence, followed by quick, harsh demands by a confused goonboy who assumed Kimmer was causing the fuss.

Kimmer smiled at the protests that the carboy had seen a man, not a woman, and trusted Rio to be behind cover, not hesitating in her own mission. She slipped around into the open office—Bruce had been in here, it seemed, filling it with the cigarette smoke she'd smelled. Behind her, a flurry of shots rang out. It was impossible to tell who was doing the firing, except that she heard someone scream and it wasn't Rio.

She closed the door partway behind her, crouching now that it wouldn't draw attention—and now that the visibility through the office windows could do her in. She duck-walked to the blinds, cheap plastic things already yellowing with age, and twisted the rod to close them. A good number of the slats had been bent or twisted, but it was enough. She handled the other blinds and stood, and when she looked over to the desk again, a carboy popped out of the foot well, a cash box in his hand and astonishment on his face.

Caught looking for candy, are you? Kimmer took a long step, swung her leg into an arcing kick, and connected toe-to-chin; the man's head cracked against the desktop and he dropped to the dirty linoleum with a clatter of the metal cashbox. A quick frisk proved him without a gun. "Careless of you," she murmured, and relieved him of the giant ratchet wrench he'd stuck into the side cargo pocket of his coverall leg, tossing it far out of reach. Then she jammed the desk chair back into the foot well. It wouldn't keep him there, but he'd make plenty of noise getting out of it. If he was smart—with the gunfire spattering to life in the garage and Kimmer's ire awaiting him from the office— he'd just play possum and stay safe. "Be smart," she told him, just in case he could hear her. "Stay put and stay out of my way."

When she jerked open the correct desk drawer, she found the key to the little prison right where it had been. Goonboy of very little imagination, that was Bruce. Like his friends who'd come after Kimmer in Watkins Glen, they'd underestimated her. Big surprise. All they knew of her had come from Hank, until their pals had started dropping off the radar in the southwestern tier of New York. And Hank, no doubt, had colored his descriptions of Kimmer with a smear of disdain.

Which suited Kimmer just fine, if it gave her any advantage at all. She slipped a hand into her sling, checking the exact position of the S&W and its hollowpoint load, and slipped into the nook that led to the tiny back room. She fumbled slightly with the key—*losing that second wind*—and cracked the door open just enough to say, "It's That Bitch Kimmer. I've come back for you."

After the slightest of hesitations, Karlene's voice said, "Okay."

Ohh, yeah. Definitely cut from the same cloth as her Auntie Kimmer.

Kimmer found them behind the cot, which they'd tipped over to act as a shield against stray bullets, the blanket spilled across the floor before it. They peered up above the mattress, regarding her warily, flinching at the continuing if sporadic gunfire and the goonboy shouts that were slipping from demand into panic. She gave a nod of approval at their thoughtfulness, even if that paper-thin mattress wouldn't have stopped a bullet thrown by hand. "You wanna get out of here?"

"Where's Mommy?" Sandy asked.

Not a question Kimmer cared to contemplate, since *in handcuffs and custody* was the only acceptable answer. "Safe," she said. "All the way back at the house." Best guess, anyway. But at the look of woe on Sandy's face, Kimmer added, "If she'd come here herself, these men—"

"Big smelly men," said Karlene.

True enough. "—would have hurt you. She's trying to keep you safe."

"*That's* why she never came!" Karlene exclaimed, standing up from behind their shelter.

"That's why," Kimmer agreed. So the carboy had been right. Susan had lied and she hadn't even cared enough for the lie to trigger Kimmer's knack. *Chimera, do your thing. Make these kids believe.*

And though they both squinted at her for a moment, hesitating as though there wasn't a gunfight just beyond this stinky little room, in the end they crept around the tipped-over bed and stood obediently before her. Karlene wrinkled her nose. "You smell, too."

Kimmer stifled a laugh in spite of the anxious circumstances. "Don't I, though." Blood and sweat, both dried now. "I think we could all use a bath."

"And a Band-Aid." Such wise children.

"Maybe two Band-Aids." She herded them around with her good arm, peeking out the door. From the darkness of the desk foot well, the pale whites of the carboy's eyes flickered; she barely made out his hunched figure, arms hugging his knees. She pointed a finger at him and said in a low voice, "Stay put."

The blinds worked both ways. Kimmer had no idea what was happening out in the garage, other than that she hadn't heard Rio shout for help and she hadn't heard him cry out in pain. *He could be dead on the floor.*

She wasn't prepared for the gasp of pain the thought wrought, and she bit her lip, closed her eyes and gave herself a mental slap. That sort of thinking wouldn't help anyone. She eased to the office door, her hand held out behind her to stay the girls at the little entry nook. From there she saw…

Nothing.

Everyone had taken cover, aside from one who sprawled across the floor in so much blood he couldn't possibly still be alive. Kimmer heard a few desperate whispers and smiled; inexperienced shooters wasted bullets fast, and these wannabe-goonboys had shot themselves out of ammo.

And Rio was still out there, or they wouldn't care.

She briefly contemplated calling to him, letting him know she was on her way out, getting a quickie report…but she'd give herself away if she did. She'd give the girls away. She looked back at them—huddled in the relative safety of the nook, their eyes big and faces pale beneath grime, their chins set and their quivering lips giving away the game.

They'd think of this as the day they grew up.

With a swallow against the tightening anger in her throat, Kimmer gestured them forward, and then herded them before her. "We're going to walk down low, like ducks," she said to them, whispering. If she'd heard the desperate exchange about empty guns, they could hear her just as well. Outside the office, the stalemate held; if anyone had ammo left—and she'd bet that at least Bruce the boss did—they weren't ready to give themselves away, but they'd sure be alert to any sign of movement. Kimmer and the girls would take the slinky way out.

She crouched, showing them the duck walk posture. With mock sternness, she whispered, "No quacking." And then she herded them out, a duck chivvying her ducklings.

They didn't get nearly far enough.

Halfway to the shelves, a gunshot shattered the stalemate.

The girls jumped, losing their balance. Kimmer hustled them behind the barrel of rags and looked out to see, if not what she dreaded most, a near thing.

Bruce turned out to be a wiry man, tall enough so it didn't look good on him, in slacks and a crew neck shirt instead of coveralls. A multitude of short black braids sprang from his head, gathered in a thick, barely there stub at the back of his head. His skin and hair texture weren't quite dark enough to support the look. But with the gun in his hand, none of that mattered. With Rio slowly rising to his feet from behind several free-standing car seats, the SIG in his hands in the middle of reload, none of that mattered. A carboy appeared on the other side and held out his hand for the SIG.

Bruce made a demand that Rio hand the gun over. Kimmer didn't listen to the exact words. She pulled the .38 from her sling, ignoring the gasps of her two little charges and eased farther into the open. The bad guys could have seen her from the corners of their eyes…if they'd been paying attention.

Rio saw her just fine.

Rio casually completed reloading the SIG, his movements careful and exaggerated, pushing the magazine home.

Or not.

My God, he knows the P226. He knew the extent of the force necessary to shove the magazine absolutely home. He knew that if one stopped just shy of using that force, the magazine would look like it was home when it wasn't—when it wouldn't feed ammo at all. He handed the carboy a useless gun.

That left only Bruce.

And Kimmer had Bruce. Bruce, who was mouthing on about how the chief would fry Rio's balls on a stick for a special City Chicken meal, how Rio would pay for the damage he'd caused, and then at second thought who the hell was he, anyway? That was all the time Kimmer had, for by then the carboy struggled to rack the slide and chamber the first bullet, and Rio had caught Kimmer's eye across the twenty feet which separated them, starting to make his move. Kimmer dropped to one knee, propped her elbow back against her numb hand in the closest thing to a Weaver stance she could manage. With no qualms whatsoever, she shot Bruce in the back.

To be more precise, in the ass.

Bruce went down with a startled shout, his muscles so shocked by the impact that they gave way beneath him.

Falling on the wound probably wouldn't do his mood any good.

Not that Kimmer cared. Not when she had the gun trained on the goonboy, and not when Rio had already snatched up Bruce's weapon and trained it on the carboy— who'd gone for the SIG's safety in case that was the problem, but only ended up stubbing his thumb against the slide stop and now stared at the P226's lever arrangement in complete frustration. Not when Rio turned to give her that guileless grin—

Except it faded instantly to alarm. And since Kimmer was neither spurting blood nor spouting horns, she whirled to look behind herself, imagining the girls felled by a stray bullet, imagining their latest carboy captive freed and coming up behind her…imagining anything but what she saw.

Hank.

Hank, standing awkwardly and yet still with an expression of relieved victory. Beside him, a middle-aged woman with near-black hair, a sleek business coif, and an expertly tailored suit slimming hips gone just a touch beyond pleasingly plump. Although her face—touched with just the right amount of makeup—was serene enough, her brown eyes snapped with annoyance. Beyond annoyance.

But this woman was more than confident. This woman commanded.

Goonboss.

And she saw Kimmer recognize it in her. They exchanged a long, steady glance, sizing one another up. More than just the physical aspects of the other…the emotional. The underpinnings. The grit.

She did, of course, have a gun. A petite lady's gun, a SIG Sauer P230 as sleek as her hair. Nor did she have it pointed at Kimmer—but at Hank's daughters. Two little girls who'd turned to throw themselves in their father's arms and who had been frozen by his warning gesture now looked to Kimmer for guidance instead.

Kimmer could do nothing but give them the merest shake of her head, making a shushing sound that was meant to be soothing but came out soundless from a suddenly dry mouth. And there stood her brother beside this woman, showing no concern whatsoever.

He didn't understand. He *couldn't* understand. He thought he had some kind of influence with this woman.

He didn't.

Not over the chief. The goonboss.

Kimmer didn't bother to ask her name. If Dave hadn't been close to nabbing her, the goonboss wouldn't be here. Bugging out. And carboy had been right, Bruce hadn't shared his situation with her. She'd been taken completely by surprise at the little war waging on her turf.

"This," the woman said in a voice tight and angry, "is not what I expected to find here."

Bruce, until now absorbed in his private agony, snapped his head up, looking at her with alarm of which Kimmer took note. "You…I…I can explain—"

"Shut up, you fool. Do you have any idea what's happening in the city?"

"I—" Bruce said, but evidently wasn't going to get any further.

"I do," Kimmer said, clear and strong. "And I don't care. I only want the girls."

The woman turned her gaze on Kimmer, a hard, searching examination. "You aren't what we thought you'd be," she said. "You've been very inconvenient."

Kimmer shrugged, easing herself from her crouch down to her knees. She still held the gun, but with a carefully casual grip, still pointed more toward Bruce than anyone else. "You can blame him for that," she said, indicating Hank with a lift of her chin. "He never knew me as well as he thought he did." *What does she want? What the bleeding hell could she possibly want?* She should have turned and left once she realized the situation in here, dumping Hank along the way. They'd come in the back; they'd had plenty of chance to assess the chaos. Plenty of chance to turn around with no one the wiser.

The woman gave Hank a derisive look, a slight flare of nostrils, a bare tightening of her mouth. "So I see."

"The wife—" Bruce started, and the fearful contortion of his face told Kimmer just exactly how dangerous his goonboss was beneath her executive lawyer look. "The Reed bitch—"

"Ah," the goonboss said, her voice like a knife. "We're all bitches to you when we get the better of you, is that it?"

Damn, she's going to—

The goonboss shot her own goonboy.

Rio flung himself aside in reaction, but Kimmer was already in motion, somersaulting backward and ignoring the blaze of fiery pain in her arm as she came back to her feet. Still crouching, the gun still in her hand—now aimed at the goonboss. She should have taken her shot right then, should have given this cruel, cold-hearted woman no chance at all.

If only the dark eye of the little SIG hadn't been pointed straight at the girls.

In that moment of hesitation, Kimmer lost her advantage. She didn't know where Rio was, couldn't tell if he had any kind of angle on the woman. And though she'd normally count herself able to drill her target right through the eye at this range, these circumstances were far from normal. Her thighs burned from her awkward position, fast heading toward rubbery. Her hand...

It trembled.

And the goonboss saw. She smiled. She nodded imperiously to Hank, gesturing him to join the girls, both of them now crying and desperately trying to hide it, to be silent. "A father should be with his daughters."

At first Hank took the direction as triumph. So deluded...so full of his own cleverness even as his world fell apart around him. He tossed Kimmer an "Oh, well, too bad for you" look and started to move the girls out of there.

"Not yet," the woman said.

Hank frowned at the aim of her gun, the first doubt crossing his face. "Look," he said. "We gave you a place to work. We're no part of the rest of it."

"You became a part of 'the rest of it' when you tried to deflect your punishment to your sister." Her eyes narrowed slightly. "I'm the only one who's allowed to kill my people."

"It was an accident—"

She cut Hank's bluster in midword. "Don't bother. I can't believe a word you say." And then she turned to Kimmer. "You see the situation, I think. Behave yourself, or the girls die. Let me walk out of here, and you can lick your wounds and fume over letting me slip through your fingers."

"I still don't understand why you walked into this place at all." Kimmer slowly shifted one knee to the dirty concrete. Her pulse pounded faster than the situation demanded. Weakness. Loss of blood. What energy reserves she'd had were quickly slipping away.

The woman's face twisted in an expression of pure disgust. "Why do you think you didn't hear me coming? Even with the idiocy going on in here, someone would have noticed if I'd driven up to the front. Car trouble, that's what. And so I need the keys to something that works."

The carboy made a stuttering noise. A raised eyebrow encouraged him to use actual words. "Everything's torn down," he managed. "Except what's out front. And that's all—"

"Stolen," the goonboss finished for him. "Well, we'll just have to do something about that." The look she shot Kimmer was less conversational. "Now it's time for you to hand over your gun. And for your friend to slink out in the open."

"Actually," Rio said, his voice coming from an angle that made Kimmer give an internal cheer, "I like it where I am. And I can see you just fine."

"Oh, please." She snorted delicately. "You hero types don't shoot anyone in cold blood, never mind a woman."

"There's always a first," Rio suggested.

But Kimmer didn't believe him. And she knew the goonboss didn't, either. She shifted uneasily, equally aware that this woman had no such compunctions. As for Kimmer...

she'd do it. If only she had the aim. If she wasn't about to pass out. She'd do it. *Oh, yes.*

"Game over," said the goonboss. Her face grew hard, her voice likewise. "The guns. Now."

Kimmer hesitated. She was loaded with weapons; giving up the gun didn't mean that much. Except that the gun was the only thing she had the strength left to use at all.

The goonboss lifted her gun slightly, off the girls and onto Hank.

She pulled the trigger.

Kimmer startled at the sound, stared aghast as Hank fell into the barrel of rags and slid to the floor. *In front of the girls. She did that right in front of the girls—*

But no sense of loss. Nothing but that strange, empty place she'd felt with the news of her father's death…the realization that the void within her would never be filled. Not that particular void. She made an unconscious move toward the girls, their small forms flung over their father's, sobbing, trying to pat him back to life. Then Kimmer froze, suddenly aware of the goonboss again. Equally aware that her actions would have released Rio to make his own shot, but not certain he had the range to make a clean one. To keep the girls safe.

"No," she said, loud and clear—and talking to Rio even as she met the woman's dark, hard gaze. "I have car keys. It's my car. It's not stolen, but there's a warrant out for it. You should know all about that. All you have to do is make a phone call and pull that warrant. Unless you've lost even that much influence."

The woman's face opened with surprise. "I can't say I expected this of you. Not after what I've heard. What I see."

"There's a catch," Kimmer told her bluntly. "The girls stay here. Everyone stays here. You're on your own. No hostages. No more dead bodies in your wake."

"Kimmer…" Rio said, and then stopped himself. She knew what he had to say. That this woman needed to be caught. To be stopped. But Dave had flushed her out, hadn't he? And Kimmer and Rio had destroyed what was left of her operation here, leaving her no bolt-hole. Nowhere to hide, not even for the time it took to prepare a real escape. Her life, like Kimmer's, had been torn down to its roots.

Not complete justice. But a form of it nonetheless.

And one that would keep the girls safe.

The rest could come later.

It's about who you are. And even with the need for retribution burning in her chest and throat, even with years of swift, ruthless action and no regrets, Kimmer found she was not someone who could put these girls in danger.

Her nieces.

The goonboss watched her, suspicion writ clearly on her face. "The girls come with me as far as the door."

But there were other things written on her face, too, written where Kimmer could see them clearly. "Didn't Hank tell you?" she said, a soft, menacing voice, resisting another glance at her dead brother. "There's no point in lying to me. In trying to fool me." In planning to jerk at least one of the girls through the still-open door with her. "Take one girl. Five feet from the door. Then you let her go. If you scuttle down real low, she'll still be good cover while you run off to save your sorry ass."

The woman hesitated.

"Five feet," Kimmer repeated.

And Rio said nothing, knowing he didn't have to. Knowing that they'd both open fire if it came to that. Trusting Kimmer to read this woman right.

"It's what you want," Kimmer said. "True, it leaves me alive. But I could say the same about you."

The woman took a deep breath, letting it trickle out again through those flared nostrils. "Another time, then."

"Probably." Kimmer watched her another long moment, waiting for the acquiescence. The truth of defeat. Then she said, "The keys are in my pocket. I'm going to get them with my left hand." Pulling the arm from the sling popped sweat out on her face, felt like she was tearing the limb in two. It took several tries for those numb fingers to extract the keys without bringing an incidental weapon along. Finally she tossed them out on the floor, offering quick instructions as to the car's location.

The goonboss instructed Karlene to bring the keys. Karlene glanced uncertainly at Kimmer, her face tear-streaked among the filth. Kimmer said quietly, "She chose you because she thinks you're the easiest," and was rewarded with a glint of defiance. Steadily, Karlene retrieved the keys and handed them to the goonboss, standing just within reach. It didn't stop the goonboss from grabbing her hand along with the keys, or from pulling her along to the door, her gun held far too close to those grimy curls.

"There," Kimmer said, loud and clear, as the woman closed in on the door. *"Now."*

The woman hesitated—of course she hesitated, calculating her odds. Kimmer raised her pistol, both hands to steady it this time. "Do you have any idea how easy it is to read you? Try returning the favor. Take a good look at me and ask yourself if I'm going to let you get through that door with her."

Shaky. Pale. Bereft of the life she'd built and standing on nothing but the decisions that had brought her here—here to help family, because it was the thing to do regardless of who those people really were. Here to save her nieces even if it meant losing the quarry she'd come after. Finally certain of herself.

Solidly Kimmer.

The woman's face changed. "Another time," she said, and abruptly pushed Karlene away as she leaped for the still open door.

And Kimmer let her go. She turned instead to the angry, crying and grieving youngster between them. She met Rio there and gathered Sandy up along the way.

Time to start again.

Chapter 17

They took her by surprise.

They grabbed her while she checked the mail in the early dark of midwinter. Leo Stark's muffler-challenged car started up and swooped in behind her as her oldest brother popped out from behind the huge maple and snatched her arms behind her back. He kept his face averted from her instant reaction, having learned from experience that her head was harder than his nose and lips. "Let's go, Kimmerbitch," he said, grunting as she slammed a sneakered foot back into his shin but not loosening his grip. "Time for you to become a woman."

She froze in an instant of animal fear, knowing things had been building to this moment. She recalled Leo Stark's increasing leers, the escalation of his attempts to grope and fondle her, his easy recruitment of her brothers. In that moment, they tossed her into the backseat of the big old Ford. It wal-

lowed on old shocks beneath her, then sank into the laboring acceleration.

She didn't bother to demand where they were going, even had she the breath. She knew well enough she couldn't afford to arrive there, wherever it was. Someplace with a dank mattress, probably out in the woods. One of their spots. *Boys will be boys,* her father always said when they came home reeking of beer and strutting their stuff.

Leo must've been in the back already. As Kimmer struggled to sit up, already fumbling for the door handle in spite of their speed, he threw himself on her. Already aroused, already pressing against her. Kimmer wanted to spit.

But her mouth was dry.

"Don't bother," he told her, jerking his head at the broken door handle, his blond hair reflecting dully in the dash lights. The car bounced over a dirt road pothole, jostling them into even closer contact. Kimmer squirmed beneath him. He thought it was an attempt to get away; he grabbed her hair to pull her closer, promising crudities and thrusting at her through their clothes.

It suited her fine. He never realized what she was really doing—that she'd grabbed her unblooded war club. That even as he licked her neck, she pulled the weapon free.

She jammed the handle into his ribs, three fast hammer blows and by the last he was retching atop her. Her brothers—all four of them, planning to watch, no doubt—turned to check on this unexpected noise.

If they'd anticipated screaming, they'd been so wrong. Kimmer flipped the club around and bashed it backhand, up and over her head, hunting window glass. The first blow cracked it; at the second, it collapsed on itself and rained glass along the road. One more blow to Leo, a hard smack

*with the business end of the club somewhere on his back, and
Kimmer shimmied out from beneath him. By then the car
was slowing, and that, too, suited her fine. She snaked out the
window and landed hard on the dirt road, trying to roll but
losing every bit of air from her lungs anyway.*

*She scrambled to her feet still gasping for air, heading for
the woods. They'd never find her, no matter how quickly they
followed. She'd make it back to the house, grab the stash
she'd packed months ago and make her way out of this place.*

Free.

Finally free.

Free.

Of what, Kimmer wasn't entirely sure. Not of the interrogations still ahead and the two-state investigation still going strong, hampered and slowed by the need to ferret out the goonboss's many associates. Not of the sling around her arm, torn muscle and impinged nerves healing just fine but not fast enough to suit her. Not of the trouble the situation had caused Hunter, even if fingering Paula Romajn—high-powered criminal attorney in high-powered city society—as goonboss offset much of the bad PR. Rio had even signed on the dotted line the day before: part-time operative.

Certainly not free of the knowledge that Hank's girls had seen their father killed, seen their mother taken away in handcuffs as Dave—a tad battered himself—arrived on the scene with his trusted police detective friend. The girls were in foster care now, but reportedly happy to see the letters Kimmer sent them while she investigated other possibilities. Closer to home possibilities.

Family might just be a part of her life after all.

And meanwhile the world went on. Shara Ingleswood at

WEFL was happy as a pig in slop, following the dots she'd been given to build a big-crime story with connections to Watkins Glen—the Hunter Agency had been kept out of it, but not Hank. Not Susan.

Hank had done it to himself. So had Susan. Their decisions…their consequences. Kimmer had merely tried to make the right choices in their wake. Her own choices.

Free.

That was it.

Free to make her own decisions untainted by her family past. Redefining herself on her own terms. Kimmer, showing herself a different way to live.

She sat against the hood of Rio's Element, went to cross her arms, and compromised by tucking her good arm under the bad. Rio settled onto the hood next to her and gazed up at the house in whose driveway they parked. "Well?"

"I haven't even seen the inside."

"You can't just tell?" He pretended astonishment.

"That's with people," Kimmer informed him, haughty as she surveyed the place. Not nearly as old as her old home. Big enough for two.

Big enough, actually, for four. It needed landscaping, and it needed to lose that wretched fake well out front. She'd wait till her arm was better and take an ax to it. Kimmer fished for her camera.

"Aha," Rio said, straightening to attention.

"Doesn't mean anything." Kimmer moved off to better frame the picture.

Their real estate agent, hanging quietly in the background, stepped forward. "Why don't you let me take it—then you can both be in it. Even if you don't like the interior of the house, it'll make a cute picture."

Cute. Just like the woman, a petite, rounded person with a pixie-short haircut and an ever-present cell phone. Maybe she'd give Kimmer tips on keeping it charged. Or on keeping it away from goats. Maybe she'd know of a cute replacement for that last one. *Cute* was one of her favorite words.

But Rio cocked his head and gave Kimmer a nudge, one of those guileless and unselfconscious things he did. Goofball-speak. "C'mon," he said, and the sunlight hit his brown eyes just so, to light them up from the inside out.

She returned his look most thoughtfully, enough of a smile coming through so he grinned back, and finally nodded. "Okay," she said.

Maybe one day they'd even make a memory book.

* * * * *

There's more Silhouette Bombshell coming your way!
Every month we've got four fresh, unique and
satisfying reads that will keep you riveted....
Turn the page for an exclusive excerpt from
one of next month's releases

ULTRA VIOLET
by Ellen Henderson

On sale October 2005
at your favorite retail outlet.

"**M**s. Marsh?"

With a gasp, Vi whirled around.

Then she blinked. Even with her heart suddenly pounding in her throat, her brain still had time for a *hello, handsome!*

Which he was. Spiky, dark hair, chiseled face, deep green eyes, all attached to a long, lean, hard body in a black T-shirt and faded jeans. She swallowed hard.

Of course, the fact that he knew her name meant that he either worked for Gideon Enterprises, which made him a scary mercenary, or that he'd been spying on her independently, which made him just plain scary.

"Are you Violet?" he asked. His voice was low and terse, a little gruff.

Willing herself to stop noticing things about him, she drew in a breath.

"Are you Gideon?"

He smiled a little at that, the barest quirk, but he turned his head to the side as he did, as if the smile wasn't for her because she didn't know the joke.

"No," he answered. "But he's here. I'll take you to him."

He lifted an eyebrow. A beautiful, silky eyebrow. *Stop noticing.*

"You sure you want to go through with this?" he asked.

She frowned at him. But she didn't see any reason to lie.

"No," she answered.

He smiled again, and this time it was for her. For just a moment, she felt like a normal twentysomething single girl, standing in a park getting fluttery over a hot guy's sly smile. Then—

"Well, honey, it's too late to turn back now."

Vi turned again to see Natalie walking up to them, her hands tucked into the pockets of her denim jacket.

"Nice of you to show up," Vi said, scowling at her.

Natalie shrugged. "I could hardly get here first, since I had to follow you."

"You followed me here?" Vi shook her head. "Seems like a bit of overkill. After all, you already knew where I was going."

"Had to make sure no one else was on your tail, now didn't I?"

Vi frowned, not sure whether to believe that or dismiss it. Natalie started walking again.

"Well, come on. Let's go see Gideon." She looked back over her shoulder. "Jackson, you want to take this side, and I'll go south?"

Mr. Hot & Scary—Jackson—gave a curt nod and half-turned away, his eyes scanning the park. With a strange reluctance, Vi stepped away from him and followed Natalie toward a string of benches near the statue.

As they drew closer, she spotted a man sitting on one of

the benches, looking completely at ease with his ankle crossed over his knee. He was in his early forties, she decided as she stepped toward him, noting his salt-and-pepper hair and the crinkly crow's-feet around his blue eyes. His gray suit looked expensive, his manner exuded confidence, and while he wasn't as drop-dead gorgeous as Jackson, he was still pretty damn good-looking.

Vi thought about Jackson, flicked her eyes to Natalie and looked back at what must be Gideon. So what—did you have to be hot to be a spy? Was it some kind of prerequisite? Did Gideon Enterprises double as a modeling agency?

Whatever it was about, it was damned annoying. She was dealing with a personal crisis, and she didn't need to have her average looks thrown in her face on top of everything else.

Natalie stopped in front of Gideon.

"Here she is, boss," she said, then she turned and winked at Vi and walked away, toward the end of the park that Jackson wasn't covering.

Vi stopped, feeling awkward and hoping it didn't show.

Gideon smiled at her—an interesting smile. Sort of sad and wise and kind and cold, all at the same time. It made her instantly suspicious.

"So," he said, "this is Violet Marsh."

She nodded. "And you must be Gideon."

"Mal Gideon. Malcolm," he added with a smile. "But you can see why I don't use that."

Uh-oh. Self-deprecating humor. He could be dangerous.

"I'm glad you're here," he said. "I've been wanting to talk to you."

That was better. Now she remembered exactly why she wasn't going to like this guy.

"Yeah, I kind of figured as much when I found out you'd

set a spy on me. You know, when you want to talk to some-one, it's customary to pick up the phone, maybe write a note."

He grinned at her. "True. But this situation is a little un-usual, wouldn't you say?"

"You tell me. I don't have a clue what you're up to. And honestly, I don't care. I just want to know whatever it is you know about me."

For the first time, he stopped smiling. His eyebrows drew together in concern. "Yes," he said, then sighed.

"Why don't you sit down?" He gestured to the opposite end of the long bench he sat on.

Trying to move with assurance, she sat down on the edge of the bench, as far from him as possible.

Gideon dropped the foot that had been resting on his knee and leaned forward on the bench. "What I know…" He shook his head. "There isn't a good way to say this, so I'll just say it. Something has been done to you."

A prickling sensation rushed over her scalp. She didn't un-derstand, but she didn't like the ominous sound of his words. "What do you mean?"

"You've been sick."

She nodded, eying him warily. He must know already. "I just got out of the hospital."

He shook his head again, slowly. "I'm afraid not, Violet. Where you were was no hospital."

Icy prickles poked at her stomach, and she suddenly felt light-headed. She wished she'd eaten more that morning. She'd been too nervous to eat as much as her body seemed to be de-manding, but now she knew she could've used the fortification.

"Let's just say," she began, trying to keep her breathing under control, "that I believe you on that for the moment. Where was I, and how do you know about it?"

He looked slightly pained. "I can't tell you everything. There's…something else at stake. What I can tell you is that there's a…facility. We've been watching it for the past few days for another purpose. Three days ago, we saw you taken out of that facility under very suspicious circumstances. We thought there might be some connection to the case we're working on, so we tracked you down and watched you."

"And?" Her skin had gone clammy, cold, and her mind felt cold, too—almost numb.

"And what we've seen since has convinced us that…" He paused, watching her closely. "We can't be sure at this point. But given what we've seen, it seems likely that you've undergone some kind of genetic enhancement."

INTIMATE MOMENTS™

From *New York Times* **bestselling author**

Sharon Sala

comes

RIDER ON FIRE

SILHOUETTE INTIMATE MOMENTS #1387

With a hit man hot on her trail,
undercover DEA agent Sonora Jordan
decided to lie low—until ex Army Ranger
and local medicine man Adam Two Eagles
convinced her to look for the father she'd
never known…and offered her a love she'd
never known she wanted.

Available at your favorite retail outlet October 2005.

Where love comes alive™

Silhouette

BOMBSHELL™

COMING NEXT MONTH

#61 FINDERS KEEPERS by Shirl Henke
Straitjackets, blindfolds, restraints—Samantha Ballanger used any means necessary to rescue deluded people from dangerous cults. So when she retrieved a man from a kooky commune at the request of his wealthy aunt, it was a routine grab—until Sam realized she'd slapped her straitjacket on a Miami investigative reporter working a big story on the Russian mob. Oops! Now some powerful people wanted Sam and this man dead....

#62 FLAWLESS by Michele Hauf
The It Girls
An elite jeweler had been shot, diamonds embedded with secret military codes were up for grabs...and the übersecret Gotham Rose spies were on the case. Jet-set gemologist Rebecca Whitmore blazed a trail through London, Paris, New York and Berlin with her partner, British MI-6 agent Aston Drake, to track down the stones and snag the shooter. Could she stop the codes from falling into the wrong hands...before it was too late?

#63 STRONG MEDICINE by Olivia Gates
The Global Crisis Alliance had been field surgeon Calista St. James's *life,* until she'd been blamed for a botched humanitarian mission and dismissed as a loose cannon. Now, years later, GCA wanted her back for a delicate rescue operation in rebel-controlled Russian territory. Could Calista work with the man who'd fired her to free a group of hostages, or was this a prescription for disaster?

#64 ULTRA VIOLET by Ellen Henderson
Forget lost weekends—Violet Marsh couldn't account for five whole days! But when security firm Gideon Enterprises warned her that during that time she might have been subjected to genetic experiments without her knowledge, Violet dismissed it as nonsense...until she discovered her enhanced strength and sprinter's speed in a fight with a strange assailant. Who would do this to her? Violet wanted some answers—fast.

SBCNM0905